HOT DOGS are Diet Food

Jennifer Bogart

Hot Dogs are Diet Food
by Jennifer Bogart

Print ISBN: 978-0-9949593-4-8
Digital ISBN: 978-0-9949593-5-5

Originally published as "Reflections"
copyright 2012 by Jennifer Bogart

Copyright 2017 by Jennifer Bogart
Cover design copyright by Joanne Kasunic 2015
Book design by Morning Rain Publishing
Book cover author photo by Olga Makridina-Bhalla
Inside author photo by Gerri Photography

Acknowledgements

Sharon, for listening to me babble constantly about imaginary friends as though they are real, your enthusiasm, editing skills, reminders, encouragement, and most of all, your friendship. I'm privileged to have you in my life.

Kirstin, for helping me research fad diets, providing insight on good nutrition and keeping me, and so many others, motivated at the gym.

Joanne, for all your creative energy. I still hold you responsible for this journey I've embarked on.

Susan, Kim, Melissa, Clair, Andrea, Jennifer, Jo, Sharon, and Mary: my Beta Readers. You're a special group and I couldn't have polished the book without you.

Jaime and Riley, the two most beautiful models.

Olga, for making me look good.

Special thanks to all my wonderful friends and family who helped along the way, with support, encouragement and patience.

Dedication

This book is dedicated to all the wonderful women
in my life.

You are strong, intelligent, giving, loving,
beautiful people who never cease to amaze me.

~

Also, to my wonderful family.
Your love and laughter keep me going.

~

Most importantly for my husband.

I love you.

Chapter One

True Lies I Tell Myself

Today, my thirteen-year-old daughter caught me struggling to fasten the stubborn button on my once-favourite jeans. I was lying on my bed, squirming my way into the stiff fabric and sucking in my jiggling belly fat in the hopes of being able to mush it into the way too tight waist-band. This was not the first time she had been the unfortunate witness to the ongoing conflict with my wardrobe. Last week I had fought with a side-zipper in a simple black dress. I only conceded that battle when the zipper pinched the delicate skin along my ribcage, leaving an angry welt. The real kicker was that I had only worn the dress once. It must have shrunk in the wash.

"Mom," Calleigh said gently. "I think it's time to go shopping."

I sighed and struggled into a sitting position. Even unfastened, these jeans were something less than comfortable. "I have other jeans," I replied. "I just really like the look of these ones."

Calleigh lifted one golden eyebrow in a look that clearly stated disbelief. I knew my thighs looked like two over-stuffed sausages in their too-tight casings; I just refused to believe they would not look less ridiculous once I got the jeans buttoned and I was in a standing position. Surely gravity would help to even things out.

"Look, they're just a little snug. I think I might have put them in the dryer when they should have hung to dry. They'll stretch out."

If possible, that one eyebrow lifted higher into her fringed bangs. She's such a pretty girl. To this day I'm not sure how I ended up with this lovely thirteen-year old. I might not have done much right in my life, but this one accomplishment was something, or rather someone, I could take pride in. There are days when I look at her and wonder how she could be a part of me. We are nothing alike. Where her hair is golden, mine is mousy-not-quite-blond. Where her eyes are a light sky-blue, mine are a murky blue-grey, where she is slender and petite, I am frumpy. It's almost as though upon her birth all the beauty that might have been a part of me surged forth to create this lovely fairy-tale princess.

"Let's go on Saturday," she suggested, as she leaned forward and pulled me to my feet. "I need a few things for school, anyway."

"Okay, okay. But remember, we're on a budget. I'm not buying designer jeans for you."

"This trip isn't for me," she pointed out as she watched me shimmy out of my too-tight jeans. Damn dryer. I could feel my thighs wobbling as I wriggled and twisted until I was free of the offensive material. I would need to go to plan "B" for today's outfit.

Satisfied, Calleigh left me to my sadly lacking wardrobe. I assumed she headed down for breakfast.

At thirteen I hardly needed to monitor her every move. Having an independent child was such a relief. So many of my friends have little ones who require constant attention, and while I remember those days fondly, I'm also glad to be out of that phase of my life. I honestly can't remember the last time I fixed breakfast for my daughter on a school day or even made her lunch. Often, she would gobble up some sort of cereal and clear away her dishes long before I ever made my way to the kitchen.

I glanced at the clock on my bedside table and kicked myself into high gear. I would be late again, I wasn't exactly making a good impression during my first month of work. Lucky for me no one really cared what I looked like at this new job. I grabbed a pair of dress trousers, a turtle neck and matching jacket. The ensemble was probably a better choice than jeans, even if today was casual Friday. Plus, the elastic waist meant I would be comfortable all day, and the long jacket would camouflage any wayward bulges that were threatening to appear under my clothes. One week before my period was about to start and I was already feeling bloated. Being female was just so much fun.

There wouldn't be time for breakfast, so I grabbed a banana and a yogurt tube and stuffed them both in my purse. For good measure, I also tossed in a chocolate dipped peanut butter granola bar. One of the benefits of having a growing child in the house was that we always had easy snacks on hand. This sure made breakfast on the go so much easier.

My drive to work took a bit longer than usual. I munched on my banana, slurped back the yogurt tube and decided to save the granola bar for later. Of course, I wasn't counting on getting stuck in traffic. While my car was idling, and I was getting more and more fidgety with the delay, I decided to occupy myself with the chocolaty treat. Of course, we all know that chocolate is actually good for you. It comes from a bean. Beans are legumes: legumes are like vegetables and therefore full of vitamins and nutrients your body needs. One could almost call it a healthy start to the day, much better than all those sugary cereals that are on the market.

Upon arriving at work, I booted up my computer and quickly checked my phone messages. I have this great new job. I can already see there may days when it could be a little on the boring side, but for the most part it's almost a luxury compared to my last place of employment. I have this little cubicle all to myself, very neat and tidy because we aren't allowed to clutter it up or have any personal items showing. It's almost like it needs to look like you aren't working, even though you are. It's a bit refreshing to look at in the morning, since it is the complete opposite from the chaos of my house. I guess the idea is you can focus more on getting your work done than on other small distractions, like pictures of your family, religious symbols or any hobbies or interests that might you have.

"You're late, and we have a meeting in ten minutes," I heard from the other side of my cubicle. Lucy was already hard at work; she had probably arrived an hour early and was busy preparing her day. I have never in my life met anyone more efficient or organized. It scares me, how orderly she keeps everything. After knowing her for just one month I knew there was no way our personalities would ever mesh. She is far too systematic in her ways and I'm simply a muddled mess of confusion.

"I know; there was traffic." I could just hear her thinking, 'There is always traffic, that's why you should give yourself extra time.' But the disembodied voice from the other side of the partition stayed blissfully quiet.

"Okay," I announced, "I'm ready—let's go."

Lucy magically appeared in front of my cubicle. In addition to being freakishly organized, she is also very fast, (probably because she is so very organized—but I would hate to admit it). She handed me a folder from out of my own in-box, one I would have forgotten and had to return for, then led the way towards the meeting room. Not only did she take care of her own business, she was perfectly capable of handling other people's as well. There were times when I wondered if she was even human.

"I finished the edits on Drew's piece, but there's so much missing. It makes me wonder if he even looked at the specs," Lucy commented as we navigated the maze of corridors. "I hate receiving work that's so unprofessional. He's been hired to do a job, so he should do his job."

"Hmmm…" I had no other response for her. She had yet to edit any of my work, since I was relatively new to the company, but I knew my day was coming. I was dreading getting feedback from her on my own writing since she had an awful lot to say about those whose work she considered to be sub-par. This was my first office experience since Calleigh's father died; until now, I had conveniently been working freelance from home. For all I knew, Lucy was right about the quality of the writing she had been reviewing; she usually ended up with editing assignments submitted by the most junior writers. While I came with years of experience, I was still nervous about the quality of what I put forward.

As a technical writer, I am used to spending my day relaxing at my desk, and working on documentation that is thrown my way. Working in an office environment isn't so very different from working at home. The primary difference is the in-person interaction that happens on a daily basis. We have regularly scheduled meetings to discuss how any given project is going and what direction to take with various issues. These meetings tend to run into lunch, and because we are working so hard without time for breaks, lunch is ordered in. The trend lean towards healthy choices, like Deli sandwiches, complimented by pasta salads and veggies and dip. The best lunch so far was when we ordered Italian on Tuesday. I think Italian food has to be my absolute favourite. All that yummy, fresh pasta, flavourful cheeses and scrumptious sauces— it's just plain irresistible. I was hoping today would be a Cheese Cappelletti day.

It turned out it wasn't a Cheese Cappelletti day, but we did have donuts and café mochas, which was an equally nice treat to break up the morning. Actually, it was Lucy who suggested the fancy coffee, which was a bit of a surprise. I had pictured her as a water or milk kind of girl. Slim, lithe and attractive with her Asian features, there was no way I pictured her as the kind of person who would be lured by decadent treats. Of course, mocha is just another word for chocolate—and we all know that chocolate comes from a bean...

"Hey Foxy-Roxy, what's for dinner," Chris asked as she came in through the front door. I was standing at the stove, stirring a pot of spaghetti sauce. It wasn't my first choice, but it would do.

"Spaghetti, garlic bread and Caesar salad," I answered absently, ignoring her use of my childhood nickname. Very few people could get away with using that one.

"Ugh," Calleigh grimaced. "Can I just have the salad? I don't feel like spaghetti tonight."

I'll admit it, my daughter is spoiled. When Calleigh was small, I would often make her completely separate meals because she was such a picky eater. As she got older, my concessions leaned more towards 'make your own dinner if you don't like what I have slaved over after a full day of work'. Of course, since it was usually just the three of us, I rarely made something she found unappealing. Chris never complained about my cooking, she was happy to eat whatever was put in front of her provided she was expected to cook it.

"Whatever makes you happy," I sighed, it wasn't worth the fight with a teenager. If she wanted to starve herself, that was her problem. Like all children, she would eat when she was hungry.

I set the steaming plates on the table and inhaled the sweet smell of tomato sauce. Spaghetti is a comfort food.

Like a hearty stew, it's just perfect on a brisk January day.

"Smells good," Chris said as she piled her plate high. I smiled fondly at my sister, older than me by only four minutes. She was almost my opposite—taller, slimmer, darker—and she ate whatever she wanted without regret or conscious. Of course, her body type allowed for it, whereas mine—well—let's just say the expression 'once on the lips forever on the hips' really does apply. Unfortunately, cooking is a bit of a passion with me, so it's far too easy for me to over-indulge in my favourite foods.

"The sauce was in the freezer, so it was an easy meal for a busy day," I commented dismissively. "How was your day?"

Chris shrugged her shoulders, "Same old, same old. Not really much to say."

She is a teacher at an elementary school, so even if she did have something to say, I probably didn't want to hear about it anyway. I love my own child, but can just as easily do without other people's kids.

"You?"

"Mmmm… it was ok—another long meeting that didn't go anywhere."

"I got ninety-six percent on my math test," Calleigh announced through a mouthful of romaine lettuce. I looked at her with such pride, I'm sure my heart was about to burst. She really was a special kind of kid; always striving for perfection and often succeeding. "But… I didn't do so well on my English essay—only got an eighty-two."

"That's ok, honey, you'll do better next time," Chris acknowledged.

I looked at her in astonishment. Eighty-two was perfectly acceptable, she didn't need to do better, even though I knew she would work harder on the next one.

"Well, I'm proud of you. In fact, I think marks like that call for chocolate cake. I'll whip one up right after supper!"

"Oh, Roxy… I don't think it's necessary—we have some low-fat yogurt in the freezer, that'll do nicely for a little celebratory dessert," Chris countered. "Especially after a hearty meal like this one."

"It's okay, mom, I don't want chocolate cake. I would rather just have some fruit."

Was she insane? Since when did thirteen-year-olds choose fruit over cake?

"Sounds like a plan to me," Chris agreed with a nod of her head. "We do have fruit, don't we? It's been awhile since that fruit bowl has been filled…"

"We have fruit; it's just in the fridge. I don't buy a lot of it this time of year because it's not very good quality;

it's expensive and doesn't keep very long. Besides, nobody eats it very quickly."

"No big deal, it was just a question," Chris insisted as she polished off her spaghetti. It turns out we didn't have any "fresh" fruit in the house. I tried to remember when I last bought groceries, we couldn't be out of all the fresh stuff already, could we? It turned out we only had one can of fruit salad hidden at the back of the cupboard. The fact that the fruit had all blended into a nondescript mass of yellow mush didn't put Calleigh off at all, but I found it sadly unappealing. I'm not at all sure how she managed to down the three spoonfuls she did before proclaiming she was full.

"Popcorn?" Chris asked me, glaring at the offending bowl. I sat on the couch beside her with a warm bowl of the fluffy white stuff. The salty smell of the butter had me drooling. An icy coke to go with it would be fabulous, but we were all out. I had considered hot chocolate, but decided that I didn't need the caffeine so close to bedtime.

I shrugged, "We'll call it dessert. Besides, I can't watch my show without popcorn. I made enough for two."

She reached over, took a handful and kissed my cheek all in one fluid motion. "That's one of the things I love about you, Roxy."

I looked at her questioningly. "You don't stress about how you look, or what other people think about you."

"Ah… well, I do care," I insisted as I curled my feet up under me and snuggled under an old blanket. "But I also know there are some things I just can't change."

Menu du Jour

Breakfast: yogurt tube, banana, chocolate dipped granola bar and 2 cups of coffee

Mid-morning snack: donut, café mocha

Lunch: Deli Sandwich (and a healthy selection of salads—macaroni, coleslaw, potato)

Mid-afternoon snack: bag of chips and a coke Late-afternoon snack: 3 cookies, coffee (in my defence, it was a long afternoon)

Supper: Spaghetti, garlic bread and Caesar salad

Dessert: Fruit Salad from a can (in light syrup) Early evening snack: popcorn

Bedtime snack: 2 cookies

Total Calories consumed: 4104 (huh?—according to a calorie counter I found on the internet)

Total Calories burnt: 1426.75 (that's it? I guess typing doesn't take all that much energy)

Chapter Two

Mirror, Mirror on the Wall

I stared at my butt in the warped glass of my bedroom mirror. There was nothing to do for it. Every pair of jeans I tried to squeeze into just made the gelatinous mass worse. You know when you get that little roll that seeps over the edge of the waistband—it kind of looks like cake batter that has expanded past the edge of the pan? Except, with cake batter, you can scrape off the excess and salvage the cake. There was no hope for these jeans, or any other in my wardrobe. Calleigh was right; it was time to go shopping.

I sighed as I squirmed out of the offensive jeans and tossed them into the growing pile for the Salvation Army.

There was no point in keeping clothing I would never be able to squeeze into again. Let's face it, at some point a woman's middle-aged body just spreads and spreads and spreads - especially one who has had kids. I am short and frumpy, as my mother had been before me, and her mother before her. I just hope that Calleigh will have better luck as her body matures. Maybe she will be lucky and take after her Aunt Chris.

"You need an intervention," Calleigh declared as she entered the bedroom and took in the pile of discarded clothing. She looked very sweet in her stylish leggings and long sweater which she had layered with a contrasting long vest. Somehow, she had developed a great sense of fashion, which did not come from me. Even when the clothes are set out in perfectly matched sets in the store, I can't possibly throw a decent outfit together. Of course, if I wore an outfit like that I would no doubt resemble a walking rolled up ball of wool that was unfortunately cinched at the middle.

"Be nice," I admonished. She might be right, but she was still my daughter and needed to be respectful.

Calleigh gave me one of those teenager-looks that basically said: 'C'mon, mom, that was nice.'

"You two going shopping today?" Chris asked as she came into the room. She had been out shovelling the driveway. Her cheeks were rosy, her hazel eyes sparkled and her dark blond curls had that tousled look models sport in magazines, only Chris' were a result of the wind. Even dishevelled she looked good, which made me feel all the more dowdy.

"Yup," Calleigh cheered. "Mom needs new clothes." "Yes, she does," Chris agreed as she took in the growing mountain of cast-offs. "A few things that fit better would be good. Lucky for you, our little mall has a pretty good selection of plus-size and full-figure boutiques."

Ouch. I know she didn't mean it, but it hurt when those comments snuck out. I have a mirror; I can see what I look like. The last thing I needed was my genetic nemesis pointing out my shortcomings.

"Oooh, you should try this on," Calleigh insisted as she held up a hot-pink, jersey-knit shirt for my perusal.

I shook my head at her bizarre taste in clothing. "I don't think so, sweetie."

The shirt would be cute on her, but on me I would only look like a giant wad of Hubba Bubba Bubble Gum. I was examining a plain black pair of trousers, size 10. Not exactly "plus-size", but this was my first venture into trying on double digit clothing and I was devastated. Why couldn't clothing sizes be consistent? All my life I have fluctuated between a generous size six or eight. Just the thought of that double-digit number dampened my spirits and put a pall on this entire shopping trip.

What made matters worse was that my thirteen-year-old was having trouble finding things that fit because she was just too thin. Who decided to create a clothing size '00' anyway? It was just absurd—how could you physically be two times less than zero? And did anyone ever stop to think about how that would affect the moral of the mommy who was wading through the double-digit dress sizes? Of course not.

"How about these?" Calleigh suggested. She was holding a pair of brown cords. They were plain, wide legged and just the thing I thought I was looking for.

"They have your size, even."

"My size—great," I muttered. I took them from her and examined the cut. They looked really, really low at the waist. You know, the 'I don't dare bend over for fear of showing my panties, or revealing a plumber's crack' kind of low rise. Why wasn't this expression gender neutral? Today alone, despite the bitter cold outside I had seen more pastel pink and blue thongs than one person should have to endure while shopping.

"Just try them on," my daughter urged. She held up three more pairs of non-descript trousers. At least she wasn't trying to squeeze me into leggings. I had already done leggings in the early 90's. At 33, I'm way too old to pull them off now.

I took the pants into the change room and grimaced as I shimmied out of my too-tight jeans. The button had left an indentation on my soft belly, and I rubbed it in an attempt to smooth away the angry mark. The cords were a disaster… The promise of a wide leg was nothing but an illusion. I could barely get them over my hips. Just in case, I double checked the tag and then frowned in dismay. Size 10—they had to be mislabelled. Or maybe they were an off-cut and that's why they were marked down so much.

Determined, I tried on the other three pairs of trousers, but with no luck. There was something wrong with all of them, either that, or there was something horribly wrong with me. How had I gotten here; sitting half-naked on a stool in a dingy changing room, nearly in tears because my middle-aged body just didn't want to conform to the fit and cut of mainstream clothing? Had I let myself go that much? Well, that decided it. I would take the plunge and do what I had never done before. I was putting myself on a diet. I never wanted to have a repeat of this disastrous shopping spree again.

I decided some research was in order before I jumped into anything too radical. I mean, I probably only needed to lose ten pounds or so to feel better about myself. Plus, I would save a ton of money by being able to ease back into my existing wardrobe. There hadn't been a real need for a shopping spree. What I needed was a wake-up call. Those size 10 plus jeans had opened my eyes to the reality of my situation. I was obese—no question about it, and the perfect diet was out there waiting for me; I just had to find it.

There were so many diet plans out there to choose from I hardly knew where to start. I purchased a selection of women's magazines boasting various fool-proof diets that worked in no time at all. 'Lose 10 pounds in just two weeks!' one proclaimed. Another boasted, 'Melt away unwanted flab in only 7 days!' And yet another featured a well-known starlet who announced: 'I lost ten pounds in just three days, and you can too with my simple plan!' I could stick to a diet for three days, no problem. I felt better already, knowing I had so many options.

"What's all this?" Chris asked as she took in the montage of weight-loss magazines I had scattered across the family room floor.

I shrugged my shoulders in response; I didn't want to get into it with her. I was seriously considering the lose ten pounds in just three days option. The faster I got rid of the blubber, the better.

"You going on a diet?"

The thing with Chris is once something has struck her interest, she's hooked and just won't let go of a subject. Without any encouragement, she'll be offering advice and looking for the best diet plan for me. The last thing I needed was weight-loss advice from someone who had never had to struggle with it before in her life. What would she know about feeling fat and cumbersome all the time? She had been blessed at birth with a natural athlete's build.

"Mmmm…" I didn't want to commit to anything, just in case things didn't pan out the way I hoped. "Just want to shed a little winter weight that seems to have settled in."

"Well," she continued conversationally, "I'm glad to see you are starting to take care of yourself. I was getting a bit worried about you."

That got my attention. She was worried about me? I was fine, really. Nothing to worry about here—just an overweight mommy who let things get a bit out of control in the past few years.

"What do you mean by that, exactly?" I asked her. "Nothing, really. I'm just glad that you aren't fixing the problem by going out and buying new clothes because by this time next year everything will be too small all over again."

I took a deep breath. Who needed a mirror when one had the brutal honesty of a loving twin sister? If she was so worried, why didn't she say something sooner? And then it struck me, she had been hinting at my increasing weight. Not outright, like just now, her observations had been subtler. Things like: 'Are you sure you're comfortable in that?' and; 'It's too bad those jeans are too tight, they looked good when you first got them." She had been giving me hints for the past year or so, only I was just too obtuse to figure them out.

"Well, we'll see," I said noncommittally. "I know I've gained weight over the past few years, but it's not easy, you know. The stress of Damian's death, raising Calleigh on my own and having a desk job—it's not like I planned all this."

"We could start simply, just by going for family walks after dinner," she suggested. We? What was this we-thing she was talking about? This was going to be my thing. I didn't want her hounding me about it. I needed to do this on my own. Since Chris started living with us aster my husband's death, she had fully integrated her life into mine. What was meant to have been a temporary arrangement had grown into a lifetime partnership.

"I suppose. But—" I didn't want to hurt her feelings. She looked at me questioningly, waiting for me to finish. "Never mind. I was just thinking that it's super cold outside and Calleigh has a ton of homework during the week. Maybe when the weather warms up a bit."

The look she gave me can only be described as exasperated. I chose to ignore it. The whole idea of fixing what I thought couldn't be fixed was overwhelming enough. I didn't need her advising me on how to go about it. I'm a grown, educated woman. I would figure this one out on my own.

So, here I go—day one of my three-day diet plan. If all goes according to plan I'll be back into my favourite jeans before the weekend. No walks, no long-term commitment, and no more hating myself every time I look in the mirror. Three days—anyone can commit to something for such a short period of time.

Breakfast was easy enough, although it felt a bit strange. I can't remember the last time I sat down and ate breakfast. After half of a grapefruit, one slice of toast with Nutella (it was supposed to be Peanut Butter, but we were all out) and coffee I actually felt full. The bigger challenge was getting to lunch. By 10:00am I was starving. I'm used to snacking my way through the day, so going without a snack was truly a challenge. The thing with working in an office like mine is that there is always something to snack on. Temptations abound and you just can't hide from them. By lunch time I was light-headed, but determined to see the day through. I could do this—I had will-power!

Lunch was probably some of the blandest fare I have ever tasted. Dry, tasteless and unappealing, but I was so hungry I didn't care.

Lucy, on the other hand had something that looked absolutely scrumptious. I could smell the exotic mix of spices as they wafted towards me across the table, making me drool over flavours I knew I wouldn't get to experience anytime soon. Then I reminded myself that I could do anything for three days. In the grand scheme of things, three days is nothing.

"Do you want some?" she offered, forcing me out of my daydream of delectable Chinese delicacies. I shook my head as though to clear it. I wished I had a nose plug. The smell of her lunch was driving me crazy.

"I'm good," I said with a smile that I'm sure came across as a grimace. I was eating my toast and tuna as slowly as possible, trying to trick myself into thinking it was more than it was because it was taking so long to get through it. The guidelines for the menu didn't specify if you could use butter to make the toast less dry, so I had only used the smallest amount, and it was still difficult to swallow.

"Okay." She speared a crisp broccoli head that had been stir fried in some fabulous sauce and ate it with relish. I think I started to truly hate her in that moment. Not because she was eating a delicious meal in front of me with such gusto, but because she could. Where was the justice in that? "But you're gonna be hungry in an hour."

I looked at the scattering of crumbs on my plate and resisted the urge to lick it clean. I was hungry now. "I'll live. I'm trying to lose some weight," I offered.

She nodded, bit her lip, but didn't say anything.

"Just a few pounds," I continued casually. I didn't want to make it into a bigger thing that it was. "You know, I'm fighting the winter bulge—I think it's my age."

Lucy frowned and stopped chewing. "How old are you?" she asked, looking somewhat confused.

"Thirty-three," I answered. "Almost middle-aged."

She laughed at that. "You mean you don't plan to live longer than the ripe old age of sixty-six? Wow."

I shrugged my shoulders. When she was my age and had a child or two, she wouldn't be laughing. Out of curiosity, I asked her, "How old are you?"

"Thirty-two," she answered. I would have choked if I had anything left to eat. She looked so much younger than that.

"Kids?" I asked, hoping I could salvage some of my self-respect. If she had kids I would hate her all the more for being so perfect.

"Three," she answered, with a smirk. In that moment, I was torn between hating and idolizing her. Sometimes life just wasn't fair.

Menu du Jour

Breakfast: ½ grapefruit, 1 slice of toast with Nutella, coffee

Mid-morning snack: glass of water

Lunch: 1 slice of toast, ½ cup of tuna, coffee Mid-afternoon snack: coffee

Late-afternoon snack: Nada

Supper: about 3 ounces dry chicken breast, 1 cup of yellow beans, ½ banana, 1 small orange,

Dessert: 1 cup of vanilla ice cream Early evening snack: glass of water Bedtime snack: more water…

Total Calories consumed: 1000 (this can't be enough for an average person—went to bed hungry)

Total Calories burnt: 1426.75 (what I burn just by breathing—that makes a difference of 426.75 calories!)

Chapter Three

Hot Dogs are Diet Food

It's rare that I wake up hungry. But that three-day diet does something to your mind, not to mention your stomach. The more you tell yourself that you can do anything for just three short days, the longer those days dragged on. My new mantra became "I can do this; I have willpower"; which even I knew was an out and out lie. Willpower? This diet was going to take far more than that. I was, of course, looking forward to supper today. Hot dogs for supper! No buns, mind you, but still; how cool was that?

It suddenly occurred to me that if I was going to lose 10 pounds in just three days that perhaps I should weigh myself. Granted, the weigh-in would be a day late, so I would have to add a few pounds of weight loss for good measure. I had never bothered with scales before. Either my clothing fit, or it didn't. I didn't need an archaic mechanical instrument to tell me I look awful. It was only recently that everything was unbearably too tight.

I began to wonder if we even owned a scale. I didn't remember packing one when we moved out of our house in the country. I wasn't about to ask Chris—she would probably just laugh at me. She already thought I was off my rocker, trying to lose ten pounds in only three days. What did she know anyway? It wasn't like she had ever had to worry about her body image. After searching in vain for an hour, wasting precious time in the morning when I could have been sorting laundry and cleaning the kitchen I decided I would just buy a new scale during lunch. After all, it would take no time at all to choke down my one slice of cheese, hard-boiled egg and five saltine crackers that would comprise my meal. The walk through the department store and change of scenery would no doubt help me forget about how deprived I was feeling.

The problem with buying a new scale is that you can't test it before bringing it home. They are all neatly packaged with all kinds of nifty features. Did I want a digital one? Did I want something that measured BMI? I didn't even know what BMI was! I settled on one with extra large, easy to read numbers that was pink in support of Breast Cancer research. It may as well be pretty if it was about to become my new best friend.

The minute I got home from work, I ditched my shoes and jacket, said a hasty hello to Calleigh and ran up the stairs to the bathroom to try out my pretty new toy.

It must have been broken… or maybe it just needed to be recalibrated.

There was no way my body weighed that much. I thought back to the last time I had stepped on a scale—it must have been at the end of my pregnancy with Calleigh. I couldn't possibly weigh more now than I did then, could I? My five-foot three-inch frame couldn't possibly support that much weight. I was going to have to be on this three-day diet forever because I had far more than ten pounds to shed.

Calleigh found huddled in the middle of the bathroom, clutching the pink scale to my chest, rocking back and forth and fighting back tears. I was so hungry, my head hurt, my stomach ached and now my heart was broken. How could things have gotten so out of hand?

Some things in life just aren't fair.

"Mom?" Calleigh approached with caution. She had the look of a frightened deer caught in the headlights about her. Poor kid, she just caught her mother in the midst of an all-out temper-tantrum. What kind of role model was I that I would let her see me crumbled on the floor having a hissy fit over a broken scale? I needed to pull myself together.

I sniffed, grabbed a wad of toilet paper, wiped my eyes and nose and did my best to pull myself together.

"It's ok, honey. I'm just having a rough day."

She nodded with understanding. "Want me to make you a cup of tea?"

Was I allowed to have a cup of tea? Really, it's just water and caffeine. I wouldn't put sugar in it, and I was allowed to have it at lunch. *Why did tea have to be so complicated?* For some inexplicable reason, I started to cry all over again. What on earth was wrong with me?

"I just need a few minutes," I hiccupped, thoroughly embarrassed that I couldn't get my unruly emotions under control.

"I'll go put the kettle on," Calleigh said before practically sprinting from the bathroom. Poor girl; I probably traumatized her for life.

Not only did Calleigh put the kettle on, she emptied the dishwasher, cleared away any left-over dishes from the morning chaos and wiped down all the countertops. I was blessed with an angel of a daughter—well, for today, anyway.

She placed a steaming cup of tea in front of me and those damn tears threatened to spring forward again. I wondered if crying burned more calories.

"Thanks hon," I choked, trying to hide the ensuing waterworks behind a sip of the hot liquid. Tea and biscuits are the cure-all in our house, a tradition passed down from my grandmother and probably her own grandmother before her. Whenever someone needed comforting, companionship or conversation, tea was at hand and so were those delightful little digestive biscuits, you know, the kind you give to babies that dissolve when you dunk them in hot liquid. I was just about to head to the cupboard to grab a handful when I remembered that I wasn't allowed. Even the comfort of tea would evade me today.

"I was thinking," Calleigh started, almost hesitantly. "Maybe we should do this diet thing together—that way you'll have support."

I looked up at her in astonishment. How did she know I was doing a three-day diet? I hadn't exactly shared my plan with her. "Calleigh, you're too young to worry about your diet."

Calleigh shrugged her shoulders in response and took a sip of her own steaming tea. "It's only for another day and a half, it's not like my whole life is going to revolve around food, or anything."

She had absolutely no idea. In this moment, my very life essence was revolving around food, or the lack thereof. In fact, I was now counting the minutes until I could devour those two spindly hot dogs for dinner. I was wishing I had made a trip to the grocery store to purchase ball-park dogs so it would be worth my while to eat them.

"It probably wouldn't hurt, but I think you need more calories, you're still growing." I think at this point I was only going through the motions of arguing with my daughter because I knew in the end she would probably join me in this craziness. She was just that kind of kid.

Calleigh shrugged, "I suppose. But I could do the bulk of it with you—and really, a couple days of supporting you isn't going to hurt me."

Her comment made me stop and think for a moment. The question was: would three days help me in the grand scheme of things?

Menu du Jour

Breakfast: 1 egg, one slice of toast, ½ banana, coffee

Mid-morning snack: 2 glasses of water

Lunch: 1 slice of cheddar cheese, 1 hardboiled egg, 5 saltine crackers, coffee

Mid-afternoon snack: coffee

Late-afternoon snack: Nada

Supper: 2 hot dogs (no bun), 1 cup of broccoli, ½ cup of carrots,

Dessert: ½ banana, 1/2 cup of vanilla ice cream

Early evening snack: glass of water Bedtime snack: more water…

Total Calories consumed: 1100 (even with hot dogs!)
Total Calories burnt: 1426.75 (because this number will never change)

The hot dogs didn't do the trick, and neither did the ice cream. By the time the third day of the diet rolled around, I was ready to commit mass murder for any speck of food left on a plate. Three days turns out to be a very long time when you're hungry. Calleigh seemed to manage alright, but then again, she was probably sneaking food at school and just not telling me so that I wouldn't feel bad. Although Chris was mostly supportive, I could tell she wasn't buying into this three-day diet thing. She kept looking at my half cup of tuna like it was a mound of wet dog food. It wasn't like I was forcing her into participating in my folly; I was still making her meals so she wouldn't go hungry.

I'm pretty sure my pink bathroom scale was broken.

When I stepped on the scales the evening of the third day I was dismayed to find I was only down two pounds. And then I remembered that you typically weigh more in the evening than in the morning. Plus, my body hadn't had time to metabolize the final days' caloric intake, so I would probably be happier with the morning results.

I was so anxious for my morning weigh-in that I hardly slept all night. When I did, I dreamt of dancing hot dogs and ice cream cones with smiley faces. It was like one of those concession stand cartoon movies they used to play at drive in movies, to get you to buy popcorn and drinks. I also dreamt that my pretty pink scale had a little gremlin inside. Every time I stepped on it, he would add ten pounds to the electronic measure. I think I woke up from this one in a cold sweat, damn that little pink Barbie-like gremlin who was so well camouflaged in my scale!

The results: I lost seven pounds. It wasn't the full promised ten, but it sure was nice seeing a slightly lower number on that scale. I guess the gremlin had decided to give me a break. I felt so great I decided I would treat myself to a nice little breakfast of fried eggs, bacon and toast. Three days on a limited diet sure made for a ravenous appetite!

Chris came into the kitchen just as I was taking the bacon from the pan. It was maple flavoured, so the salty-sweet smell of bacon was wafting through the air, beckoning all within olfactory reach to make their way to the table.

"This is a treat," she said with a smile. "What's the special occasion?"

I smiled up at her and continued with my task. "This morning we're celebrating. I lost seven pounds."

"Good for you. Are you sure you want to wreck it by eating such a heavy breakfast?"

I'm sure she meant well with her question. I'm sure it wasn't meant to come out sounding snide and unpleasant.

"I have hardly eaten anything for the past three days, give me a break—one decent breakfast isn't going to pack the pounds back on," I retorted.

She only shrugged her shoulders in response. Well, I didn't care. I was starving and nothing was going to take away my enjoyment of this breakfast. Besides, if I went to work with a full stomach, I would be able to resist the temptation of donuts that were sure to arrive at this morning's planning meeting. I knew that I would have to be careful or I would be sure to gain the weight back straight away; I wasn't that deluded into thinking a three-day diet would last forever. It was just the first step to getting me on my way.

Unfortunately, donuts did not accompany our morning meeting. Donuts I would have been able to resist, they were a common enough occurrence. Instead, we were treated by scrumptious pastries: flakey, jam filled delicacies lightly glazed with honeyed icing. The smell just about drove me from the room in tears. I had deprived myself for three entire days; never straying from the diet. One little treat couldn't hurt in the long run, could it? I would have salad for lunch and watch what I had for dinner. No problem.

"These little pastries are going to cost me an extra hour at the gym," Lucy commented as she polished off a cherry filled delight. I very much doubted it would cost her anything extra. She ate constantly and always looked slim and trim.

I sighed, looking longingly at the yummy confections. Just one couldn't hurt. I did deserve a treat, and I would forgo popcorn tonight, even though my favourite show was on and I never missed an episode with the buttery comfort of popcorn.

"I wish I were more like you," the words popped out of my mouth before I could stop them. Obviously being deprived of nourishment for the past few days had affected my brain cells.

"Huh?" Lucy looked at me curiously. "What do you mean?"

Well, I was in it now; may as well serge forward. "It's just that it seems you can eat whatever you want and you always look great." I hoped I didn't sound like I was whining.

Lucy laughed. "No, no. I have to be careful like everyone else. Plus, I do go to the gym."

"When do you have time? With work, and kids? I just couldn't find the time."

"Sure, you could. I either go before work or at lunch time. I just leave the house an hour early, do my work out, shower at the gym and then I'm good for the day. It doesn't take any time at all once you get into the routine."

"Well, I have to get my daughter off to school," I offered as an excuse.

Lucy nodded, "Yeah, it can take a bit of wiggling with schedules. But it's doable."

Our conversation was cut short by Mitch who walked into the room with his laptop and stack of official looking papers. We settled back into our seats, notebooks open and ready to listen and plan for the next two hours. Every so often the scent of the pastries would float through the air to torment me. I did try to resist the enticement, knowing I would hate myself for giving in. I wanted to keep those seven pounds off for good. If I could do that, I would be inspired to lose more. Before long I would be the one enjoying sweets and being the envy of other overweight, middle-aged women.

Menu du Jour (After the Three-Day Diet)

Breakfast: Bacon, eggs, toast, coffee

Mid-morning snack: lemon Danish smothered in honey glaze

Lunch: Cheese Cappelletti

Mid-afternoon snack: cherry Danish smothered in honey glaze

Late-afternoon snack: 3 coffees

Supper: pork chops, rice, corn, tall glass of chocolate milk

Dessert: apple crisp

Early evening snack: popcorn & soft drink

Bedtime snack: water

Total Calories consumed: the first day after finishing a diet the calories shouldn't count.

Total Calories burnt: 1426.75

Chapter Four

An Apple a Day Keeps the Weight Gain Away

One week after the three-day diet event and I was back up the seven pounds I had fought so hard to lose. Two weeks later, I was up fourteen. To quote one of my young daughter's favourite expressions: "What the hell?" What had been simply too snug before was now absolutely unyielding. Between the dryer shrinking everything, and the little pink gremlin in my scale, things were getting decidedly worse. Even my more comfortable, elastic waistband pants were being stretched at the seams. Maybe it was a health issue, so I decided to make an appointment with my doctor to make sure I didn't have some life-threatening, weight-gaining disease. "You're fine," Dr. Patterson insisted. "Your blood pressure is a bit higher than I would like to see, but that's nothing a little exercise won't take care of."

Exercise. Right. I could just see myself in a tight little yoga outfit, blobs of excess flesh hanging over the top of the pants or bunched up in the confinements of the bra, stretching and toning with a bunch of svelte twenty-year-olds. Before I was ready for a public appearance at a gym, I was going to have to work a little harder at losing some weight.

"But what about all the weight I've gained over the past year or so?" I asked. Surely there was some medical reason she was overlooking. Maybe I had a fifty-pound tumour that had gone unnoticed, which was rapidly expanding, especially in my abdomen. I think it may also have spread across my butt. Maybe it wasn't one tumour but a cluster of them making me all lumpy and bumpy. It was possible; I've watched enough medical mystery shows on TV to know it wasn't in the realm of the impossible.

"Well, you could stand to lose some weight if you are feeling uncomfortable. Again, it's easily accomplished through diet and exercise. You aren't morbidly obese; you've just managed to pack on a few extra winter pounds. Nothing much to worry about."

So—my frumpy-dumpy body was nothing to worry about? I could go back to eating buttery popcorn, flakey pastries and pasta in rich sauces guilt-free? I loved this doctor! Of course, I wasn't loving my body so much, but I could learn to live with it.

"You could also add a bit more fibre to your diet, that would also help to regulate a few things," she suggested helpfully. "You know, choose fruit and vegetables for snacks instead of sweets."

Okay, now there was a suggestion I could run with. I do like fruit; I just never think to reach for it when I'm in a hurry and hungry.

"What's that?" Lucy asked as she peered over my shoulder. I jumped. I was doing a little personal research on weight-loss and feeling a bit guilty. At least when I worked from home I never had to worry about someone peering over my shoulder. Even though my doctor had assured me that small changes would make decent results I still felt I needed something more. There had to be an easy way to shed the excess weight. After all, it had accumulated easily enough. I already knew that I had some difficulty sticking to a diet that didn't fill me. And of course, the end result had been weight gain because I had ended up gorging myself afterwards to make up for calories not consumed the three days previous.

"Nothing," I muttered, quickly moving to a new tab in Explorer. Lucy was nice enough; she didn't appear to be a gossip, but I didn't need her letting our supervisor know that I had indulged in a few moments of personal research. It's not like I was playing on Facebook, but still, we did have company rules.

"Is that a diet gimmick?" she asked, leaning casually against my desk. As usual, she was stylish in her trim-fitting trousers and a fitted long-sleeved t-shirt with a scarf around her neck which pulled the entire ensemble together. She looked casual and elegant all at once.

I shrugged my shoulders. "It's really more of a suggestion on how to increase fibre in your diet, and maybe lose some weight in the process."

Lucy reached around me, took control of the mouse and clicked back to the page in my web browser. She gave a soft laugh and started to read aloud:

"Are you tired of traditional diet plans? Do you find that you are always hungry, and your cravings never really go away? No time to hit the gym? Then we have the solution for you."

She paused and looked at me with a smile, "Sounds good so far—except for the typo, they spelled gym wrong, it has a 'y' not an 'i'."

I laughed; trust Lucy to point at the flaws! She continued to read through the advertisement:

"The Apple diet is a simple solution that will help you lose weight, feel good about yourself, and help you look younger. This guaranteed plan is so simple; you'll wonder why you didn't try it sooner. No need for lengthy work out routines at the gym, forget about complicated meal plans and never feel hungry again."

She sounded like an announcer on one of those infomercials; her voice rising in excitement as she got closer to the big reveal.

"All you need to do is eat an apple before every meal to be on your way to guaranteed weight loss. The Apple Diet works because of the high water content and rich fibre content that naturally occur in the fruit. Basically, you are 'eating water' which allows you to consume more while taking in fewer calories. Apples contain about 5 grams of naturally occurring fibre which is essential for any weight-loss program."

It all made sense to me. The expression should have been an 'apple a day keeps weight gain away'. The two most appealing aspects of this plan were not being hungry and not needing to exercise. Perfect for a busy girl like me.

"It sounds reasonable," Lucy commented after she finished perusing the page in silence. I looked at her in surprise. She was the last person I would have expected to get hooked on fad diets. "Let's do it."

"Really?" I asked. Secretly, I was pleased that she wasn't laughing in my face. Chris would have scoffed at it and insist that I need a "life style change", and apples would only play a small part in it.

"Sure, it can't hurt. We'll have to go shopping for apples at noon." She slipped out of my cubicle and made her way around to her side of the divider. "We can walk up to the market, get some apples, have lunch and then make our way back. It'll be good to have a supply of fresh fruit in the office to off-set all the baked goods that come in here."

"Great, I'll see you for lunch, then," I called over the wall. Having someone to do this experiment with might be just what I need to keep me on track. Not that Lucy needed to add fibre and water to her diet—she already looked fantastic.

Lucy's lazy stroll to the market was more like a quick sprint for me. For each of her long-legged strides, I had to speed walk with two uneven steps to keep up. She directed me to a produce place I had driven by many times, but never actually entered. It had the look of a dingy warehouse, rather than the clean brightness of a traditional grocery store. As we picked through the makeshift aisles I have to admit I was overwhelmed by the selection of produce I couldn't actually identify. The hand-written signs read: guava, cactus pears, Cherimoyas, tomatillos, and Meyer Lemons. All this time I had thought a lemon was a lemon. I didn't even know there were so many unexplored foods out there, and I had thought I knew a little something about cooking. The smells of all the overripe produce blended together, making for a strange, intoxicating effect and I found that I was hungrier than ever.

"So, what do you want for lunch?" Lucy asked as we piled apples into bags. We decided to purchase a variety so we wouldn't get bored with just one flavour or texture.

"I don't know. Something fast, though, because we don't have much time."

"We could get Lebanese and take it back to the office."

I love Lebanese food: all that garlic, those tasty spices, humus, falafels, Shish Taouk, shawarmas… it's all so delicious and flavourful. Granted, the downfall is that you stink like crazy afterwards. Lucky for us we didn't have any afternoon meetings planned, so I would be tucked away in my cubicle all afternoon, free to expel my brimstone breath as much as I needed.

"Terrific," I agreed.

What I hadn't factored in was the additional ten-minute sprint to the restaurant because we had already walked to the market. In order to get back to the office on time, we had to hike the twenty minutes back at full speed. By the time we arrived, I was winded and my arms were starting to ache from carrying loads of apples and Lebanese food. Lucy, on the other hand wasn't even out of breath. Her long black hair was windblown, her cheeks were rosy from the cold, and she looked fresh and alert. I was sticky and sweaty from the exertion and no doubt I looked as dishevelled as I felt. Keeping up with her was going to take an effort.

As soon as I sat down at my desk I reached for the still warm take-out tray of Shish Taouk. Lucy stood behind me and cleared her throat. I looked up to see her smiling and holding up a perfectly red McIntosh apple. It was huge—almost as big as my head. If I ate it, I probably wouldn't have enough room for my delicious lunch.

I sighed, accepted the apple and took a hardy bite. My teeth sank into the crisp skin much like a vampire's would pierce soft flesh. The sweet juice burst forward in a shower of flavour. I had forgotten how sweet and delicious apples could be. Not to mention, I was so hungry from all that walking and consequently late lunch that just about anything would taste good. Before I knew it, I had consumed the entire apple. Lucy had also devoured hers, after placing the bowl, pilfered from the cafeteria, filled with a colourful selection of the yummy treats before me. I just hoped that no one mistook me for being a teacher when they saw all those apples on my desk!

My take-away was now lukewarm, but still delicious. As hungry as I was, I only managed to consume about a third of it before deciding I was too full to polish it off. This felt good. Apples are tasty, so no complaints in that department. The added bonus of them being filling, but with fewer calories, would be an asset in the weight-loss department. Plus, with the added benefits of important vitamins, minerals and nutrients I would be less stressed about making sure I was eating all the right things. Not that I had ever worried about it, but I was starting to be concerned.

No doubt Calleigh would appreciate the leftovers for her own supper tonight. Chris had some art show at the school tonight, after which she planned to go out with a couple friends from work. I was so stuffed I would be fine with a bowl of soup, and an apple, of course.

"I'm not hungry, mom, I had a big snack after school," Calleigh answered in response to my offer of today's lunch leftovers.

This was happening a lot lately. I would come home from work and she would have already eaten. It wasn't like her to pass up a treat like Lebanese food. "Are you feeling alright?"

Gently I placed a hand on her forehead to see if she might have a fever, but she seemed just fine. A little pale, which was to be expected with her fair complexion in the middle of the winter, but otherwise she was just fine.

"I'm alright, maybe a little tired," she offered. "Anyway, I have a ton of homework so I had better get to it."

That was my girl, beautiful, bright, independent and dedicated to doing well. She never ceased to amaze me.

"I have some work to do too," I said as I cleared away the dishes I had set out for her supper. "Maybe if we both get it all done we catch something on TV. We'll snuggle up with a bowl of popcorn, just the two of us since Auntie Chris is working late tonight. It will be just like we're back in our old house."

Calleigh gave a noncommittal shrug. "Sure, if I get it all done. It seems like we have a lot projects this year and I want to make honour role."

"I know, but don't burn yourself out; you still have time on the weekend to finish things off. If you want me to edit anything, just let me know."

"I will." She gathered her books and disappeared to her bedroom. Shortly afterwards I heard the hum of dance music escaping through her door.

I actually had my own deadline to meet. I was used to working from home, on my own time, so writing at night wasn't much of a hardship for me. Lucky for me, my work would only take me about an hour and then I would have the rest of the evening to enjoy the company of my daughter.

Sighing, I switched on my laptop and patiently waited for it to go through the motions of loading all its mysterious background programs and files. The house was quiet with Chris out for the evening. Lately, she was spending more and more time away, and while I knew it was ridiculous for me to be jealous of her social life, I still felt an emptiness I just couldn't explain. She should be out with friends, dating and getting on with her life instead stuck here, looking after her widowed sister and adorable niece. Her life had been put on hold for far too long.

I wasn't hungry for soup, so I decided to treat myself to a bowl of ice cream. I had only had a third of my lunch today, so I wasn't feeling too terribly guilty about skipping supper completely.

Menu du Jour

Breakfast: yogurt tube, banana, chocolate dipped granola bar and 2 cups of coffee

Mid-morning snack: donut, coffee

Lunch: gigantic apple, 1/3 of a Shish Taouk plate

Mid-afternoon snack: too full for an afternoon snack

Supper: chocolate ice cream

Early evening snack: popcorn

Bedtime snack: apple

Total Calories consumed: 1603

Total Calories burnt: 1426.75 + 79 (for walking…

that's it?) = 1505.5

Jennifer Bogart

Chapter Five

Warning Bells

Calleigh and I stood side by side gazing into the dressing room mirrors. I was grimacing over the fit of the size 10 jeans I had finally decided to purchase. They looked alright, they weren't particularly fancy or anything, but the fit was pretty good. She was scowling over the fit of the size 0 jeans she had on. It was hard to believe my daughter was developing into such a beautiful young lady. She was too slim for standard girl sizes and tall enough to fit lady's petite. Her hips were just starting to round out, which was quite obvious in the new jeans.

"They make my butt look big," she commented. "I don't like them."

I frowned at her. My butt was easily twice the size of hers. Rationally, I knew it should be; I'm twice her age. She had nothing to complain about, she was perfect.

"What are you talking about? They look great!"

Calleigh gave me a patronizing look that clearly indicated she thought otherwise. Of course, what would I know about fashion? I was only her mother.

"I hate that I went up a size," she sighed, turning away from the mirror.

"I hate that I went up a size," I echoed. "You're supposed to be growing and filling out. You're not done growing yet, you know. Besides, you can hardly consider going from a double zero to a zero going *up* a size."

I'm guessing that was the wrong thing to say to my daughter as she nearly burst into tears. I was going to have a hard time getting used to the hormones that were obviously taking root. Between her body developing and her emotions erupting, it was like I had a totally different child to deal with.

"Calleigh, honey, you're beautiful," I insisted, but her tears continued to flow. This was far worse than dealing with a two-year-old's temper tantrum in a store. A two-year-old can be consoled with candy and hugs, teenagers not so much. I was mortified that I had made her cry like this.

"It's just that I'm already one of the tallest kids in my class," she hiccupped. "And no other girls have to wear a bra. Some of them do anyway, but they don't *have to*!"

"You should be glad for your height. It's not like you're going to be a giant, it's not in your genes. Aunt Melanie is the tallest female in both our families and she's only five-foot seven. That's actually considered to be average." I wasn't sure if she was even listening to me, but I felt compelled to continue. "As for the other, well you'll be grateful for that in a few years, trust me."

She glared at me before yanking open the change room curtain and disappearing from view. "I don't care about in a few years. I care about now," I heard her mutter as she changed into her regular clothes. When she emerged from the change room, she dumped a pile of rolled up jeans into my arms and walked out of the store without a word. So much for a fun afternoon of shopping and mother-daughter time...

Apologetically, I handed the rolled-up bundle to the sales lady and proceeded to chase after Calleigh. From behind me, I could hear someone calling to me frantically, but I didn't stop to listen. My daughter was far more important than anyone in that store. As I exited the doors, alarm bells went off, followed by a rainbow of flashing lights.

I was going to kill her. My mortification at her emotional outburst in the dressing room quickly turned to outrage at her adolescent eruption and the consequent display I made of myself as I chased after her. She didn't care that I was horribly embarrassed by her behaviour; she was already halfway down the corridor of the mall. In fact, she was so self-absorbed she didn't even look back to see what all the commotion was about.

"I'm sorry ma'am," the sales lady said breathlessly when she caught up to me. "But you need to pay for those jeans, or take them off."

Part of me wanted to take them off right there in the middle of the mall corridor. Let them all get a good look at my granny-panties and butt-jiggle while I chased after my distraught daughter; at least then there would be something worth staring at. Rather than take the time to change, I hastily paid for the jeans, gathered up my old clothes, impatiently waited for the sales lady to remove the security tag and then went in search of my troubled daughter.

Calleigh wasn't far. She had just made her way to a nearby bench, where she sat with her head buried in her lap. My heart was breaking for her. I remembered being about the same age and not wanting to grow up. Quietly I sat down beside her and just waited for her to acknowledge my presence. I watched the crowds wander past: teenage girls in groups of five or six, mothers with small children, young couples holding hands—in general, happy people. We were supposed to have been among the happy people today, but somewhere along the way it all went wrong.

Finally, Calleigh lifted her tear stained face and gave me a long, hard look. "I'm sorry," she mumbled. I guess she figured she was in trouble because she quickly looked away and started fidgeting with the strap of her little purse.

"It's ok, sweetheart. Why don't we go get some ice cream and then call it a day?"

Calleigh shook her head, "I'm not very hungry, but you go ahead if you want it."

I remembered the shopping trips where she begged me for ice cream as a special treat for behaving so well.

Maybe she felt her behaviour was unworthy of the sweet treat. "C'mon, my treat," I insisted.

But Calleigh held her ground, "Really, mom, I just want to go home now. You can't fix everything with ice cream; I'm not a little kid anymore."

I sighed. Ok, we would go home and I would indulge in ice cream there and try to figure out what was going on in my daughter's head. My return to work and Chris's more frequent absences were no doubt taking their toll on Calleigh. She was accustomed to having two doting parents on hand at all times, with all the changes over the past few weeks, she was probably feeling as though she barely had one.

It turns out that the apple diet does work, sort of. Just as the internet advertisement claimed, one apple before every meal does fill you up. Of course, you have to remember to bring apples with you wherever you go. It was easier to keep a supply of them at work than to lug the cumbersome things back and forth. The only problem was that I had officially become the apple lady. Whenever someone was looking for a tasty treat, outside of donuts and pastries, they would stop by my desk to snag an apple. One at a time, it didn't seem like all that much. But one at a time, up to ten times a day, meant a daily walk to the market. Upon arriving, Lucy and I would purchase a variety so that we were sure to please everyone: Red Delicious, Golden Delicious, Granny Smith, Spartan, McIntosh, Royal Gala, Lobo. You name it; we bought it. But it all disappeared so very fast.

The constant foot traffic was wreaking havoc in my work space. I'm easily distracted, and with so many visitors on a daily basis my productivity dropped considerably. Because I'm such a stickler for deadlines; I ended up bringing home a ton of work.

Poor Calleigh now had to deal with me actually leaving the house every morning and then being unavailable to her at night. Not that she wanted to spend much time with me; she usually disappeared to her room to attend to homework. She had an awful lot of it these days.

The other thing was the daily apple run was eating into my grocery budget. Now, don't get me wrong, I make a decent salary, and sharing some living expenses with Chris was helpful, but still—I wasn't earning enough to feed the entire office building.

"Why don't you ask them to replace the donuts and pastries with fruit platters instead?" Lucy suggested as we hiked our way up to the market. "We could still get our daily walk in to the market to pick them up. And the fruit platters from here must be less expensive than the boxes of bakery items they bring in everyday."

I shook my head. I felt I was far too junior an employee to suggest even subtle changes to the office environment.

"I'm not so sure they would go for that. A lot of people go looking for the pastries. And I still enjoy a donut or Danish during early morning meetings."

"I'm just saying," Lucy continued, ignoring my protest, "that it would be a good idea to suggest. Maybe they could alternate? Or order in half baking, half fruit? At the very least, I'm pretty sure they could handle an apple budget."

"Or, we could figure out approximately how much one apple costs and just put a jar beside the bowl and hope that everyone contributes. It's less than fifty cents an apple. . ."

"You could try that, but people in this office aren't used to paying for their treats."

That was true. "The bigger problem is that the apples are living on my desk; which is completely against the rules."

She laughed at that. "If anyone has a problem with that, I'm sure they would have mentioned something to you by now. Even Carl has come by to sneak an apple, and he's head-honcho."

"No, he didn't," I said. "I would have noticed if he came by my cubicle." Not only would I have noticed, I probably would have had a panic attack!

"He did," she insisted. "I think you were in a meeting, or maybe in the bathroom. Anyway, if you just ask I'm sure he'll agree it's a good idea."

"Yeah, well, I'm still considering moving the apples to the staff room."

"You know what will happen if you do that?"

I looked at her quizzically and shook my head. I had no idea.

"You'll forget about them. You'll go for lunch and just devour everything in sight because you didn't have your preventive medicine."

"Nah, I wouldn't forget." She was crazy. I hadn't forgotten all week. I was starting to get a little sick of apples, even with all the variety we had been purchasing, but this was by far the easiest diet I had ever heard of. No special preparation, no counting calories and no starving yourself.

She gave me a look that clearly stated she didn't believe me. "I'm starting to get to know you, and I have a feeling you're the 'out of sight—out of mind', kind of person."

"Well then, I guess you don't know me very well yet, do you?" I shot back. I would show her, I would continue this apple diet and be as slim and trim as she was by summer. Lucky for me I had several months to go.

"Come on, Calleigh, you have to have more than a salad," I insisted. We were sitting in what had to be the noisiest section of *East Side Mario's*. It was Friday night, and I had thought it would be a nice idea for Calleigh and me to go out for dinner so that we could perhaps start to reconnect. After last weekend's episode in the mall I had hardly seen her. I wasn't sure if she was angry with me, or just too embarrassed to be in the same room with me. Besides, we deserved our mother-daughter time in a nice little restaurant.

"I'm not very hungry," she insisted. We both loved this restaurant, the noise of the crowd, the garlicky smells and the crazy decor. Normally she ordered a plate of pasta, complete with salad and garlic bread. Tonight, she only wanted the salad and a glass of water.

Well, I was ordering a good dinner. I had behaved all week, making sure I had an apple before every meal and only indulging in one donut or pastry each day. The description had insisted you needn't change anything in your usual routine; just add the apple before the meal. It had been easy to follow; almost too easy. Not to mention, I had added a daily walk to my formerly non-existent exercise routine. I was due for a little pampering tonight.

"Well, I'm having Cheese Cappelletti," I announced. I had been craving it for weeks now and decided that I finally deserved the treat.

"You always have that," Calleigh commented with a smile. Something about her tonight wasn't right.

She was quieter than usual, almost subdued.

Before I could ask if anything was bothering her, the waiter arrived. He was an attractive young man, probably in his early twenties with dark hair and flashing dark eyes. His smile lit up the room and certainly did wonders for Calleigh's disposition when he directed it at her. Maybe that was the problem. Maybe there was a boy at school she was having troubles with. I wasn't sure if I was ready to deal with all the complications and heartache of boyfriends. Why, oh why did my little girl have to be growing up?

In the end, Calleigh did order a Mediterranean salad which looked plentiful and quite delicious. It was a meal by itself, which made me feel better about her food choice.

"Mom, can I ask you something?"

Uh oh, I thought, here it comes. She is going to ask me about whatever is bother her and I am going to have to be the all-knowing mom and give her sound advice.

"Of course, sweetheart, you can ask me anything. You know that."

"When you met Daddy. . ." it was definitely going to be a boy question. Mentally, I prepared myself with an appropriate answer. ". . . were you chunky?"

"Huh?" the sound just escaped my lips without warning. So, she wasn't ready to open up to me after all, she just wanted to know about my own weight issues. Quickly, I tried to cover up my blunder with a chuckle. "Calleigh, when you're only five-foot three, you tend to be curvier than the average person. I guess you could call it chunky if you wanted. You've seen pictures."

The truth of the matter is that I hadn't been all that chunky. I had certainly weighed significantly less than I do now, at least twenty to thirty pounds less.

"I know that I need to lose some weight now, and I'm working on it."

Calleigh looked pointedly at my cheese stuffed, cheese smothered, cheese dusted pasta and then looked back up at me. Her clear blue eyes said it all. She was embarrassed by her chubby mommy.

"I am working on it," I insisted. "Everyone deserves a treat once in a while."

"Right," was all she said.

So much for having a heart to heart conversation with my daughter. She picked through her salad, glancing occasionally at my plate of pasta. I would have liked to say I lost my appetite, but my disappointment in our evening out together overrode my hunger filters and I ended up devouring my entire plate, along with a hearty helping of chocolate mousse cake for dessert.

Menu du Jour

Breakfast: apple, yogurt, toast, cup of coffee

Mid-morning snack: donut, coffee

Lunch: gigantic apple, Deli Sandwich

Mid-afternoon snack: apple

Supper: Cheese Cappelletti, chocolate cake, small dose of humility

Evening snack: popcorn

Total Calories consumed: 1858 (thought it would be more because of self-indulgence)

Total Calories burnt: 1426.75 + 79 (for walking) = 1505.5 (does being hurt by your daughter because she is embarrassed by you burn extra calories?)

Chapter Six

Beware the Thunder Thighs

I love weekends. Especially when there is nothing in particular that needs to be done. I putter around in my pyjamas until well after noon; watch a bit of home improvement television; fold a couple loads of laundry; maybe read a few chapters of my favourite book. When Calleigh was little we would sprawl on the floor together, engrossed in princess colouring books or dressing Barbie in the latest fashions. Thinking about her curled up with her little bottom sticking up in the air; clad in pink Polly Pocket PJ's brought a wistful smile to my face. I did miss those days. Until recently we would even curl up on the couch together, sharing a blanket, each of us engrossed in our own book.

Today, however, was not one of those lazy Saturdays. My parents were coming for dinner. That meant the house needed cleaning top to bottom, groceries needed to be purchased and a four-star dinner cooked up to perfection. I love my parents, but they have standards that had to be met. Once, when Damian and I were first married, we made the colossal mistake of inviting them over and ordering in Chinese food. To this day they still talk about the poor service, the cold noodles and the headache they both developed as a result of all the MSG. I learnt my lesson after that one dinner—my parents expected home cooked.

But not just any home cooked meal, it had to be good, almost professional quality cooking. No cheap ingredients, no slapped together stir-fries. They felt they were entitled to roasted potatoes, braised beef, steamed vegetables, fancy salads and decadent desserts. The more dirty pots and pans to scour, the better the meal would be. I learned early on it was better to invite them on a Saturday so that I could spend the Sunday cleaning up the kitchen aftermath.

"So, what are we cooking up today?" Chris asked as she sauntered into the kitchen. She had been out until well after midnight, yet looked fresh and ready for the day. As usual, we had planned that she would get the groceries while Calleigh and I scoured the house. Of course, Calleigh had yet to make an appearance this morning, so I had a feeling I would be doing the cleaning on my own for this visit.

"I haven't decided on a menu yet. Is there anything in particular you would like?"

Chris shook her head, "Nope, you know me, as long as I don't have to cook it myself, it's all good."

Great. Cleaning, planning and cooking all on my own. What a fabulous way to spend my Saturday. The chores weren't what disappointed me; it was the alone part that I couldn't stand. I have a pretty solitary job where I sit alone for most of the day. At home, I like to be surrounded by family. One of the benefits of having Chris live with u s meant there was always adult company in the house.

"Fine, I'll flip through my books and see what I can come up with," I sighed. Chris poured herself a cup of coffee and refreshed mine before sitting across from me with her bowl of Froot Loops. I did wish I had her metabolism; she could eat like a kid and never face any consequences.

Calleigh slugged her way into the kitchen, looking around her with half-dazed, sleepy eyes before depositing herself on a chair and flopping over on the table like a rag-doll. Her hair spilled across the table in a waterfall of blond silk.

"If you're so tired, why don't you go back to bed?" Chris said to her through a mouthful of crunchy cereal. Not only did Chris eat kid-foods, she also had kid manners. No wonder she was still single.

Calleigh lifted her head just enough to peer through her tangled mass of hair. "I have too much to do," she muttered, before plunking her head back onto the table, looking as though she had the weight of the world to carry on her shoulders.

"Right," I said with a bit of sarcasm. "A thirteen-year-old with too much to do? Wait until you're my age with real responsibilities."

She mumbled something unintelligible which I chose to ignore.

"Well, if you aren't going back to bed, get yourself some breakfast and you can help me with the clean-up. Grandma and Grandpa are coming over for supper."

I think she might have moaned; it was hard to tell with her face buried in her arms.

"Come on, Calleigh, we really don't have time for your dramatics today."

That got her attention and she jerked her head up in a motion that must have made her dizzy with its abruptness. "I told you have I have a lot to do," she insisted. "I'm just going to grab a yogurt and then get to work on my project."

I looked at her quizzically. "I thought you finished your project."

"I did," she looked me straight in the eye, "and now I have another one. I told you, I have the teacher from hell."

"What is this one on? Maybe Aunt Chris or I could help you?" Having a teacher in the house did have its advantages. The two of them already had a special bond, probably because Chris didn't have any children of her own.

"It's French. Aunt Chris doesn't speak French, and neither do you, so it's not likely either of you can help me much." She stood up and stretched and I noticed that she must have grown yet again. Her Pyjama bottoms gaped slightly at the waist, and were floating above her ankles. Too bad last week's shopping spree had been cut short; she was going to need new clothes soon if she kept sprouting up like this.

"Okay, then. Get yourself organized, eat, shower, and get some work done. School is important but so is this family, so I expect you to be your bright and sunny self when your grandparents arrive at four."

She shrugged her shoulders, grabbed a low-fat yogurt from the fridge and disappeared to her room. I should be glad that she is so concerned with doing well in school, but something about her attitude was niggling at me. Oh well, I didn't have time to sort it out right now, I had family to entertain and only a few hours to prepare.

"Just look at you, Calleigh," my mom exclaimed as she walked into the house, dropped her purse at the entrance and immediately enveloped my daughter in the kind of hug only a grandma could get away with.

Calleigh returned the hug with much less enthusiasm.

"Oh," my mom pulled away for a second and took another good look at her granddaughter. "You're nothing but skin and bones! We need to fatten you up a bit with a good dinner!"

I smiled at my mom. It was just like her to come into the house and take command over everyone and everything, all the while blatantly ignoring her hosts. She hadn't even acknowledged Chris and me standing in the entrance.

My dad gave me a warm hug. The smell of his aftershave was overpowering, but that was all part of his charm.

"Smells good," he commented. Although how he could smell the roast lamb over his own overwhelming scent was beyond me.

"Thanks, Dad." I ushered them into the living room where Chris had already started to poor drinks for everyone: Cosmos for mom, Chris and me, whisky for himself. Calleigh was treated to a soft drink in a fancy glass, as she had been since she was a toddler. As an only child, she was very adult oriented and had always been included in the pre-dinner drink ritual.

"How's school going for you? Into report cards yet?" my dad asked Chris after taking an appreciated sip of his drink.

Chris shrugged her shoulders in response. "Well, to be honest work has been a bit overwhelming lately. Lots of late nights with extra-curricular activities. I'll be happy for spring break to come around."

Dad nodded, as though he had a complete understanding of all things academic, when he had barely completed high school before finding his first factory job.

Dad turned to Calleigh who was still being smothered by my mother. "And how's my girl?"

Calleigh smiled at her grandfather. There had always been a special kind of bond between them. "I'm good.

But school is crazy right now."

Dad nodded in understanding. "You just keep on doing what you're doing and I know you'll be fine in the end," he encouraged.

Calleigh placed her untouched soda on the table before taking a seat on the arm of the sofa. There was a time when she would have downed the soda and asked for seconds before anyone else had even touched their drinks. She was turning into a young lady.

The conversation was probably boring for her. Dad had started to discuss politics with Chris and mom was interjecting where she felt appropriate. I decided to give Calleigh a break. "You can take your drink into the other room and watch TV until supper time," I whispered in her ear.

She looked up at me gratefully, and very quietly left the room. No one noticed her leave; although I did notice she forgot her soft drink on the table.

My parents were their usual talkative selves. They chatted about their neighbours, friends and people I had known while growing up. They were genuinely interested in our own daily lives and routines and much of the conversation centered on our careers and Calleigh's interests.

"Roxanne, there is something different about you that I just can't put my finger on," my dad insisted as he piled sour cream onto his baked potato. "There's a glow about you. You're not pregnant, are you?"

I nearly choked on my wine when I heard those words. Did I look pregnant? "Do I look pregnant?" I asked in disbelief.

"Well, honey, what your father means to say is that your complexion is nice and clear. You've always been on the portly side, so it's a natural assumption."

Horrified, I was torn between fleeing the table like a distressed teenager and wailing in protest like a temperamental toddler. Before I could explode Chris decided to intercede.

"Roxy has been trying to lose weight. The glow you see is just the natural effects of daily walks and healthy foods." This wasn't exactly the kind of help I had been expecting.

I wasn't sure if I should be grateful for what sort of sounded like a compliment, or mortified that Chris had pointed out my intentions while I, myself had loaded my plate with calorie laden nourishment. My cheeks had started to lose their flushed, angry feel, only to flare up again in mortification.

"Is that so?" my dad asked. "You always were a pudgy little thing. But so cute, with those pinchable cheeks."

"Oh, Dick, remember that name her cousins used to call her... now what was it... sort of made me chuckle a bit every time I heard it." My mom was laughing softly to herself now, oblivious to the fact that I was definitely not laughing. "Something like thick thighs..."

"No, no... it was more like ample ass." Thank you, Chris, for that one, I thought wryly.

"Oh! I know!" my mom crowed, waving her fork in the air for emphasis. "It was Thunder Thighs!"

The adults at the table were all peeling with laughter, oblivious to the fact that this was not a happy reminiscence for me. Calleigh was strangely silent, either not listening or horrified that she might be following the same path as her mother.

"Thanks, Mom," I said, forcing my voice to be steady when what I really wanted to do was screech at her for being so insensitive. "What I remember most, was asking you to tell them all to stop, and your turning to your brother and sister and repeating the horrible name. And then all of you laughing at me."

"Oh, honey, we weren't laughing at you," she insisted as she patted her eyes with her napkin. She had been laughing so hard her eyes were tearing up. "We were only laughing at the creativity of the name they came up with."

"Right," I said. "Anyway, that was years and years ago. And for the record, I was not fat as a child. It wasn't exactly my fault the rest of the cousins were giraffe-like in height which made them look so skinny in comparison."

"No, you weren't fat, exactly," my dad agreed. "Always a bit on the chunky side, but definitely not fat."

"Lucky for Calleigh she's more like the rest of the family: tall and slim," my mother pointed out. "She won't have to deal with any weight issues."

"I didn't have any issues," I protested. Well, no issues other than the name-calling episode one summer when cut-off jean short shorts were very popular and I made the mistake of trying to wear them.

My mom looked at me knowingly.

"There was one other thing that seemed to be a bit of an issue, dear," she insisted. Her eyes travelled from my face to my ample bosom. I had forgotten about that. By age eleven I had been forced into wearing bra. It had been awful. I was the only girl in grade five whose mother had taken her to the lingerie department of Sears and forced her to try on a multitude of scratchy, uncomfortable braziers, as my mother had called them.

"Well, Calleigh seems to be taking after you in the bosom department," he pointed out with raised eyebrows. My dad obviously didn't want to be left out of the conversation.

I couldn't believe he had just done that. Calleigh is a sensitive thirteen- year-old who is not at all comfortable with her body. My mom knew this as I had told her about last week's shopping episode. I assumed she would have had a conversation with my dad so that something like this wouldn't have been discussed in front of my daughter.

Calleigh looked up from her plate. She had done little more than push the food around on her plate and I couldn't say as I blamed her. I had lost my appetite with all this nonsense and that almost never happened.

"Dad, I think we should talk about something else now."

He waved his fork in Calleigh's general direction.

"Okay, but I can't help it if your daughter suddenly grew boobs. She certainly didn't look like that when we were here last month."

Before he had finished his sentence, Calleigh's fork landed on her plate with a noisy clatter and she ran from the room. I could see unshed tears glistening in her eyes.

My dad took a hefty mouthful of the roasted lamb and exclaimed, "What?" As if he didn't know.

Chris looked from me, to my parents, not sure of what to say. My mother was also speechless. While she had had no trouble ridiculing me, she drew the line at upsetting a child.

"Richard, we talked about this."

"Oh yeah," he said through another mouthful of food. "I forgot. Must be mad cow, or something."

I sighed. There wasn't much that could be done about it now. We would finish supper and then I would reheat Calleigh's dinner for her after my parents left. I was pretty sure she would be too discomfited to come out of her room while they were still here, and I didn't know if I had it in me to kick them out.

Menu du Jour

Breakfast: apple, bacon and eggs, coffee

Mid-morning snack: too busy cleaning to snack

Lunch: apple, grilled cheese sandwich, coffee

Mid-afternoon snack: too busy cooking supper to snack

Supper: roasted lamb, baked potatoes, glazed carrots and a huge helping of embarrassment

Evening snack: chocolate bar

Total Calories consumed: 1892

Total Calories burnt: 1426.75 (for being alive) + 895 (for cleaning the house & making a gourmet dinner) = 2321 (is it possible to burn more calories when you're angry?)

Chapter Seven

Super Sleuth

So here we are. Calleigh is distressed that Grandpa noticed she has boobs, and I'm dismayed that Grandma pointed out my thunder thighs. We are quite a pair. My parents were well-meaning, good people; they just hadn't put their best faces forward during dinner. We all knew they were a little rough around the edges, but last night had been jagged to the extreme.

"Calleigh's a tough kid," Chris said as she poured herself a cup of coffee. "She'll bounce back to her old self in no time."

I looked at her thoughtfully. The problem was, Calleigh hadn't been her old self in ages. In fact, I was beginning to believe that her old self had disappeared completely. She had very little contact with her friends, she spent most of her time hiding away in her room and she always looked stressed and tired. The more I thought about it, the more I began to piece things together. Her lack of appetite, her constant need for privacy, her strung out appearance… I think perhaps it was time for a search of her room. She was awfully young to be involved in drugs, but I had heard that kids were starting earlier and earlier.

Even though we had talked about the dangers, she was just a normal, curious girl. Under the right circumstances she could have been persuaded to try something. Maybe my return to work had been a lot more difficult for her than I thought it would be.

"You don't think she's on drugs, do you?" I asked Chris.

"Who? Our mother? If she isn't, then she should be!" She laughed at her own joke and didn't see that I was frowning at her. I was trying to be serious here.

"No, you dolt! Calleigh—all the signs are there ..."

Chris gave me a look that clearly said I had gone off the deep end. She ran a hand through her dark blond hair and sighed heavily. "You worry too much, Roxy. Calleigh isn't taking drugs. She's a good kid. I do think that she's stressing too much over school, but then she has always been like that."

I nodded. That was true. Even in grades one and two she would worry over her spelling tests being perfect. Sometimes she would worry so much she made her stomach ache. She just didn't seem very happy lately and I couldn't see a magic solution anywhere in sight.

"Well, it might not be drugs, but there's definitely something."

Calleigh chose to enter the kitchen at that ill-timed moment.

"Drugs? You think I'm on drugs?" Disbelief was written all over her face.

She walked over to the fridge and helped herself to a 0% milk fat, sugar-free yogurt. I didn't remember buying them, but maybe Chris had picked them up by mistake on her grocery run yesterday. They were the usual brand we bought, but the packaging was obviously different.

"No Calleigh," Chris interjected before I had a chance to respond to her. "Your mother does not think you're on drugs. She's just worried about you."

Calleigh shrugged her shoulders, "I'm fine."

"See, she's fine." One of the things I both love and hate about Chris is that she isn't a fan of conflict. This means she tries to smooth things over as quickly as possible. It also means that she has a tendency to gloss things over instead of digging deeper. Well, I was going to dig deeper and take a little hunt around that girl's room if she ever left it long enough so that I could.

I ended up taking a "sick day" in order to get access to Calleigh's room. I was afraid that if she knew I was going to be taking a peek, she would hide things that she might have otherwise left out as evidence. Of course, I didn't even know what I was looking for; I was just searching for a clue to where my daughter might be headed while travelling the road of adolescence. A part of me felt a tremendous sense of guilt over invading her privacy, but I just couldn't see any other way of figuring this out.

What I did find shattered my heart into a thousand tiny fragments.

At first glance, there was nothing unusual to note. Her bed was haphazardly made, with the pink comforter spilling onto the hardwood floor. Her dresser was a cluttered mess of barrettes, hair clips and head bands. A few pictures of her with her friends lined the mirror and I could see where she had been trying out a few different shades of make-up. She wasn't allowed to wear it to school, but I was all for practicing technique now so she wouldn't look like a clown later.

Her desk was very tidy and organized. All her papers were neatly stacked in baskets that were labelled with various projects she had on the go. The shelves above held the usual reference books, dictionaries, and a few outdated textbooks. On the floor beside her bed was a small pile of trade paperbacks she was probably working her way through in her spare time. She always had been an avid reader. Although her closet doors were closed, I imagined I would find a disarray of clothing falling off hangers and a mishmash of shoes littering the floor inside.

I was mildly surprised to see her closet was spotless on the inside. Shoes all neatly lined up, clothing hanging straight and sorted by colour. It all looked strange and at complete odds with the rest of her room.

Years ago, I had had custom shelving installed in an attempt to keep all the clutter under control. Calleigh's closest was a study of the little girl she had been and the young woman she was growing into. One shelf was overflowing with boxes of stuffed animals and beanie babies. They were so cute with their little heads peeking over the top. Another shelf held book series she had read over and over again: *The Magic Tree House, Narnia,* and *Little House on the Prairie* just to name a few. She was well past these books, but obviously wasn't ready to pass them on to charity.

I was about to shut the closet door when a shiny corner of a magazine page caught my eye. There was nothing particularly notable; I think it only attracted me because the torn page was so out of place in the otherwise orderly closet. My original intention was to toss it in the recycling, but the image on the page was mildly disturbing. It was of a young model, walking down a runway, scantily clad in lingerie. She was so thin her knee joints were wider than her upper thighs and you could literally count every rib that showed through the thin silk of the lacy top. Her cheeks were hollowed shadows and her eyes had a distant look of distraction and something else, maybe fear. It had to be the most awful picture I had ever seen.

Obviously, Calleigh didn't value the image or it wouldn't have been crumpled on her closet floor. To be certain there weren't more like it, I bent down on hands and knees and pulled at the first neatly labelled box. The tag read 'Research Projects', but the box was about a quarter full of torn out magazine pictures. They were all of young girls who were thin to the point of emaciation. In my mind, these images were grotesque and highly unappealing. The make-up was garish, highlighting the gauntness of the models' features. The clothing was skimpy, showcasing jutting corners where there should have been soft curves. Why on earth would Calleigh have these pictures? Was she doing a paper on anorexia?

I could barely stomach looking at these poor girls, but I found myself drawn to their images, unable to look away from the disaster they had made of their young bodies. I thought I had issues with being slightly overweight in my mid-life crisis. These girls were in crisis and they had barely begun their lives. Carefully, I placed the pictures back in the box with more care and respect than these girls have ever shown themselves. Until I knew for sure what I was dealing with, I didn't exactly want my daughter to know I had been snooping through her things.

Calleigh had received a lovely journal for her birthday from one of her best friends. Even though I knew with every fibre of my body reading it would be wrong, I was beginning to wonder if it might hold the key to what was going on in her head. I peered under her bed, which was an obvious hiding spot, but only found a few dirty socks and a discarded towel. Her desk drawers were equally empty of anything that might point me in the direction of her thoughts. I did notice another glossy page she had torn out of a cooking magazine. It was a recipe for some kind of soup. Strange that she would have kept something like that, but nothing to worry about, I was sure. It wasn't like it was an advertisement for diet pills or anything like that.

I had no clue where she had hidden her diary, and going on a full-scale search was not part of my plan. As concerned for my daughter as I was, I wasn't ready to throw thirteen years of trust into the trash just yet. She wasn't on drugs and as far as I could tell she wasn't doing anything illegal. She might be struggling with her body image because she was quickly approaching adolescence, and we would deal with that. Having an overweight mother probably wasn't helping either, but that was something I was addressing.

Remembering how I would often find her pyjamas stuck between the headboard and wall, I reached my hand in to see if there were any wayward bits of laundry there. Since I was home on a weekday, I fully intended to catch up on laundry and house work. May as well make the best of my sick day. I didn't find any clothing, but I did dislodge a scrap book that had been wedged back there. It fell to the ground with an audible thump that startled me.

I told myself I only found it because I was collecting laundry. I also insisted that I had not expected to find anything more than a pair of forgotten pyjamas. I wouldn't have looked at the contents of the book if it had landed on the ground shut, but the pages had flipped open and I just couldn't help myself.

The magazine pictures had been sad. This scrapbook was devastating. Calleigh had taken full length pictures of herself and replaced certain body parts with images cut from the magazines. Seeing her sweet, smiling face above the skeletal frame of an undernourished model made me gasp in shock. Why would she do that? Why would she want that? It didn't make any sense.

I flipped through the pictures, studying each one of them and willed myself not to cry. Some of the pages had notes scrawled down the sides; they were reflections of what she liked and what she didn't. There were a few ramblings about feelings and control. There were notes that could have been termed poetic except for the raw pain I saw reflected in the words. She couldn't possibly think she was fat, or in any way overweight, so what was the draw to all these images? I thought of all the times she had left the house with me thinking she had eaten breakfast and then I thought of all the times she had skipped supper because she just wasn't hungry, or wasn't feeling well. Did she even bother with lunch at all during the week? It had been eons since I had packed her a lunch; she was such an independent child.

I spent a good hour reflecting over where I might have gone wrong. I was hurting for her, but I did know that sitting on her bed crying wouldn't do her any good at all. I needed to come up with a plan so that this didn't progress any further than it already had. Thank goodness my Dad had mentioned her sprouting breasts last night. If he hadn't, it might have been weeks until I started to take her erratic behaviour more seriously. I only hoped that it wasn't too late.

I was sitting at the kitchen table with a plate of freshly baked, still steaming, chocolate chip cookies and two glasses of skim milk in front of me when Calleigh breezed through the door. She looked up, startled to see me home, and then put on what I could see was a brave smile. She knew I knew. I'm not sure how my brain made the connection, but I was certain she was aware I had been in her room.

"Hey, sweetheart," I said with my own false smile. "Come tell me about your day."

After hanging her jacket in the closet, she hesitantly took her customary seat at the table. The sweet smell of the cookies was driving me to distraction, so they must have been some kind of a temptation to a girl who had potentially been starving herself for the past few weeks.

I pushed the glass of milk towards her and offered her a cookie. Calleigh bit her lip and gingerly accepted the treat.

"Why are you home?" she asked. "Did you get fired?"

I laughed at that. "No, I took the day off. I woke up with a pounding headache and couldn't bear the thought of sitting in front of a computer all day. When I started to feel better I decided to give the house a good cleaning."

Calleigh nodded, and then took the smallest bite possible of her cookie. "It looks nice."

It was my turn to nod. "It does. I was pleased with how clean your room was, I hardly had to do anything at all. Just cleaned out some laundry from under the bed and straightened up your dresser a bit. When did you become she such a neat freak?"

Her blue eyes were beginning to take on a troubled expression. "I've always kept my room pretty clean. Maybe now that I'm older there is just less to manage."

"Maybe," I agreed. I reached behind my back and gently placed the scrapbook in front of her. "I found this when I was cleaning, it fell from behind your headboard." It was a partial truth, it had fallen and that's all she needed to know.

A look of pure panic played across her beautiful features. She was like a deer caught in headlights and didn't know which way to turn.

"I'm not going to pretend I know anything about what might be going on in your head," I said to her in all sincerity. "I only know that it broke my heart to look through it. This isn't a healthy body image."

Tears started to slip down Calleigh's cheeks. I wanted to pull her close and wipe them away for her, but I had a feeling that it wouldn't do either one of us any good.

"I'm sorry, mom," she whispered. I could tell she wanted to flee, but her sanctuary had been disturbed and she had no other place to run.

"So am I," I returned softly. I could feel the burn of my own tears threatening.

"I'll stop." It couldn't be that easy, could it? "I haven't been starving myself; I don't think I have the will-power." For good measure, she took a big bite of the cookie, chewed slowly and swallowed it down.

"I know, but you are well on your way. Being too thin isn't healthy, or attractive." I looked at her pointedly, almost daring her to point out my own weight flaws. "So, from now on you're going to eat breakfast and supper with me. No more hiding in your room or telling me you already ate. As for lunch, I think we'll start packing that the night before, so I know that it's done."

Calleigh nodded. "Okay." She polished off the cookie and glass of milk. "Can I go now?"

I shrugged. I didn't have anything else to say just now. We would talk more later when we were both ready. Calleigh took my shrug as a yes. Although she glanced longingly at her scrapbook she left it on the table before disappearing to her room. I was sure she was taking an inventory of all that I might have seen or disturbed. Although I had searched the rest of her room more carefully after discovering the scrapbook I hadn't found anything else that would indicate she had gone too far. I just hope I wasn't too late in my discovery.

Calleigh's Menu du Jour

Breakfast: 0%, no sugar added yogurt

Morning snack: water

Lunch: apple, salad

After school snack: 1 chocolate chip cookie, 1 glass of skim milk

Supper: 1 chicken drumstick (no skin), a bit of rice, left-over glazed carrots

Dessert: banana

Calories consumed: 368—a growing teenager needs a minimum of 1800 a day to stay healthy Calories burnt: 1826 just breathing.

Chapter Eight

Peering Through the Fog

As I drove into work, the fog lifting from the snow created that eerie grey effect you only see in horror movies. After yesterday, I was beginning to wonder if my world was turning into one big horrific event. Logically, I knew that force-feeding my daughter a chocolate chip cookie was not going to make the problem go away. If anything, I might have made it worse. Although, when I studied her closely this morning, she was her usual spunky self. She looked healthy. Her skin glowed; her hair was silky and shiny. Although a little on the thin side, she had curves where a growing adolescent should. She had always been one of those awkward skinny kids, so I didn't expect to see any excess weight on her. Maybe it was something that had caught her attention, but had quickly lost its appeal. The magazine clippings had been at the bottom of her closet, and the scrapbook looked as though it had been abandoned behind her headboard. It had even grown a layer of dust along the spine that had been facing upwards.

"You look like you're a million miles away," Lucy said as I came into the office. "And you're late."

I smiled. At least one thing in my life was consistent. "I know. I'll be late for a while; which means I'll be staying late."

Lucy looked at me quizzically, but didn't say anything. That was one of the things I was quickly growing to like and respect about her. She didn't pry. She was curious, and I think she was genuinely concerned, but she wasn't going to try to drag anything out of me if I wasn't ready to share.

"I replenished the apple bowl yesterday, but they went fast," she said as she took a Golden Delicious and sank her teeth into it with relish.

I looked at the bowl which was just a symbol of my desperate attempt of tricking myself into believing I was in control of my own weight situation. This wasn't a diet plan. It was fun and had created a social atmosphere in a place that had been boring and dry. It had helped me to find my place in this office environment, but let's face it— my weight wasn't going to budge by eating apples.

"I see that," I said with a wry smile. "I guess that means another trip back today."

"Yup."

I nodded, switched on my computer and opened my drawer in search of the file I was supposed to be working on. "Okay then, let's get to work so we have time to go."

Lucy hopped off my desk in a fluid, athletic motion. "See you a few," she said as she slipped around the cubicle walls to her own side. Soon after, I heard the steady clicking of her keyboard as she set to work on her own document.

Unexpectedly, her head popped up over the cubicle wall, startling me out of my reverie. "You know, when you're ready, I'm all ears."

I smiled up at her—she must have been standing on her desk to be able to lean over the top like that.

"Thanks," I said with genuine appreciation. "Now get down, before you fall down. I'll see you at lunch."

"You need a stress release," Lucy commented as we marched up to the market. The walk didn't feel nearly as cumbersome as it had a week ago. Maybe I was getting into better shape, although I couldn't imagine a daily walk would have that much effect already.

"I do," I sighed. "Up until now, my stress release has been chocolate, popcorn, chips… not very good choices."

"You could come to Yoga with me."

I shook my head. My body was not designed for Yoga. I'm pretty sure my arms and legs were far too short to contort themselves into pretzel-like positions. "I don't know; I don't really have much time right now."

At least that was a complete truth. I didn't have that much time. I would be coming in late every day so I could ensure Calleigh had a decent breakfast and a packed lunch. After work, I would be rushing home to make sure she had a healthy supper. I couldn't monitor her in-take all day, and I didn't want to become overbearing, but there were small changes we could make as a family that might help. I had wrongly assumed that my daughter was ready for her independence, but I was beginning to think I had let go just a bit too soon.

"It's an hour-long class, I go Monday evenings." Lucy had picked up her pace and I matched it, although I was now breathing a bit harder.

"Let me talk to Chris and see what her schedule is like, maybe she won't mind helping out a bit," I answered.

Yoga might not be such a bad idea. If it were in the evening I might be able to squeeze it in. There wasn't anything good on television Monday nights anyway. "What time is it at?"

"Oh, it's pretty early. It starts at 7:30. We finish by 8:30 and then you're free for the evening. I think you would like it. It's just stretching and relaxing."

I nodded. I could use some stretching and relaxing. "Hmmm… I'll think about it."

My drive home was similar to my drive into work. As I peered through the fog, all I could focus on was how to fix things with Calleigh. When I had talked to Chris about it, she had shrugged it off as just an adolescent phase; something Calleigh had got caught up in with her friends for a short time and that like all other stages in life, it would pass—no real harm done. I felt I didn't know enough about it to determine exactly what it was at this point.

"You know mom, leaving a plate of cookies and a glass of milk already poured in the fridge isn't going to help," Calleigh said to me as I walked into the house. I had planned to be home before her, but my meeting had run late so she had had about an hour to herself before I walked in the door.

"Well, hello to you too," I said in reply as I hung up my jacket. "And how was your day?"

Calleigh scowled at me and returned to her task at the table. I was surprised to see her doing homework in the kitchen. Lately, she had been hiding out in her bedroom after school and avoiding me. Maybe I couldn't fix things with a plate of homemade treats, but I was doing something right. Part of me wanted to remind her she would have to clean up her mess before supper, but the sane part of me knew that a comment like that would only serve to push her away.

"I don't understand why we have all these ridiculous projects," she complained. "It's too much work."

I glanced over her shoulder to take a peek at what she was working on. It was a simple research project on environmental change. There sure was going to be some environmental changes in this house. I frowned as I read over the directions.

"It's a group project," I pointed out the obvious. "Are you each doing your own part at home and then getting together on the weekend to put it all together?"

Calleigh shook her head. "Nope. I got permission to do it alone. I don't like group work and having to rely on someone else. And then, when they don't do their part, I have to share their bad mark? No thanks."

That made sense, but still, in the real world there was group work everywhere. My job, as solitary as it could be, was all about group work. For now, I would let it go. We had other battles to deal with.

"Want to help me make supper?" I asked. When she was very small, Calleigh used to love to help me in the kitchen. She would put on her frilly pink apron and stand beside me on her princess stool. I would give her a vegetable peeler and she would chatter away while peeling her one carrot. She was also very good at stirring sauces and pouring batter. We hadn't talked about much of anything, but it was time spent together with giggles and love. Afterwards, she would devour whatever we had made. The whole process had been a great way to get her to try new things because she always wanted to be the first to try her concoctions.

"I have a lot to do," Calleigh insisted, gesturing towards her papers.

"So, do I," I countered. "If we do this together, supper will be on the table that much faster and we can both get back to our work. We might even have time to watch some TV together."

I could tell by her expression that she wanted to argue, but she also knew that after what I found in her room yesterday she was walking on thin-ice.

"I guess I could give you fifteen minutes," she offered as she stacked her papers and books into a haphazard pile.

As I started to pull ingredients out of the fridge I could feel Calleigh watching me closely. My plan was to make a hearty lasagna and salad. We would throw everything together and then pop it into the oven so it would be ready when Chris got home. It was cold and damp outside and I was craving the comfort food of pasta.

"You know mom," Calleigh started hesitantly. She was chewing on her bottom lip, a new habit that clearly indicated she was nervous. "I don't really feel like lasagna tonight."

I took my head out of the fridge. I could just imagine the view she had of my derriere sticking out past the fridge door while my head was buried inside searching for the ricotta cheese. "Too bad." I returned to my search. Lasagne just wasn't the same without all the different kinds of cheeses.

"It's so heavy, and greasy," she whined.

I handed her a head of Romaine lettuce, "Here, clean the lettuce for me."

I wasn't arguing with Calleigh about food. She would eat what was put in front of her and that was that. I didn't expect her to eat like a line backer for the Montreal Alouettes, but did expect her to have a decent meal with her family.

Calleigh sighed and marched over to the sink. I heard the thud of the lettuce as she practically threw the vegetable into the sink. Her temper was by far easier to take than her storming off to her room. I should have been frustrated; instead I was happy that she wasn't running off to hide from me.

I started chopping the vegetables to add to the meat sauce. We worked in silence, but at least we were together. Every so often, Calleigh would nibble on a piece of lettuce, or pop a mushroom in her mouth. When she was younger she would have gone straight for the grated cheese, which is what I was snacking on. Maybe she was grazing because she knew I was watching her, or maybe she was grazing because she was genuinely hungry. I had no idea, I was just glad to see that while she had passed on the plate of cookies, she was munching away on veggies.

Once the lasagna was tucked away in the oven, I set to work cleaning the kitchen while Calleigh resumed work on her project. She was a bit of a workaholic, my daughter. From what I had gleaned when I had looked over her work she was nearly finished all the research. She still had a week come to complete the good copy and hand it in. In a way, I wished I worked more like she did; I had a very bad habit of leaving things to the last minute.

"Something smells fabulous," Chris announced as she walked through the front door. Anyone looking in through the frosty windows would see a blurred image of perfection. The table was set, Calleigh was curled up on the sofa reading a book, I was sitting at my desk working on a cross word and Chris was home with her usual infectious smile. I had even turned on the little gas fireplace to help chase away some of the chill that had settled into the house. In all, it was a very cheery scene.

"Lasagna," Calleigh said without looking up from her book. "Mom and I made it together."

"Lasagna is one of my favourites, especially when it's made by my favourite niece." She looked up at me as if to say, 'I told you so', then tousled Calleigh's hair so that it fell into her eyes and obscured her view. Calleigh just ignored her aunt's playfulness and returned her attention to her book.

I put my pen down and stood up and stretched. Why was it she could get away with teasing while I had to take care of all the serious stuff? I wasn't going to ponder that just now. I was starving. Forcing myself to exert self-control and not snack on junk food while the delicious smell of the lasagna permeated the house had just about driven me insane.

I opened the oven and a hot, burst of heat escaped, quickly followed by a billow of steam. The smell of supper intensified and my stomach rumbled in appreciation of the meal to come. As much as I was anticipating the delicious dinner, I was also looking forward to having some peaceful family time. I waved away the steam and placed the lasagne pan on top of the stove. Calleigh was right; it was a rather greasy looking meal. The oils from the cheeses had separated and floated to the top. It would taste fabulous, but it made me think of all the extra calories that were probably lurking in what I had previously thought was a relatively healthy meal.

I left the lasagna to settle while we enjoyed our Caesar salad. Calleigh had done a great job with it, as good as any restaurant.

"This is fabulous, Calleigh."

She smiled and took another bite of lettuce. She had insisted on using a low-fat recipe she had tucked away in her room. My initial thought had been, no way, but then I had decided that it was only salad dressing and why shouldn't she use a recipe of her choice. I didn't know that low-fat could taste so good.

Chris nodded her approval, "It is good."

Had anyone decided to peek through that misty window they would have seen a loving family relishing a perfectly prepared supper. They might have even been envious that we were smiling and chatting and obviously enjoying each other's company. That is, until the main course was served.

Calleigh took one look at the lasagne and declared, "I'm not eating that."

I looked at her steadily, but refused to acknowledge her statement.

"Why not? It smells delicious." Chris didn't know to leave things well enough alone. I had only planned on serving her a small piece. I had watched her fill up on salad so I knew what she was up to.

"Just look at all the grease floating on the top," Calleigh pointed out. "What's the point in using extra lean ground beef if you're going to use all those fatty cheeses? I can feel my arteries hardening just looking at it." She gave a little shudder to help illustrate her revulsion.

Chris pondered her statement for a moment. Her next words made me want to throw the entire dish at her. "I see what you mean, sweetheart."

I took a deep breath. There was nothing wrong with this lasagne. It was the same recipe I had been using for at least ten years, and they both loved it. Calleigh gave me such a look of satisfaction I was ashamed to admit I wanted to slap her.

"Maybe you could use low-fat cheese next time," Chris suggested. I'm guessing she didn't realize that I was getting more and more upset by the second. Being my twin, you would think she would be more in tune to my emotions.

"It's for your own good, mom," Calleigh piped in. "Just like you want me to be healthy, I want you to be healthy too."

I had completely lost my appetite. Was this what all this was about? She was worried about my health. I was healthy; I had even been to the doctor who had said there was nothing wrong with me.

"Besides, if we all keep eating like this, we'll be as big as elephants," she insisted.

I bit my lip and refused to answer. So that was the real issue. She wasn't worried about me on a personal level. She was worried that she might end up like me.

I dished out moderate servings of the lasagna and practically threw the plates at my family. "This is dinner.

Take it or leave it, I don't really care."

My anger must have registered with both of them on some level, because they chose to take it, in silence.

From outside that foggy window, we still looked like a perfect family. You just needed to look a tiny bit closer and you would be able to see all our flaws.

Menu du Jour

Breakfast: apple, yogurt, granola bar, coffee

Mid-morning snack: banana

Lunch: apple, Deli sandwich, tart

Mid-afternoon snack: couple handfuls of goldfish crackers

Supper: Caesar Salad, Lasagne

Dessert: a hefty helping of frustration & anger

Evening snack: popcorn Total Calories consumed: 1776

Total Calories burnt: 1426.75 + 79 (for walking) = 1505.5

Jennifer Bogart

Chapter Nine

Through the Looking Glass

Could it be possible that Calleigh was afraid of growing up and turning into me? I thought back to when I was a child. How many times did I say I would never be like my own mother? But I had usually threatened that in terms of her parenting skills, not her looks. I don't think I had ever registered that my mom may have looked any different than a mom should.

That brought me to the question of whether or not Calleigh was ashamed of me. I know I need to lose some weight, I have a mirror and it talks to me every day. I know that I am not the most attractive woman in the world, perhaps a little on the plain side, and probably not all that fascinating. But I'm not that bad either. However, the more I looked at myself through the reflection of Calleigh's eyes, the less I wanted to be me. I just didn't think there was all that much I could do to change the situation. Perhaps if she had two parental role models instead of just me, she might see things differently.

For as long as I could I remember I had struggled with my weight. My own twin is taller, slimmer and far more vibrant. Calleigh takes after her in physical build and height, which was a good thing. She did get the best of the best when it came to the more attractive genetic traits of her parents.

I stood in front of my floor length mirror, naked, contemplating my portly image. Starting with my toes; short and stubby—they were a prelude for the rest of my body. I had never been able to wear those sexy knee-high boots as my calves were just too chunky. My thighs, well, 'thunder thighs' was a pretty apt term despite its cruelty. With age, and probably inactivity, they had developed that lumpy bumpy look from cellulite deposits. I couldn't remember the last time I willingly wore a short skirt or shorts that didn't reach all the way to my knees. Who would want to get an eyeful of cottage cheese as I jiggled my way down the street on a hot summer day?

Hips are aptly named, for mine certainly make me look more like a hippo than a woman. The one good thing about having wide hips is that they narrowed nicely into the curve of a waistline. Of course, my waistline is in desperate need of toning and has been so stretched and skewed by pregnancy, that it's not much to brag about after all. My breasts, well, they were always too big, and I don't say this just to make those not so blessed feel better. With age comes the sagging and dragging and all things nasty that gravity inflicts over time. Whenever someone complains that they are too small up top, I just laugh. They have no idea. Boobs are a nuisance and it is nearly impossible to find a pretty bra to contain, lift, support and keep them in the right place for very long. Wonder Bra, Playtex, Warner's, you name it—I have tried it. La Senza has a pretty decent selection, so does La Vie En Rose and of course Victoria Secret—but they are all designed with young, perky women in mind. In the change room, everything fits fine, with all the bits tucked into the right place, firmly supported with no unsightly bulges or ripples; but the moment I went for a walk, they would just jiggle out of place, resulting in a hideous lump otherwise known as bubble boob.

Of course, we can't forget my arms. Winter is a blessing in disguise. I get to wear long pants, long sweaters and long-sleeved shirts. What I don't understand was why all elegant formal wear is sleeveless. Don't designers know that chunky women like to hide their flaws, not showcase them? Of course, maybe like all the pretty lingerie, formal wear is only meant for skinny young things.

My face is nothing special: grey-blue eyes; average skin; and mousy hair that is neither brown nor blond. It was confused, just like the rest of me. My parents had insisted on braces when I was a teenager. At the time I had been horrified, but now I am forever grateful. At the very least I have straight white teeth and a good smile. All in all, I was a pretty sad sight, standing there in front of my floor length mirror naked. My flaws are my own, and the last thing I wanted was for Calleigh to think she would end up like me.

I love my daughter, and the fact that she might find me lacking in some capacity hurt me more than I had thought possible. For her sake, and mine, I needed to take a stand and either accept who I am or make the necessary changes so I could like who I am. While sifting through Calleigh's drawers, I had come across a number of low-fat recipes and diet plans. None of which she had had the opportunity to try. They weren't suitable for a child like Calleigh but there was no reason a grown adult like me couldn't follow one of them with success.

I needed something to jump-start my metabolism into losing weight. After that I would be more sensible in meal choices so I could keep that weight off. I might never be a beauty queen, and I may never have that celebrity sparkle but I could certainly do with many improvements.

It turns out the soup recipe I found in Calleigh's desk was part of a diet plan. The Cabbage Soup plan, to be precise. There are many versions of it kicking around, but they all follow the same basic format. You make yourself a big pot of Cabbage soup, full of nutritious vegetables and flavoured with spices so it's not too terribly bland. You are not supposed to let yourself get hungry. The first day you eat all the fruit you want and as much soup as you can stomach. The second you eat all the vegetables you want, and of course all the soup you can stomach. As the week progresses, you add in proteins and different combinations of food, never forgetting to eat that cabbage soup. After seven days, you should have melted away ten pounds. When you resume eating a regular diet, they encourage you to watch your portions and the kinds of food you choose to eat. Then, if you want to lose more, after a week or so, you just repeat the diet.

The web sites that claim to be very concerned for your health also encourage you to take a multi-vitamin to ensure you're getting important nutrients that you might be missing out on. I appreciated this bit of advice. You would think that by eating so many fruits and vegetables all day long, and never actually letting yourself get hungry that you wouldn't need anything extra. But then we forget about important things like iron and calcium. I was determined to lose the weight so that I could feel better about myself and so that Calleigh would not worry so much about ending up looking like me as she grew up.

I didn't want her to think that you didn't have a choice in the way you look. You might not get to choose your hair colour (but you could always fix that), or your eye colour, or if your nose is crooked; but you do get to choose what type of body you have.

I was going to choose skinny. I had seen enough reality TV to know that it was absolutely possible. I was a closet watcher of the *Biggest Loser*, and *You Are What You Eat*. They all push for healthy diets and exercise. I could do that. I was already planning to try out yoga with Lucy on Monday. Not a big work out, but it was a start.

Once I was on my way to successful weight-loss I would add more workouts into my schedule. I was very self-conscious about hanging out at a gym and having all the beautiful fit people watching me struggle to keep up. The last thing I wanted was to make a spectacle of myself.

"You want to get lunch?" Lucy asked as we made our daily trek to the market. I had started to look forward to that little jaunt. It broke up the day and gave us an excuse to enjoy the bright sun on a cold winter day. Getting up to a dark sky and driving home in the gloom gave me an entirely new appreciation for the little bit of sun I could steal during the day; especially when I didn't even have a window to look out.

"I brought my lunch," I said. I wasn't sure I wanted to share my new plan with Lucy. She was always so encouraging with the walking and little things like the apple diet, but I wasn't so sure she wouldn't be judgemental of my choice of diet. Logically, I knew it could be a gimmick similar to that hot-dog diet I had tried a few weeks ago. But in my heart, I really wanted to believe that this would be the lucky break I needed.

Lucy nodded. "Are you trying a new diet?"

I hesitated before answering. Her intuition was remarkable. Why not tell her? She was my friend; a new friend, but so far, a good friend. "Yeah—I'm kick starting a weight-loss plan with the Cabbage Soup Diet." "Okay." That was it, no comment or criticism.

"It's pretty simple, and you get to eat as much as you want, but you have to stick to the plan." I shrugged my shoulders as though to say I didn't have a vested interest in it. "If I lose, great; if not, well at least I didn't starve myself trying to lose."

"It could work. I've heard of it before. Someone I know lost ten pounds." Lucy's words made me feel very hopeful for all of five seconds. "But then afterwards, when she started eating her regular food, she gained back the ten pounds plus another five or six."

That wasn't a surprise to me. I had done enough reading to recognize how easy it would be to gain the weight back. The thing you had to remember was not to over-indulge afterwards. I would have to keep reminding myself that if I did lose the ten pounds, I would deserve a reward, but that reward would not be food.

"I know, I'll be careful. The best thing is that I won't be hungry. I was so hungry when I tried that ridiculous three-day diet. It was insane."

"Well, I would have told you it wouldn't work, but I didn't want you to think I was being snotty about it," she said with a little laugh. "It's hard to believe you thought you would lose weight eating hot dogs and ice cream."

I laughed too. Even though it had only been a few weeks ago, it felt like a lifetime. "Yeah, well I think there was a lot of wishful thinking going on. I was living in a fairy-tale world."

"If you want to get in shape you should join a gym," Lucy pointed out.

I shook my head. "I'm not sure I'm ready for that kind of commitment. I'll try the yoga, and maybe sign up for a class, but I don't think I'll go to a gym enough to warrant paying a yearly membership."

Lucy shrugged her shoulders and picked up the pace. "Well, if you change your mind, just let me know. The one I go to has a lot of great classes and instructors."

"I am trying the yoga," I reminded her. I didn't want her to think that I was against going to the gym. I just needed time to adjust to the idea and perhaps lose a few pounds before I even got there. I didn't want to look like I needed to be going to the gym.

The cabbage soup was not a great success with my family. I had made a pot of the stuff early in the morning and let it simmer away in the Crockpot all day in the hopes it would create a more flavourful soup. It didn't taste bad at all, it just wasn't what my family was accustomed to eating.

"What is that smell?" Calleigh asked me, her pert little nose wrinkling up in disgust. "Is that our supper?"

I nodded. "It's cabbage soup. Doesn't it smell great?"

"Um… no, mom. It's a bit like that old food smell that lingers in the hallway of old apartment buildings."

It did have that quality about it, but I wasn't going to admit to it. "Well, it's your supper for tonight. If you don't like it, you'll have to make yourself a sandwich. Besides,

I got the recipe from your stash of diet plans, so it won't hurt you to try it."

She looked up at me, startled. Had she really tricked herself into thinking I had only found the scrapbook? She had to know I would have gone searching deeper, even if I hadn't pointed it out to her.

"You went through my desk?" she accused. I could see anger starting to spark in her ice blue eyes.

I nodded. "Calleigh, I was worried about you. I'm still worried about you. Maybe it was wrong for me to invade your privacy, but I needed to know what was going on in your head."

She gave me a look that clearly indicated I had no right to her personal space, but she knew better than to argue with me.

"So, it's okay for you to try all these radical diets and I'm not allowed?" she countered. I could almost see the attitude rolling off her like steam from a boiling pot.

"There is a big difference between you and me," I pointed out. "The most obvious one being that I actually need to lose weight, and you don't. The second is that I'm an adult and have a pretty good idea of what is good for your body. This diet doesn't promote self-starvation."

Calleigh sighed and sniffed the air, "It might not say it's making you starve yourself in the literature, mom. But it sure does smell like that's the plan."

She gathered up her books, stuffed them in her school bag and marched to her bedroom. I just didn't have it in me to correct her rudeness tonight. At least we were talking—well, arguing. Any kind of communication was better than no communication at this point in the game.

Menu du Jour

Breakfast: apple, orange, coffee (although this might have been forbidden) Mid-morning snack: apple

Lunch: Cabbage soup, apple

Mid-afternoon snack: apple, Cabbage soup

Supper: apple, orange, Cabbage soup (I wasn't hungry, but I was going to have get a better variety of fruits and vegetables!) Dessert: pear

Evening snack: Cabbage Soup

Total Calories consumed: 773—no wonder you're supposed to lose weight on this diet

Total Calories burnt: 1426.75 + 79 = 1505.5 (although I'm sure it doesn't matter, with all the fibre I took in)

Chapter Ten

Survival of the Fittest

This was the longest week of my life. First there was the episode with my parents, then my discovery of Calleigh's dangerous dip into depravity, and then my own revelations about my body image. Since I had decided to commit myself to the yoga class as a form of exercise, I was planning a little shopping trip to get some appropriate workout attire. As much as I knew I would look like a newbie the minute the instructor started talking about creeping cobras, playful puppies and bouncing babies, I didn't need to look like someone who didn't have a clue. Besides, I didn't have anything suitable to wear. Anything I did own in the way of workout clothing was faded, torn and most likely covered in paint. Lucy had told me I needed a mat, unless I didn't have an issue with borrowing one from the studio. The problem with that was I wasn't too keen on sharing someone else's DNA via old sweat that might be on that mat. She had also insisted I needed a good bra and exercise shirt—or a combination of the two.

"There's a lot of stretching and bending in yoga. You don't want to be falling out of your shirt, or have it hanging over your head."

I grimaced at the thought of my rolls hanging out for everyone else to see. I also shuddered to think of the view the person behind me would get when I did attempt Downward Dog. My butt sticking up in the air in ill-fitting, paint splattered cast-offs from my late-husband would certainly leave a lasting impression, even if my total lack of balance and coordination didn't.

First, I needed to get through a few more days of Cabbage soup hell. The first two days were somewhat bearable—lots of fruits and cabbage soup the first day and lots of vegetables and cabbage soup the second day. Not too difficult to manage, and if I found myself getting hungry, I just poured myself a cup of what I was hoping would be a magic elixir. The third day of the diet was more soup of course, with a mix of unlimited fruits and vegetables. By this point, my body was screaming for protein but that wasn't allowed until day five.

I wasn't sure I would survive day four. Both bananas and skim milk are low on my list of tolerable foods. I find that bananas have an unusual aftertaste that lingers. They are alright in a pinch, delicious in banana bread or muffins, but not something I would want to consume all day long. As for the skim milk, what was the point? It's basically cloudy water. I could get that out of the tap when the water department was flushing the system. It might even taste better too.

It was probably a good thing day four and five fell on the weekend. I was starting to get moody and irritable. I was also starting to forget things and felt as though I was easily confused. I don't consider myself to be flighty or emotional, but I felt like I had a heavy dose of PMS coupled with a feeling of being hung over without the benefit of consuming a drop of alcohol. Aside from the outing for workout clothes, I fully intended to spend Saturday sipping soup, and making banana shakes with the skim milk. Nowhere did it say you couldn't blend the ingredients together to make them both more palatable.

Sunday would give me an opportunity to get some of my equilibrium back as I would be adding real protein back into my diet. It's a beef and tomato day. Strange combination, but seriously, what did I care? Just the thought of 10 to 20 ounces of beef had me salivating like a rabid dog. The tomatoes I could do without—they're basically water, acid and colour; the savoury goodness of red meat would be a divine treat indeed.

Lucy was picking me up to go shopping. I had considered taking Calleigh to come along, but I didn't want a repeat of our last shopping experience, especially when I was feeling a little emotionally unstable. Besides, she was finally getting together with a few friends. I believe their plans were to work on a group project for school and then reward themselves with a movie and popcorn. Chris would have no trouble managing a bunch of girls for a couple hours.

To be certain I wouldn't pass out from hunger, I packed two bananas into my purse. So far, my weight hadn't changed, and I wondered if I could be eating too much soup. I had done a bit more research on it and practically everything I read boiled down to the same thing. There just weren't enough calories in this diet plan to sustain you, so your body will start to metabolise its own fat and tissue. Of course, there were a plethora of web sites outlining how unhealthy this fad diet is. The combination of too few calories, not enough protein and a deficiency of important nutrients created a health risk to anyone who followed the diet. I could see that being a concern if you did it for more than a week. I once had the stomach flu for five days. All I managed to keep down were a few saltine crackers, watered down soup and flat ginger ale. I managed to lose about five pounds (which I promptly gained back), but was no worse for wear. I figured the worst-case scenario in experimenting with the diet was that I would end up hating bananas and tomatoes more than I already did. The best-case scenario would be that I would lose ten pounds and kick start myself onto the path of healthy weight loss.

I had a goal in mind and I was determined to achieve it.

Lucy didn't take me to your average department store or sporting goods store. I was fully expecting to sort through racks at The Bay or Sears. Even though I can't remember the last time I had been in one; I knew that sporting goods stores carried quite a selection of clothing and shoes, but that wasn't on her list of destinations either. According to Lucy, there was only one place to shop for workout clothing.

The minute I walked into the store I felt intimidated. Brightly coloured tanks, tees, and sweaters lined the walls. Headless mannequins modelled stylish, form-fitting outfits. There was no way I would be able to squeeze my thunder thighs into one of those outfits. Additionally, my breasts weren't designed for such skimpy little tops. My eyes caught a glimpse of one of the price tags and I sucked in my breath. You had to be kidding me! Over fifty dollars for a little tank top? Lucy was completely insane if she thought I could afford this stuff.

"Are you sure about this?" I could feel my wallet shaking in fear inside my purse. It wasn't that I couldn't afford it. I was just appalled at the thought of spending so much money on something I was going to purposefully sweat in.

Lucy nodded and started handing me a selection of items. "I think you're about an eight in here."

"I think I'm at least a ten," I countered. She checked the tags and threw a few more items on top of my pile.

"You would be surprised."

Another tag caught my eye and I was sure I was going to have a heart attack.

"Do you think you would prefer a drawstring waist or flat elastic? I prefer the flat elastic because the string makes me look like I have a belly, but you should try both just in case."

She obviously had a passion for this because she knew exactly where everything was and what to pull out. Within ten minutes my arms were overflowing with a rainbow of colours in every possible shape and size.

The sales girl was a bean-pole with boobs. I would have hated her except she was so sweet and quite helpful. Efficiently, she sorted out my selection of special wicking fabric and gave me a handful.

I checked the tags and realized with dismay that I had been right; the first set to try on was the bigger size ten. The dressing room was surprisingly roomy. I didn't knock any walls as I shimmied into the form fitting yoga pants, or wriggled my way into the extra support workout shirt. The fact that the walls were lined in mirrors, didn't exactly make me feel comfortable until I took the time to look at my reflection in the glass. Wow.

Lucy had been right. She had told me this was the only place worth shopping at for workout clothes.

"Everyone looks good in this brand," she had insisted.

Somehow, the fabric smoothed everything in all the right places without created bumps and ripples to accommodate the fit. I could move easily and the shirt, with its built-in support was quite comfortable. I could live in this outfit.

"Are you coming out?" Lucy asked me from the other side of the door. She had picked up a couple things of her own to try on and was already waiting for me on the other side. I think this was the first time in a long while I didn't hesitate to open the door. Why weren't all clothes made to fit like this?

"Ta da," I announced as I swung open the door. I'm not model slim by any stretch of the imagination, however it sure felt good to try on clothes that not only felt good, but looked pretty good too—even if they were form fitting.

"That looks good," Lucy complimented. Then she added smugly, "Told ya so!"

I laughed, "Yes, you did."

"I still think you should try the smaller size, though," she insisted. I shook my head in response. I didn't want to deflate my ego by trying to shimmy into something too tight.

"Well, when you are pulling your pants up halfway through the workout, I don't want to hear you complaining."

The only reason my pants ever slipped down was because they were too tight, not too loose. These felt good. They hugged my hips and thighs, but weren't so tight they created an unsightly bulge over the top of the waistband. It's like they were made for me.

Lucy shrugged her shoulders in response, as if to say suit yourself. I went back into the changing room and contemplated the size eight yoga pants. It couldn't hurt to try them. The very worst that could happen is I wouldn't be able to get them up over my hips. The very best would be a bit of an ego boost if I did manage to get them on.

With some wiggling, jiggling, hip shaking and tummy sucking I did manage to get them on. Wow. They fit. They were snug, obviously tighter than the ones I had had on before, but they didn't look all that different.

Again, there was no unsightly overhang of muffin-top flab at my waistline. Everything was sucked in, all nice and tidy. I wondered if I could manage the smaller shirt.

The shirt was trickier. You have to be some sort of contortionist to be able to get the shirts with built-in support on. By the time I was out of the first one and into the second, I thought I had achieved a mini-workout already. The shirt was also a success. I was so pleased I wanted to perform a little happy dance right there in the tiny cubicle—but I contained myself and settled for a big grin.

"Okay," I called out to Lucy. "You were right, the size smaller does fit. It's a bit snug—but it's still good."

"I don't know why you bother to argue with me," Lucy answered; I could hear the smile in her voice. "I'm always right."

I laughed at that. Shopping for overpriced workout clothing had been so much more fun than I had thought possible. I needed more outings like this, if only for my self-esteem.

When I came in the door I was greeted with girlish giggles and the overpowering smell of popcorn. My stomach rumbled and I thought of the cold cabbage soup that would be my lunch. I had already eaten three bananas today; I think the limit was supposed to be eight. Compared to the salty, buttery smell of the popcorn, the pongy cabbage soup was a horrible punishment. "Hello girls," I called to them. I didn't want to interrupt Calleigh's much needed day with friends, so I continued past them to the kitchen. Too bad our house had an open concept design. The girls would have to put up with the stench of my lunch; I just hoped it didn't overpower the scent of their buttery popcorn treat.

They were all so engrossed in what they were doing they didn't bother to answer me back. It was probably just as well. Maybe they wouldn't notice me as I reheated my soup in the microwave. I would eat in my room and watch a bit of TV.

As I passed by Chris's room I took a peek to see if she was hiding from the teenagers. Her room was empty, even though it looked as though a tornado had recently swept through. That was just like her—to say she would be home for Calleigh and then take off. It was a good thing Calleigh and her friends weren't a bunch of preschoolers in need of constant supervision.

I decided to ask Calleigh if Chris had even bothered to leave a message for me.

"Oh yeah," she said through a mouthful of popcorn. I was glad to see she had resumed normal adolescent eating habits, but I wasn't so keen on her total lack of manners. "She said she had to go something up from another teacher. And then she would bring back pizza for lunch."

"Right," I sighed. Pizza and popcorn. Thinking of two of my favourite things while my defences were so low wasn't fair. Oh well, I would survive and be stronger, healthier and thinner for it. I just needed to barricade myself in my room, think of my pretty new workout clothes and the reward waiting for me at the end of the week of cabbage soup hell.

Right on cue, Chris walked in with a steaming pizza. The overwhelming aroma of cheese and pepperoni wafted through the house to tickle my nose. There was no hope. I ran from the room before the ridiculous waterfall of tears could fall. I couldn't believe I was crying over pizza.

Menu du Jour

Breakfast: banana, 2 glasses of skim milk, cabbage soup (yes, I had it for breakfast)

Mid-morning snack: 2 bananas

Lunch: Cabbage soup, glass of skim milk, banana Mid-afternoon snack: banana, more milk

Supper: Cabbage soup, banana, skim milk

Dessert: banana

Evening snack: one more banana, Cabbage soup

Total Calories consumed: 1480 (most of it carbohydrates from eating so many bananas)

Total Calories burnt: 1426.75 (I wonder how may extra calories you burn when you cry over pizza?)

Jennifer Bogart

Chapter Eleven

Some like it Hot

I was so excited about the prospect of tomatoes and beef in addition to the ghastly cabbage soup that I was practically floating as I came into the kitchen Sunday morning. I had new yoga clothes that were comfortable and made me feel good. I could see that my jeans were fitting just a bit looser around the waist; well, they were no longer straining across my hips. And Calleigh had had a good day without any ridiculous teenage angst or drama.

Chris was humming away in the kitchen, pouring coffee for the two of us. "So, what's on the agenda for today?"

"I'm not sure. I don't have any real plans aside from laundry, groceries and of course steak and tomatoes." I opened the fridge and took out the giant container of cabbage soup. I would have to replenish it to get through the next couple of days.

"You mean steak and potatoes," she corrected me. "I think that soup is starting to affect your brain cells."

I shook my head in response. "No, I mean steak and tomatoes. That's the meal plan for today. You can have the potatoes, but please don't ask me to make them for you.

You know they are one of my weaknesses." In addition to my own meals, I had still been cooking separate dinners for both Chris and Calleigh.

Playfully, Chris smiled at me, "You mean, you can't have a delicious baked potato slathered in sour cream? No French fries? No mashed potatoes drowning in salty butter? Poor you."

I glared at her, but I was not going to let her teasing affect my mood today. I was happy; today I was getting some much-needed protein and I wouldn't let her teasing spoil my mood. "It's all good. I have willpower."

"Uh huh," she mumbled through a mouthful of Coco Puffs. She didn't sound convinced.

Well, it was obvious that I did. Day five of this monotonous food and I was still going strong. So, what if the smell of it had turned me into a blubbering two-year-old who couldn't have the cookie? So, what if I had one of those headaches that sit right behind your eyes for days and days. I only had two days left and I could see the results already. Of course, the thought of making more soup today was just about killing me, but after today it should be so much easier. Day six was both beef and vegetables—no potatoes, but you could do a lot with that combination. And the last day? Carbs. Glorious, delicious, filling carbs. I would for sure be doing my happy dance that day.

Calleigh came into the kitchen looking all sleep-tussled, reminding me of when she was a toddler in her pink flannel PJ's and tangled hair.

"Do you have to buy that stuff?" she asked, motioning towards the box of Coco Puffs.

"Good morning to you, too," I said. I guess Mistress Surly was back for the morning at least. "And for the record, I don't buy that 'stuff'—your Aunt Chris buys her own junk-food cereal."

"I need a coffee," Calleigh grumbled, heading towards the cupboard where we kept the mugs.

"I don't think so," Coffee consumption had been an on-going battle between us since she started grade eight.

"I'm tired and I need some caffeine to wake up my brain," she argued.

"You're thirteen, and I said no."

Chris chose this moment to intercede. "She already drinks diet colas, what's the difference? At least with coffee there isn't any of that artificial crap in it."

If looks could kill, my sister would have a bullet hole right in the middle of her forehead. She had to be kidding me! "The difference is she is thirteen, it's a bad habit and I said no."

Calleigh turned to Chris with pleading eyes, knowing her aunt would spoil her in ways her mother never could.

She knew who was in her court for this battle and she could taste victory.

"I think there is about the same amount of caffeine in both. Besides, you aren't supposed to have coffee on your crazy diet, but you do." The girl knew her dietary facts.

"Actually, I can have coffee on my crazy diet," I argued. "It's on the list, along with tea and cranberry juice." I knew that arguing with my daughter wasn't a good idea, but something inside of me pushed me forward.

"With milk and sugar?"

"Calleigh, you're being rude."

At the same time Chris said, "I still don't see the problem."

So, my good mood today was quickly turning sour. What did I really care if she had coffee or not? It wasn't like she was drinking alcohol. Was this a power struggle I wanted to waste my limited energy on? And now I wanted chocolate. Damn.

"The problem is, she is thirteen and thirteen-year-olds don't need coffee. They need proper sleep and nutrition." I wasn't going to give on this. I had a feeling that if I did cave, there would be bigger battles I would lose and I wasn't prepared to relinquish control just yet. I did have willpower.

Chris just shrugged her shoulders, "One could argue the same for you."

She looked pointedly at my bowl of cabbage soup. I started laughing. So, the soup didn't smell great, and it was probably lacking in many important nutrients, like iron and protein, but it had to be better than the sugary, artificially flavoured cereal she indulged in every morning.

"And for you, too." I took my bowl of reheated soup and went to the family room where I turned on the TV, effectively ending both arguments.

My tomatoes and steak weren't as great as I thought they would be. Afterwards, I felt bloated and uncomfortable. The problem with the entire diet is that you eat a lot of gassy foods. That gas sits in your tummy with nowhere to go, until you—well, for lack of a better expression let loose. It's embarrassing, but if you don't it can cause cramps that are quite painful. The diet itself is very clean, no sugar, no artificial flavouring, no preservatives; so, you would think that your entire digestive system would be happy with the break from all things processed. My system did a big hiccup, backed up and left me feeling like a distended balloon.

I thought I would be looking forward to the vegetables and beef day which would follow, but after the discomfort of day five I was wondering if I might just skip the beef part. I was supposed to be going with Lucy to try yoga. If I felt as bloated as I did after the tomato and beef day then I wasn't sure I would be able to keep up with all that bending and twisting.

"Ah, you'll be fine," Lucy insisted when I voiced my concerns. "Just make sure you drink a lot of water all day because you're going to sweat a lot."

"Really?" I thought yoga was all about karma, inner peace and meditation. I had seen the yoga lady on early morning television many times, and while some of the poses looked twisted and impossible, she was never out of breath or glistening with sweat.

"Yup. You need at least eight glasses of water today. Not coffee or tea, it's gotta be water."

How did she know me so well after only a few weeks of friendship? I loved my coffee and had thought I would just substitute the flavourless water with that. After all, it is just another liquid.

"Fine," I sighed. "I'll drink water all day long. And I'll come tonight, but I'm warning you, I'm not feeling the greatest right now."

Lucy looked at me as though she were studying the results of a science experiment. "You do look a little pale. Your colour isn't right."

Great. She was supposed to be my encouraging support. What was this analysis all about?

"But you're doing great—and you'll be happy you went to yoga with me. I promise." That's what I needed to hear. "Besides, you only have a couple more days to go, you'll be angry with yourself if you quit now." "You're probably, right," I agreed.

"I'm always right," she reminded me, which made me laugh.

I thought we were going to the gym Lucy frequented, but it turns out we went to a yoga studio. It was quaint, with little carved wooden benches and the sweet smell of incense burning. There were a number of men and women already mingling in the hall and in the change rooms. The overall atmosphere was relaxed and surprisingly non-judgemental. There were people there of all shapes and sizes; none of them looked self-conscious of their bodies. Of course, there were many who had no reason to be self conscious with their slim, muscled twenty-year old physiques. But there were others who were in worse shape than I was. Or maybe, they just needed the right workout attire to suck everything in and hold it in place.

Lucy had also insisted I purchase my own yoga mat while we were on our little shopping spree. "You don't want to use one from the studio that has been used by countless others," she had pointed out with a shudder.

Upon entering the studio, I gasped as a wall of heat hit me in the face. It was like entering a sauna, hotter even than a muggy summer day. Were we expected to exercise in this? Just the thought of it made me feel dizzy.

Quietly, everyone filed into the room, found their preferred spot and laid out their mat. Some were sprawled on their backs on their mats, and others sat cross legged, waiting for the instructor to begin the class. As I glanced around at the people around me I was surprised to see many of them were taking this very seriously. Some looked as though they were meditating and others were practicing what I hoped were various breathing techniques. If they weren't, then they had some serious respiratory issues they needed to deal with.

We started the class with some deep breathing exercises, all very simple, but surprisingly noisy. The man beside me had stripped off his shirt and was practically humming every time he exhaled. Interesting. The woman in front of me forced the air through her nostrils so violently I could see them flaring in the mirror. I tried not to giggle as I focused on my own quiet breaths. Beside me, Lucy looked as though she had forgotten about me; but as the shirtless man let out another humming sigh she glanced at me and gave a little quirk of her lips. If I was going to take this class seriously, I wouldn't be able to look at her.

The first few poses were simple enough. Downward dog, child's pose—all very easy, if a little awkward. I wasn't sure how I felt about my prominent bottom pointing up in the air so much. If Chris were here, she would probably be cracking jokes about the awesome target it presented. Other than the heat, the class looked like it would be straight-forward, with a lot of stretching, focused breathing and a little musical accompaniment from the nearly naked man beside me.

Within five minutes I was sweating profusely, but I wasn't uncomfortable. The woman in front of me had lifted her shirt so that it looked more like a bra and I wondered why she didn't just come to class in the teeny tiny yoga shirts that all the twenty-year-olds were sporting. She was slim and well muscled so she had nothing to hide. But as her shirt crept up higher and higher I wondered if she were planning to take it off altogether and join my shirtless neighbour in baring it all—or most, anyway.

Within ten minutes the sweat was literally dripping off me and pooling onto the mat. No wonder Lucy had insisted I should buy my own. At this point I feared the class would magically transform itself into a swimming lesson if we were all dripping like this. I looked around to see that everyone was indeed glistening with sweat. I could see in the mirror that my face was flushed and my workout clothes had lost their splotchy appearance, probably because I had soaked through everywhere. Despite all this, and the noisy, rhythmic breathing all around me, I was still quite comfortable in the class. Some of the poses were more demanding, but there wasn't anything I couldn't handle. In fact, I felt more flexible than I ever had in my entire life.

The balancing exercises proved to be a challenge. I was wobbly and quite frankly unable to hold the poses. As I toppled over from one pose, I nearly knocked over my shirtless neighbour. I cringed as I imagined the domino effect this fall might have; and then I couldn't help myself—I giggled. The instructor gave me a warning look that clearly told me to get myself together. Lucy mimicked the look almost perfectly and I had to bury my face in my towel to keep from laughing outright. If I was going to do this again, I would have to practice the balancing poses at home. I'm sure with enough practice I would be able to become a standing tree or even soar like an eagle.

I have to say, I really did like the names of the different poses. They were descriptive and imaginative all in one. As I bent my knees and stretched my legs impossibly at the same time I did feel like a warrior preparing for battle.

When we went back to the Downward Dog position that flowed into the Baby Cobra and then back again, I was feeling quite relaxed and confident. For the most part I had been keeping up with the class with only a few minor modifications. I had been able to block out the breathing of the other participants in the class and for once I was focusing on just me, my own breathing and what my body could achieve. I was finding my own little happy place and it was fantastic.

Then I farted.

It wasn't one of those silent, sneaky ones you can pretend didn't happen. It was one of those loud, vibrating ones that echoed through the breathing sounds of everyone else. Admittedly, it didn't smell too great either. I was horrified and wanted to bolt from the room. Lucy looked at me and started to laugh silently. She bit her bottom lip in an attempt to stifle it, but I could tell it wasn't going to work. Some friend she was!

As I melted into a puddle of mortification, the instructor took this moment to impart some useful information.

"As your internal organs are being massaged, do not be ashamed of your natural bodily functions." Her tone was one of reverence, but I could see her nose wrinkling in distaste as she passed behind me. I'm pretty sure my face couldn't become anymore flushed. "This is a good thing."

A giggle escaped Lucy and I wanted to smack her. But then, I couldn't help myself and a smile of my own battled with my humiliation. It *was* funny. And I felt so much better than I had earlier. The smile slipped into a chuckle and before we knew it, both Lucy and I were laughing hysterically into our towels. The instructor chose to ignore us and carried on with the class.

Jennifer Bogart

Menu du Jour

Breakfast: carrots, cabbage soup, piece of left over steak and coffee

Morning Snack: celery, raw broccoli and coffee

Lunch: more steak, cabbage soup, leafy green salad

Afternoon snack: carrots

Supper: gigantic barbequed steak, cabbage soup, leafy green salad with cherry tomatoes, mushrooms and cucumbers

Evening Snack: Carrots and more steak

Calories consumed: 1099 (it's all in the meat)

Calories burned: 1426.75 + 955 = 2381.75 (Hot Yoga! Also wondering if you expel additional calories through flatulence?)

Chapter Twelve

Last Day of the Cabbage Soup Diet

Mornings are always difficult for me. It's not that I'm a night person; it's more that I like to sleep, especially in the winter. Just the thought of my bare feet hitting the cold hardwood floor after spending the night snuggled up in cozy blankets was enough to convince me that I did deserve the extra ten, fifteen, even twenty minutes of daydreaming I would steal in the early morning hours. I was feeling particularly rested and relaxed after the workout of the night before; that is until I tried to stretch. Every muscle in my body screamed in protest at a decibel I'm sure the neighbours could hear clearly.

This was not something I had anticipated. The yoga had been ridiculously easy. During the session, I had felt my muscles and joints relax and move with ease. There were a few poses I had found a bit difficult, but I had not felt as though I were straining or overworking anything. I had been impressed with what I was able to accomplish even though I knew I was horribly out of shape.

I also wondered if I would be able to get out of my pyjamas and into the shower on my own steam. I moaned as I carefully rolled into a sitting position. I could do this. If Lucy could do this, I could do this. If the other overweight and unattractive people in that class could function the following day, then so could I. Besides, I was on the home stretch today with the cabbage soup diet. I had a great reason to get out of bed. I just wished I had the energy and spring to achieve it.

The last day of the diet and finally I got to eat a carbohydrate. My body had gone through detoxification in more ways than one; it had been cleansed and so had my soul - as per the karma yoga from the night before. It was the last day of the diet so no protein, but as much rice and vegetables as I wanted. I had not weighed myself for seven days. Part of me had wanted to step on the scale, but I knew if I did before the week was up, and I didn't see any positive change, then I would not continue with the diet plan. I figured that by not weighing in all week, I would have a better chance of making it through the entire seven days with some sort of success.

Plus, I was paranoid that the little pink gremlin might still be hiding inside, just waiting to play tricks with extra weights. I had weighed myself the morning before I started the diet; I made sure it was before I had breakfast but after I had my shower. In order to get through this last day, I needed to know something about the diet was working. If there was absolutely no change, I might skip the final day of cabbage soup and go straight for real food. I could use a little comfort food with the way my body was feeling.

So, I followed the same routine I had the last time I had weighed myself. But I hesitated before stepping on the scale. What if, after depriving myself of real food all week, the scale measured the same weight as before? Or worse, what if I weighed in heavier?

I was tempted to call Calleigh into the room and get her to look at the scale for me, but then thought better of it. I didn't want to horrify my daughter with my naked body; she had enough issues to overcome as it was.

Gingerly I stepped on the scale; it was electronic, so there was no sound of gears sliding to signal when the measure was ready. The numbers slid by so fast, I had no idea where they would stop. It was my own private viewing of the *The Biggest Loser.* The only thing I was missing was the suspenseful background music and the dramatic cut to commercial before the big reveal.

I checked the digital display with a quick peek through squinted eyes and then opened both in astonishment. Not only had I lost the promised ten pounds, I had lost a bonus pound for good measure! I still had one more day to get through and I had just been given the incentive to keep going.

As I stepped off the scale my entire body shuddered in protest; in my elation of seeing the lost pounds I had temporarily forgotten that my body was screaming in pain. My muscles were lethargic; there was a pinch between my shoulder blades; and my thighs felt as though they were on fire. Even the little joints of my toes were achy. Lucy had warned me I would be a bit sore a day or two after the yoga workout. Well, that was a bit of an understatement. I felt as though I had been run over by a truck. And then for good measure, the damn truck backed up and did it again. I would survive, but I wasn't so sure I would be trying that particular activity again.

"Something is different about you," Lucy noted as I limped into the office. I wanted to be floating, I was so happy with my achievement, but my poor broken body just didn't have enough gumption for grace.

"Nope," I answered with a grin. "I'm the same old, same old."

Lucy studied me intently. "You look… you look happier…"

I laughed at that. "I am happier. I'm very relaxed."

Lucy nodded knowingly. "That would be the yoga. It's good for your spirit as well as your body."

Now she was scaring me. I'm not a very spiritual person. We go to church on major holidays, and when I'm in a bad way, I might whisper a hurried prayer. But doing something that is good for my spirit - well, I sure hoped that Lucy wasn't the kind of person who would try to draw you into whatever religious trend was currently most popular. She didn't strike me as the kind of person who would, but you just never knew. During the class, she had been just as amused and sceptical of the more metaphysical aspects of it as I was.

"I'm just in a good mood," I said. I didn't want to tell her about my weight loss until I was officially finished with the diet. It was my own little success and I was savouring its sweetness for just a while longer.

"Okay," she answered. This was the second time she hadn't tried to convince me to share my secrets. It almost made me want to tell her what I was so happy about. "Do you want to go again? There's another session Thursday."

I winced as I settled into my chair. "I don't know. I liked it, but I'm really suffering for it now."

"It's better if you stretch everything out again. Your body will get used to it and it won't hurt so much after the next one." She sounded as though she knew what she was talking about. "Trust me."

I sighed. "I'll let you know, I need to check my calendar."

"No problem. It's not usually full on Thursdays."

Great, I could even wait to the last minute and then let fate make the decision for me.

Hot Yoga also has a few other side effects I wasn't exactly prepared for. As they started to emerge throughout the day, I decided to do a Google search to make sure I wasn't going crazy. Aside from the expected aches and pains of muscles and joints that were worked beyond their usual capacity, I was unbearably thirsty. This would be due to the fact that I had disregarded Lucy's advice to drink a lot of water. I figured that since my diet was mostly liquid, I didn't need to increase my fluid intake. Of course, I wasn't expecting to be sopping wet when I came out of the studio, either. When we left the heated room, our feet left little puddles on the tiles in the corridor that led to the changing room.

I was also very, very, very gassy. The combination of the cabbage soup and the "massaging of the internal organs" as the instructor had so delicately put it, had created a rather noxious combo. I was almost tempted to take the day off, but I had a deadline to meet, so I made myself deal with it the best that I could. This meant frequent walks around the building. I used the excuse that I was stiff and needed to stretch my legs, but I have a feeling Lucy knew better. She didn't even suggest we go for our habitual walk during lunch. Of course, our desks are separated only by a thin partition, so she was no doubt very aware of my acute discomfort.

I was also exceptionally relaxed. Actually, I think the correct term would be lethargic. At one point, I think I even drifted off to sleep at my desk. Maybe I was snoring or something because a loud, vibrating thump startled me and I nearly jumped out of my seat. I had been dreaming of cupcakes with various fancy icings. Maybe I would treat myself and my family to a few of these delicious treats as a celebration of sorts for getting through this week. I might also have been dreaming about the details of my celebratory dinner, which made me wonder exactly how long I had been asleep.

Just one more day to get through; so why did it feel like it was taking forever?

"Cabbage soup for supper again?" Calleigh asked as she sniffed air.

I nodded, "Yes, but it's the last time, I promise. It's not like you have had to eat this stuff."

She looked at me thoughtfully for a moment. I could tell she wanted to confide something in me, but I was afraid if I pushed her, she wouldn't be so open the next time. We needed to work on our trust with each other.

"I did eat it," she finally confessed. "It was ok, kind of bland."

"Really?" I didn't quite know how to respond to that revelation. She had been complaining about the smell of it all week and making comments about the way it looked so watery and unappealing. I never would have guessed she tried it herself.

"Yeah - someone else I know went on the diet, she lost her ten pounds, but then instead of eating regular food like you're supposed to, she just continued with the diet."

This got my attention. For one week, it couldn't really hurt you, but to continue it for longer couldn't be a good thing. Where were this child's parents?

"That's not a good plan, Calleigh," I warned her. Had she followed the diet or had she just tasted the soup? I desperately wanted to ask. She looked so healthy and vibrant. I searched her face for signs of weight-loss. Her long sweater over her leggings was too baggy to give any indication of what might lie beneath.

Calleigh shook her head, "Don't worry, mom. I only tried it a couple times. It wasn't something that I could stomach. It made me feel awful and crampy."

I'm sure my relief was clearly etched across my face. I closed my eyes, grateful she had been turned off by my own folly. I needed to be careful where she was concerned.

"Well, it was an awful diet. And I did lose some weight, but it's not a long-term solution," I told her honestly. "I can't wait for a real meal tomorrow night!"

"I'm glad you lost some weight," she said, almost hesitantly. "You'll be happier now."

I thought about that for a moment. Would I be happier because I had shed a few pounds? I was happier because I had proved to myself that I could do it. But while the scale measured lighter, I didn't exactly feel lighter. Yes, my buttons had less strain and the waistband of my trousers was no longer cutting into me, making it difficult to breath. And yes, my face had a slightly slimmer look to it, but I was still quite pudgy. I would probably be happier when I had lost the entire forty pounds I knew needed to go. After that three-day, hot dog diet I had not only gained the few pounds back that I had lost, but I packed on a few more for good measure. So, in all reality, all the cabbage soup diet had done was put me back to the beginning. And that was ok. I knew I could do it; I just needed to take my time, and figure out how.

"So, what is on the menu for tonight?" Calleigh asked again.

"For you and Auntie Chris, brown rice, steamed broccoli and ham," I answered her. "For me, cabbage soup, brown rice and steamed broccoli. Tomorrow we'll have something really tasty, like pasta."

"But no more cabbage soup?"

"No - no more cabbage soup."

If I never see (or smell) another bowl of cabbage soup again I will be the happiest person in the world. Although it did put me on the right path for weight loss, I was pretty sure it wasn't the best approach. I also think this particularly nauseating diet was meant to leave a lasting psychological impression. Here is what I learned from the cabbage soup diet:

- -You can survive on only vegetables and cabbage soup and not be hungry
- -You can live without protein, but it's not ideal and you feel weak
- -You do get past cravings for sweet and salty foods - even if it's only temporary
- -Cabbage soup is great if you're on a budget
- -Baked potatoes are a luxury
- -Steak tastes best after several days on a starvation diet
- -If you have the willpower to get through this diet with your sanity, you can survive just about anything.

Menu du Jour

Pre-breakfast weigh-in: minus 11 pounds - insert happy dance here

Breakfast: Cranberry juice, carrots, brown rice

Mid-morning snack: coffee, celery

Lunch: Cabbage soup, leafy green salad, brown rice, coffee

Afternoon snack: more carrots

Supper: LAST BOWL OF CABBAGE SOUP! Brown rice, steamed broccoli

Evening snack: I wasn't hungry

Calories consumed: 933 - but, seriously, who cares? No more cabbage soup!

Calories burned: 1426.75

Chapter Thirteen

You Spin Me Right Round, Baby...

It took about three days for me to recover from that hot yoga session. Each day a different muscle group took up protest against me. At least I was able to eat regular food. After supper on the final day of the Cabbage Soup Diet, we ceremoniously dumped the left-over soup down the toilet and sent it off with a satisfying whoosh. I had lost my ten plus pounds and was determined to keep going, only with a more varied diet plan.

The problem is—I love to eat. My biggest downfall is probably pasta, and there are very few low-fat, low carbohydrate, low calorie-count pasta recipes. Oh—some of them look all healthy, with their extra virgin olive oil and fresh, colourful veggies; but let's face it—the noodles themselves are just empty calories.

I was considering taking on the Atkins diet. If I could live off little more than cabbage soup for a week, then I could probably handle a month without carbohydrates. But first, I was taking a week off from the whole dieting thing. My plan was to eat sensibly, but allow myself a few little rewards for making it through last week while everyone around me indulged in whatever they wanted.

The worst part was watching Lucy. She does just eat whatever she wants. Her metabolism must be amazing to be able to devour a full plate of pasta, a glass of wine and a scrumptious dessert without thinking twice. Maybe one day I would be thin enough to pull that off, but I knew there was something very important missing from my life. I might have lost over ten pounds last week, but with every bite of pizza, pasta and pesto I could feel the weight settling back in, especially around my waist and hips. Sometimes, life just isn't fair.

"Are you coming to yoga with me on Thursday?" Lucy asked. It was Wednesday afternoon and I was starting to feel a bit more human. At least I didn't groan every time I had to get up from my chair.

"I don't know, I'm not so sure I appreciate the after effect. Plus, after last time…" I blushed, completely embarrassed by the memory.

Lucy started laughing, "Oh, it happens to everyone at some point. Stick around a while and you'll see or hear a whole lot worse than that!"

I loved how she tried to make me feel better. "Okay, but if I feel as though I have been tortured by medieval contraptions the next day, I'm never going back."

Lucy shrugged her shoulders. "Suit yourself. At least if you go back you'll know you gave it an honest try." I nodded, that was certainly true.

"You should also come spinning with me Friday morning," she suggested. "You'll burn all the extra calories you've been stuffing yourself with this week."

If she hadn't been so sweet and well-meaning, I might have been insulted. Had Chris or Calleigh come out with something like that, I would have stormed off in a fit; angry at them for pointing out my obvious flaws when they are supposed to be supportive. I guess that's the difference between girlfriends and family; something I had never considered before. Granted, I had never had a friend quite like Lucy.

"Spinning? Like twirling around in circles?" I asked. I knew it was a stupid question the moment the words tumbled out of my mouth. What on earth was she talking about?

"It's riding a stationary bike, with an instructor and loud music. It's all about setting your tension and holding different positions. Try it, you might like it."

I thought about it for a minute. I could ride a bike. It had to be better than jogging. The problem with jogging when you are overweight is that everything jiggles and jumps and thumps and it's horribly unpleasant. At least there wouldn't be any bouncing while riding a stationary bike.

"I guess I could try it."

"The best thing about it is you can burn up to eight hundred calories if you work hard enough," she added for good measure.

So that was her secret—she burned whatever she consumed. Did that mean the more I wanted to eat, the more I would have to work out? It made sense. If I didn't change my eating habits and just added exercise to my current sedentary lifestyle I wondered if I would lose weight or just stay the same.

"Eight hundred? Really?" That seemed exceptional. When I was doing the crazy soup diet I don't think I was consuming more than a thousand calories for the first few days. "What if I can't move Friday morning after yoga?"

"You'll be fine," Lucy insisted. "Trust me."

I have to say I did enjoy the hot yoga the second time around. I felt just as comfortable and flexible as I had the first time. Lucky for me, I avoided an embarrassing repeat performance by making sure I drank plenty of water and ate only non-gassy foods before the class. Coming out of the extreme heat into the minus ten-degree weather was still a slap in the face, but it was completely worth it for the feeling of relaxation and contentment I carried with me. I could easily see how hot yoga could become a healthy addiction.

Chris looked up from her book when I came into the house and smiled. "Did you have a good workout?"

I nodded. "It was good. You should try it," the words slipped out of my mouth before I had a chance to retract them and I froze, waiting for her to respond. I love my sister, but did I want to share this with her? Would Lucy want her there?

Chris shook her head, "I think I'll pass on that one. I'm not into the whole Zen thing."

"Okay." I was kind of glad she wasn't interested in coming and I wasn't about to make the mistake of offering for her to come again. "You're home tomorrow morning, right?"

"Yes, it's a professional day for the kids, so I don't need to be there until ten or so. Why?"

"Can you see Calleigh out the door and make sure she has a decent lunch?"

She looked puzzled for a moment. I guess it was a strange request; I hadn't asked for this kind of help from Chris since I started back to work. I didn't even know for sure that Chris knew which school Calleigh went to, I guess I needed to update my emergency preparedness plan.

"I guess I can, where are you going to be?"

"I'm spinning with Lucy." I decided not to bother with a complete explanation; if she wanted to know I'm sure she would ask.

"In the morning?"

"Before work, it's the only way we can fit it in."

"You and Lucy are spending a lot of time together… I think maybe it's time you brought her home to meet everyone." Her tone was teasing, but I could tell she was serious. It wasn't like I had met all of her friends. I guess when you don't go out much, and suddenly, your life-style starts to change a bit, people get curious. "I'll invite her family for dinner sometime." I just hoped Lucy's husband wouldn't be uncomfortable with our unique family living situation.

"Sure, whatever you want." She went back to her book. I felt like a child who had been dismissed.

Getting up at five in the morning so that I could go to the gym was such a novel idea to me I practically jumped out of bed the next morning. I only had the one set of workout clothes and I was amazed that they were mostly dry after washing them the night before. I just hoped that when I tossed them in the dryer to finish them off they didn't shrink too much. Lucy had assured me they wouldn't, but I was still nervous. They might be "just" workout clothes, but they were some of the most expensive articles of clothing I owned.

I was amazed that my muscles weren't nearly as sore as they had been after my first hot yoga session. I had honestly been expecting more of the same discomfort and had psyched myself up to work through it. I was a little stiff, but it was a refreshing kind of soreness that wasn't in any way bothersome.

There was no point in taking a shower since I would probably just end up sweaty and stinky, so I grabbed a cup of coffee, a yogurt, and a banana; and waited for my workout clothes to finish toasting in the dryer. At least they would have that fresh from the dryer warmth when I shimmied back into them.

This gym looked more like what I had expected when we went to yoga. Strange-looking contraptions lined the walls, most of them resembling unusual torture devices, others I did recognize from various TV commercials. One would expect the gym to be empty at a quarter to six in the morning, but they would be completely wrong. There were men and women everywhere, many well into their workouts and others still who were ready to pack it in for the day so they could head to work. It was almost as though a totally different culture existed within the walls of this building. Strangely enough, I found it somewhat exhilarating.

The instructor, upon finding out I was new to all this, graciously showed me how to set up my bike. Apparently, you don't just hop on the bike and start peddling. The bike needs to be adjusted so that you are comfortable and can therefore get an optimum workout. At this point, my plan was simply to make it through a full hour of cardio. Daily walks with Lucy were great but I knew that in comparison, they were quite literally a walk in the park.

"All set?" Lucy asked with a grin as we mounted our bikes in preparation. I think the last time I rode a bike was before Calleigh was born. I don't even own a bike.

Sitting in the saddle felt awkward and I sincerely hoped I wouldn't fall off.

I nodded, fighting to slide my shoes into the stirrup. Lucy had these fancy little shoes that just clipped into the peddles, which looked so much easier to manage.

The music was a bit of a surprise. I was anticipating fast paced; I wasn't expecting so much variety. Much of it had been remixed to fit the needs of the class, but there was everything from traditional rock, to techno funk, and even a bit of my favourite—country. The instructor had even thrown in a track from "Phantom of the Opera" for good measure. The music was so loud, it made the walls pulsate with its varied rhythms. So far, my only gym experience has been hot yoga, and that is done pretty much in complete silence; save for the rhythmic breathing, sighing, and humming.

The instructor was this cute little young thing and although I knew I wasn't quite old enough to be his mother, it just somehow seemed wrong for him to be teaching so many middle-aged people. I glanced around the class and realized it was packed. With everyone in various forms of workout clothing, it was difficult to picture them in their real lives. Some wore expensive designer outfits that showcased strong muscles and lean bodies; others wore sloppy, worn out faded clothes that had seen better days. The trick was not to be fooled by their clothing. Just because you looked good, didn't necessarily mean you were a star athlete. I knew that I looked better in my yoga capris than I did in most of my bulky jeans, but that didn't mean I was fit.

As I was taking in the class participants, my eye was caught by one person in particular. He was tall, probably around six feet, with dark brown, nearly black hair and equally dark eyes. There was something vaguely familiar about him but I just couldn't place it.

Lucy leaned over and said something in my ear that I didn't quite catch over the music. It sounded something like "nice eye candy, eh?" but I couldn't be sure.

After the first track, I forgot all about the man on the other side of the room, even though he was clearly in my line of vision. The warm-up had me breathless and I decided I needed to focus on just getting through the class in one piece. By the third track I thought my lungs were on fire and my heart was going to take flight out of my chest. Lucy looked relaxed and focused. No one else struggled the way I did, and I began to wonder if there was something wrong with me.

Halfway through the class I knew I was having a heart attack. I could tell by the numbness in my legs. I had lost complete feeling in them and they were just spinning all on their own. I wanted to kill the instructor. And I would, if I ever recovered from this hell called spinning. He was peppy and energetic. His smile was annoying and even though he was sweating, he still looked fresh and vigorous. Unbelievable.

He kept throwing out terms like "Shotgun" and "Suicide"; which made me wonder what I had managed to get myself into. I was beginning to wish I had a shotgun—not so that I could commit suicide, that's not in my nature, but so that I could go ahead and shoot that snazzy Colgate grin off his handsome face.

My only goal was to get through the class alive, with my heart and lungs intact. I hadn't considered what it might do to my legs. When I dismounted I wasn't sure they would support me. They felt like jelly in a numb kind of way.

Lucy grinned at me as she followed instructions to stretch her quads, glutes and hamstrings. I didn't even know what those were, but I copied the instructor anyway, hoping the movements would bring some sort of feeling back into my legs.

"So… what did you think?" she asked. She looked so happy and still amazingly refreshed. I felt like I was a dripping, wobbling mess.

"It was okay." I was having a hard time responding as I was still out of breath. Part of me was elated I had made it through the entire class without stopping; another part of me knew I was going to pay for it later.

"Admit it, you like it," she cajoled. Did I? I thought about that for a moment. I felt good. I was definitely off-balance and breathless, but I felt like I had achieved something.

I nodded. "I'll let you know for sure when my body catches up with my heart, but I think I did like it."

She laughed and headed for the change rooms. It was time to shower and get to work. Amazingly enough, this would be the first time in months I arrived early and I already felt as though I had accomplished something today.

Menu du Jour

Breakfast: yogurt, coffee

Mid-morning snack: cheese, crackers, banana

Lunch: Deli Sandwich, brownie (it was a treat for burning the extra calories)

Afternoon snack: coffee

Supper: pork chops, rice, corn

Evening snack: ice cream Calories consumed: 1801

Calories burned: 1426.75 + 445 = 1871.75 (I thought the instructor said it was possible to burn up to 800 calories in a spinning class—guess I'll have to peddle faster).

Chapter Fourteen

Memory Lane

My parents were coming for their once a month Saturday dinner and I dreaded the idea it might turn into a rerun of their last visit. Calleigh and I were communicating better, and I didn't want them to do anything to upset the delicate balance we had established. She was growing and changing so fast I could hardly keep up with her socially and emotionally.

I have to admit, Chris is such a big help that sometimes I feel as though she does half the parenting. Calleigh isn't her responsibility at all, but I am forever grateful that she has been here to help me along every step of the way.

"Is everything alright?" Chris asked as she helped me set the table.

"Everything is fine." She knew me well enough that when I said things were "fine" they weren't. Everything should be fine, life was good. My job, although somewhat boring paid well enough that Calleigh and I didn't struggle for anything. Calleigh seemed to have gotten over her brief dissatisfaction with her own body image and I was working towards becoming a healthier, happier me.

"I don't think you need to worry about mom and dad. They aren't likely to make the same mistakes twice.

Besides, mom will kill dad if he so much as looks at Calleigh the wrong way."

I chuckled; Chris almost knew me better than I knew myself. One of the advantages of having a twin sister is the bond we share. We can't read each other's minds, but we can easily read each other's body language and moods.

"I know. I guess I'm just tired and could do without any drama tonight."

Chris studied me for a moment then put one arm around me reassuringly. "I could call them and say we aren't up for it tonight," she offered.

I shook my head. Then I would have them over here with bowls of chicken soup; their hearts on their sleeves and pity in their eyes. I had had enough of that kind of attention after Calleigh's father died. Every time they brought out their sympathy formula, I felt as though I were being transported back in time when I was desperately trying to move forward.

"Really, I'm just tired. I think the spinning took more out of me than I thought it would." Not to mention I finally figured out why the man with the dark hair and eyes had felt so familiar to me. I had known him in a previous life. The one where I had had a healthy, happy husband, a newborn baby and everything in the world was just as it should be. Part of my melancholy had a lot to do with being forced down memory lane, a place where I didn't much care to wander. In fact, it was a place I had pretty much stricken from the map except for emergency detours. Thankfully those were far and few between.

"Between the crazy diets and the sudden increase in exercise, you should be tired!"

"I thought I read somewhere that exercise gives you energy," I mused aloud. "I must have been mistaken because I'm whipped."

Chris smiled and patted my back. "It will probably get better, just give it time."

When I looked at Chris, I hoped she couldn't see the envy in my pale grey eyes. She didn't need to go to the gym to spin off excess calories; she didn't need to try insane diets to get her weight under control. Like Calleigh, she is tall and slender, a graceful gazelle in comparison to my frumpy rhino. Life would have been fairer if we had split the "good" genes down the middle and called it even.

Calleigh bounded into the room, bringing with her energy and sunshine. She looked very pleased with herself, and I wondered what she had been up to.

"Hey, you," I said with a smile. Her grin was infectious. "You look like you're up to something." "Nope, I'm just in a good mood," she insisted as she opened the fridge and started to root around. I almost told her no snacking before supper, but then I caught myself. Did I want to discourage her from eating? Not at this point.

Chris winked at me and I looked at her questioningly. These two had secrets, they always had, and in all the years that Chris had lived with us, it had never bothered me. Usually, Chris would cave in and confide in me, but there was something different about the two of them today. I guess I would have to wait until later to pry it out of one or both of them.

"Cosmos before dinner?" Chris asked as she started to take out the glasses.

I shrugged. "I was thinking Lychee Martinis."

"Oh, fancy." She took out five martini glasses and set them on the counter in preparation for later.

"What's with the extra glass?" I asked. Had the two of them invited an extra guest?

"You'll just have to wait and see," Chris answered.

There was no point in trying to force it out of them. When Chris decided to keep a secret, she zipped her lips and threw away the key. Calleigh was just like her.

When the doorbell rang to announce the arrival of our guests, Calleigh went tearing past me like a little speed demon. She pulled open the door and practically threw herself into the arms of the man who was patiently waiting with my parents. He looked achingly familiar and I didn't know if I should laugh or cry.

"Ryan, it's so good to see you!"

He released Calleigh and folded me into a bear hug. Years melted away in that moment.

"It's good to be seen," he said as he kissed my cheek. "I swear, Roxy, you haven't changed a bit."

"Flattery will get you everywhere," I told him as I ushered him into the house.

"Do you like the surprise?" Calleigh asked. She was practically jumping up and down in her excitement.

I smiled, hoping she could see all the love I felt for her pouring through. "I love my surprise," I told her earnestly. "It's the best surprise ever."

She grabbed hold of Ryan's hand and led him into the family room, all the while chattering about school and friends as though she had only seen him yesterday and not several years ago.

My parents followed him in quietly. "We weren't sure..." my mom said hesitantly.

"I hope you don't mind, but Calleigh insisted," my dad said at the same time.

"It's fine," I said. And this time I meant it. Seeing my husband's brother was good for my soul. The timing was strange, considering who I had run into the day before, but it was still good to see him.

"Your dad mentioned to Calleigh that he was in town for the week and she begged him to bring him for dinner," my mom explained as she handed me her jacket to hang up.

"Really, it's no problem. I'm glad she insisted."

"You know how I am with that girl," my dad added. "I just can't seem to say "no" to her."

I laughed. When Calleigh turned on her charm, even I was hard pressed to say "no" to her.

"So, tell me what you girls have been up to," Ryan said. He had forgone the Lychee Martinis and gone straight to the Jack Daniels. I had a flashback of Ryan and Damian sitting across from each other, deep in conversation, each of them nursing their own glass of the amber liquid. They had always been close so it had seemed that Ryan had been a semi-permanent fixture in our house.

"Oh, you know," Chris answered for me when she noticed I had drifted off to times gone by. "Same old, same old."

I smiled, "Yes, we're always busy, but we never seem to be doing anything."

My dad chuckled. "Life is like that when you're young, working, and raising a child. When you and your sister were young, we never had any time to do anything for ourselves. You have to take the time."

"Well said, Richard," Ryan saluted as he raised his glass. He was so much like Damian in his mannerisms I could hardly stand to look at him, yet at the same time I wanted to soak in every familiar detail of him, commit it to memory so I could refresh the old visions I held close to my heart.

"Mom has been busy with her new friend, Lucy," Calleigh piped in. "We hardly see her anymore."

"Now that's not really true," Chris said with a warning look at my daughter.

"Hmmm… it's kind of true," I finally joined the conversation. "We've been spending some time at the gym and we work together. But I hardly think I spend more time with her than I do with you."

"The gym, eh," Ryan pointed out. "Good for you. Not that you need it, you look great."

"Thanks." I'm sure Ryan was just being his usual complimentary self. The ten pounds I had shed last week were slowly catching up to me already. I wasn't gorging myself on junk food, for the most part, but old habits are very hard to break.

"Oh, you didn't tell me about the hot yoga you tried," my mom said. "Did you enjoy it?"

"I don't know if I would use the word 'enjoy', exactly. It was good and I was able to complete the entire class."

Ryan studied me carefully, "That's a pretty intense workout. What made you decide to try that?"

I shrugged my shoulders. I couldn't remember if I had actually agreed to go. It was more like I was coerced into trying it, for which I was very glad. I needed to step outside of the little bubble I had been living in for the past ten years and try a few more things like that.

"A girlfriend suggested it, it was surprisingly relaxing."

"Well, I'm telling you, you look great, so whatever you're doing, keep it up." I thought back to the last time

Ryan had seen me and realized that of course I would look better, even if I was rounder, older and flabbier. Seven years ago, I had still been a mess of unresolved anger and emotion.

Dinner was a very pleasant event. We kept the conversation light and current. There was an unspoken agreement that we would keep Damian in the past and focus on the present and future. I know Calleigh would have loved to hear stories about her dad, but she needed to spend some time alone with Ryan for those details. I had put aside the guilt and hurt feelings a long time ago, and I still wasn't ready to revisit my past. Damian and I had been unbearably young when we got married and had Calleigh. It wasn't my fault the accident had occurred, but I knew things may have turned out differently if I hadn't been so selfish at the time. The only person who knew there was more to the story was Chris, but then sisters have a way of being privy to information we wouldn't normally share with the rest of the world. Even then, she didn't know everything. What was the point? The world knowing all the gory details wouldn't change anything or bring Damian back.

"I'm so glad Uncle Ryan came to visit," Calleigh sighed, as I tucked her in. Even at thirteen years old I still enjoyed the luxury of pulling her blankets tight, kissing her forehead and closing her lights.

"Me too."

"I wish he could stay longer…"

"I think we were lucky to see him at all, he's a very busy guy." I straightened a few things on her night table and made sure her alarm was switched on. "He did say he would come by tomorrow to take you out for a bit. It was supposed to be a surprise, but I thought you would want to know."

"Really?" her blue eyes widened into saucers. She looked so much like her dad had as a young boy that I could feel the sting of tears behind my eyelids. "I better call Andrea and tell her I can't go the movies with her. Aren't you going to come with us?"

I shook my head. Ryan and Damian were only two years apart, and the family resemblance was uncanny. Ryan had matured into an attractive man, just as Damian would have. The evening had been nice. With light hearted conversation and stories of his work, Ryan had kept us all entertained while keeping the painful memories of the past at bay. I imagine him seeing us all together was just as difficult for him as it was for us. At least we had each other. After Damian had died, Ryan had disappeared to make his fortune and drown his sorrows. He kept in touch via e-mail, letters, and phone calls, but visits, until today had been just too painful to bear.

I wondered why he had decided to come back now. Other than Calleigh and me, he didn't have any real ties to this city.

"I want you to enjoy your time with Uncle Ryan, without an old bat like me hanging around."

She laughed. "You're not an old bat. You're probably the youngest of all my friends' moms."

Well, tonight I was sure feeling like an old bat. "I think you and Uncle Ryan need some private time together. Besides, I'm a busy girl and have lots I need to get done this weekend."

"Are you going to the gym again?"

"I need to clean the house and do laundry or you'll be going to school naked! Now go to sleep, tomorrow is going to be a busy day for you."

She sighed, rolled over and cocooned herself into her blankets, just as she always had for as long as I could remember. Damian used to do that too, and I would complain that I was left freezing cold in the middle of the night.

"Mom?"

"Yes, sweetheart," I was at the door, ready to switch off the light.

"I love you."

"I love you too." Quietly I closed the door and made my way to my own room. The minute I shut the door, the floodgates opened and I dissolved into a deluge of tears, grief and incredible pain. I couldn't remember the last time I had cried like that, but it felt good, almost cathartic. For seven years I had been stomping and squishing painful memories away into a box locked up tight in my heart. I hadn't had the strength to deal with them and I very much doubted I had the strength to address them now. Why had Ryan shown up now? Over the past few weeks I had felt as though I were getting my life back on track, his appearance was completely throwing me off balance.

Jennifer Bogart

Menu du Jour

Breakfast: French Toast, Fruit Salad, Coffee

Morning Snack: didn't need one, had a late breakfast

Lunch: Vegetable Soup (NOT cabbage) and a sandwich
Afternoon snack: no time, too busy getting ready for
company

Late afternoon snack: does a Lychee Martini count?
Supper: Leafy green salad, salmon steaks, rice & roasted
egg plant

Dessert: Chocolate Mousse with raspberry sauce
Calories Consumed: 2,050 calories but it's Saturday,
calories don't count on Saturday

Calories burned: 1426.75 + 516 (housework & cooking
add up!) = 1942.75

Chapter Fifteen

The Carpet Cleaners

There's only so much one person can do in a lifetime. Unfortunately, there are many days when I feel as though I'm only doing a small fraction of what could be done. When Calleigh was young I could easily use her as an excuse. She needed me, I was her only parent, I had already lost so much and I was desperately afraid to let her out of my sight. I also needed to work. As the sole source of income for the two of us, I needed to ensure I had job security and a career that I could grow into. I didn't have time to figure out who I was or what I wanted out of life. There were days I barely had time to shower or brush my teeth.

Calleigh is now on the verge of becoming an independent young woman. There will be dips and bumps along the meandering road of adolescence, but somehow, I know she'll persevere. She has this incredible instinct for survival, but then, I guess almost all children do. Calleigh can't be my excuse for not engaging in life anymore. I can't blame my excess flab on left over pregnancy weight; I can't use the excuse of no babysitter to hide in the house. It was time to face it; hiding behind my daughter was no longer an option. It was time I ventured into the big wide world and took the time to figure out what I needed out of this life.

Seeing Ryan had reinforced the fact that my individuality had slowly slip away. I had replaced it with the sole identity of being Calleigh's mommy and Chris's sister. Actually, I had insisted on this identity. I never wanted to be known as Damian's widow. Aside from the archaic terminology, the pitying looks, the sympathetic glances and the sad eyes people presented whenever they saw me made me cringe. It was easier for me to sweep the past under the carpet and forget about it. But the carpet was beginning to fray at the edges. Soon it would need replacing altogether as the occasionally cleaning just wasn't removing the stains from the past as effectively as it once did.

"Where are you?" Startled, I looked up to find Lucy standing at my desk. I had been so lost in thought that I didn't even realize she was there.

"Huh?"

"You look like you're a million miles away." She placed a stack of papers on my desk. "Stan asked me to drop these off."

"Thanks," I said absently. With a sigh, I realized I had been sitting and staring at a blank computer screen. I needed to pull myself back into the present. Somehow my musings had brought me into the past while yearning for a future that just couldn't exist.

"Are you alright?" She looked genuinely concerned.

I shrugged. "I'm alright. I had a bit of a crazy weekend and I'm tired."

Lucy wasn't buying it, I could tell by her pursed lips and raised eyebrow. "When you're ready, I'm here."

I nodded. She was doing it again; opening the door to a deeper friendship and all I could do was push her away. I wasn't slamming that imaginary door in her face; I just wasn't ready to invite her into my world. She might decide she doesn't like it there and then I would lose the only real friend I had outside of family.

"By the way, do you want to go to yoga tonight?"

Did I want to? Sure—why not? It would get me out of the house and I was pretty sure Chris was home tonight should Calleigh need an adult. I needed a distraction.

"Sure, sounds good."

"We're going to try a different one." There were different kinds of hot yoga? Surely, she was kidding me. How much variety could there possibly be. Hot was hot, and yoga was yoga. I was completely inept when it came to knowing anything about fitness trends like this.

"The one we've been going to is more Zen, it's relaxing and good for you, but I think we should try the Bikram style."

"Uh, okay," I agreed. I had no idea what she was talking about, but I would do an internet search on it. If it looked too crazy, I would just plead a headache or come up with some other excuse. After all, I was a pro at finding reasons not to participate in life.

"We need to be there thirty minutes early, so they can explain it all to us."

"You haven't done this before?" I was surprised. I had been under the impression that Lucy had done it all, and I was becoming her tag-a-long, like a puppy on a leash.

She laughed. "Nope. But I have wanted to try it for a very long time."

Great. We would be Newbie Yogi's together. "What's the difference?"

"I'm not sure. I think the Bikram is a bit longer, maybe a bit more intense. We'll have to wait and see."

Wait… I had been waiting my whole adult life, so I guess I could wait a few more hours to see what type of physical torture I would be indulging in this evening.

We basically had to sign away our lives before they would let us in the course. It wasn't a simple waiver which you signed the bottom and then were done with it. You had to read through the entire thing, initial each clause, and then sign the bottom. It was very clear they would not take any responsibility for any eventuality that might happen in the class. I found it a bit worrisome, but Lucy insisted it was the same for pretty much every kind of membership or trial class.

The karma yoga we had experienced was more like a relaxing afternoon on a warm, breezy beach. In contrast, the Bikram Yoga was like doing an intensive workout in a dry dessert with a militant auctioneer for an instructor. We were told to lay our mats at the back of the studio since we were inexperienced. There was absolutely no talking during the class, not even to ask questions. The drill sergeant also informed us that she would tell us when we could have water breaks and that if we needed to rest, that was ok, but under no circumstances were we allowed to leave the room. Lucy and I looked at each other and tried not to laugh. It was highly doubtful the two of us could go for a full ninety minutes without talking!

The room was stifling and very dark. The regulars took their places with confidence and assumed what I think were meditative poses. Lucy and I laid out our mats side by side, gingerly sat down and waited patiently. At least I tried to give the impression I was we were being patient, but I was itching to get going. The faster we started, the faster we could escape the extreme heat. I hated that there wasn't a clock on the wall. There was no way of knowing if five minutes had passed or fifteen. I only know that by the time the instructor entered the room I was already starting to feel overheated and I had done little more than wiggle my big toe.

Abruptly, harsh lights pierced our eyes that had only just adjusted to the gloom and the instructor's voice boomed out something that got everyone up and on their feet. She explained that she would not be demonstrating the moves, but rather we were to watch those in front of us for guidance. I wondered briefly how those people felt about being watched so carefully. I hoped the person in front of me knew what she was doing.

The first exercise was all about breathing. We were warming up the inside of our bodies so we would be able to perform the poses with ease and confidence. With my elbows flapping up and down above my ears and my hands clasped under my chin, I wondered if I might eventually take flight. I felt totally ridiculous and I was sweating profusely even though we were only breathing.

As my body adjusted to the heat, I found I could easily follow the verbal instructions while copying the person in front of me. The first few poses of the class were pretty simple: all positions I had done before. I wanted to drink, but she had instructed us not to and with the tone of voice she used, I was afraid to break ranks. Lucy had no qualms about doing her own thing. I only wished I had her confidence.

About halfway through the class I got incredibly dizzy. We were rapidly moving up and down and up and down again. With the extreme heat, I was sure the blood in my body was no longer sluggishly making its way through my veins, but rather it was streaming through my body at breakneck speed. I wanted to stop, but at the same time I thought that if I did, I would pass out. Beside me, I wasn't sure if Lucy was struggling too, but she gave me a look that clearly indicated she wasn't enjoying something about the class.

Our drill sergeant instructor spoke so fast we could hardly perform one pose before moving onto the next. I had thought Yoga was a slow moving, relaxing kind of exercise. This was more intense than the spinning had been.

When the nausea struck, I was deeply concerned I would vomit all over the carpet. Until that moment I hadn't paid any attention to the floor covering. Why would they line a yoga studio with carpet? It didn't seem like the most sanitary choice, but it did explain the dirty sock odour that was permeating the room. At first, I had thought it was body odour even though I had only noticed the smell when we were doing horizontal poses. Of course, once I was aware of it, I couldn't clear the stench from my head. The smell was not helping my queasy state in the least. These carpets needed a good cleaning.

I persevered, I had been through worse things in life and surely the class couldn't last that much longer.

"We are halfway through, good for you," the instructor chose that moment to point out the time. She had to be joking, but there was no way to know. I sorely doubted I would survive the class without disgracing myself. Lucy's expression clearly showed she was not impressed.

The next pose we attempted was supposed to hurt, which I thought was just insane. Why would you purposefully attempt to contort your body into a painful position? "Pain is just crystallized emotion your body doesn't know how to deal with. Accept and acknowledge it. Feel the pain and the emotion you have been pushing down so that you can find release."

I decided in that moment that she was totally off her rocker. The physical pain and discomfort I was experiencing had very little to do with the emotional anguish I had locked away safely in a box at the bottom of my heart. "Release your emotion, embrace your pain, and cry if you need to."

I would not cry. I had done enough of that Saturday night. *I would not release my emotions,* despite the horrendous nausea that continued to envelope me. I focused on the glaring light above me. I desperately wanted to sit up, and experience a cool draft. I made a forceful effort to clear my mind, and focus on my breathing. It worked.

And then, suddenly, we were done. We were instructed to lay on our backs in meditation. She praised us, told us we were so beautiful and graceful, before slipping unnoticed from the room. I was exhausted, both physically and emotionally. Before I could stop them, tears started to leak from the corners of my eyes. They mixed with the salty sweat and stung as they coursed down the sides of my face. I wanted to wipe them away, but I knew instinctively if I did, the dam would break and I would be a puddle of grief all over again. Where had this come from?

Thankfully, during the meditation at the end of the session, the instructor had plunged us back into darkness. No one could see my tears and I absolutely refused to sob opening. I would regain control before leaving the darkened studio. Beside me I felt, more than saw, Lucy pull herself into a sitting position, roll up her mat and leave the room. I was grateful she decided not to wait for me. I needed a few moments to compose myself.

When I finally emerged from the extreme heat I was back in control. I could attribute my red eyes to the heat, everyone had red eyes, and the tears had blended well with the sweat. Lucy might have been aware of my lack of composure, but she didn't remark on it. She was too busy scowling over a bitter apple someone had offered her.

"It's going to take forever to cool down," I commented as I headed towards the change room. Everyone was milling around the waiting area, drenched in sweat, eating bitter apples and chit-chatting away. One guy was even sitting in a chair, shirt off and sweat puddling at his feet. I know the chair was a faux wicker so it could easily be wiped down, but I was still disgusted. The very least he could have done was use a towel.

"You wanna go for a drink?" Lucy asked. I did, but at the same time I didn't. Something in me was searching for release and this would be as good a time as any to share. I knew she wouldn't be judgemental, but something was still holding me back from confiding in her. Maybe it was simply a force of habit that I couldn't bring myself to open up to anyone. I had been my own confidante for so long, just the thought of talking to someone else made me feel anxious.

I shook my head, "It's late, and Calleigh is home on her own."

"She should be sleeping by now," Lucy pointed out.

Her own children were younger, so naturally went to bed a bit earlier.

"She is unpredictable at the best of times, and sometimes won't sleep until both Chris and I are home." I wasn't about to explain to Lucy that the last time Calleigh had gone to bed when her parents were out, she woke up to her mother coming home in hysterics and her father hospitalized. Six-year-olds have a way of holding onto traumatic memories for a lifetime.

"So, what did you think?" she asked after a few moments. Her eyes were as red as mine and I thought for a moment that maybe she was the one who needed to talk. Lucy talked a lot, but she was pretty closed-mouthed about her personal life. She talked about her sons constantly, she occasionally mentioned her husband, but for the most part, her conversation was light banter.

I shrugged my shoulders, "At one point I thought I was going to throw up. I'm still a bit queasy."

She laughed at that. "Yeah, I was pretty sure I was going to pass out, I got so dizzy."

"I'll let you know how I feel tomorrow, when I can't get out of bed, if I want to do it again. That was far more intense."

She nodded in agreement, which surprised me. I had expected her to breeze through the class, making it look as effortless as everything else she did. "It won't look very good if we both call in sick."

"Nope," I agreed. "Hey, if you don't have any plans on Saturday, do you want to bring your family over for dinner?"

She thought about it for moment, then said quietly,

"Well, Devin and I might have plans because it's Valentine's. I'll let you know for sure later in the week."

"Oh yeah, I forgot. We can do it next week then, if that works better for you."

This was the first time I had extended an invitation for dinner outside of immediate family in seven years. I hoped that I could come up with a reasonable meal to serve.

Menu du Jour

Breakfast: yogurt, apple, cereal bar, coffee

Morning snack: coffee, muffin

Lunch: Cream of chicken soup, grilled cheese sandwich

Mid afternoon snack: cheese, crackers & coffee

Supper: small portion of grilled chicken, broccoli and rice

Dessert: thought I would save it for after yoga, but it turned out I was just too hot to stomach food

Calories Consumed: 1669

Calories burned: 1426.75 + 715 (during Bikram Yoga— who knew?) = 2141.75

Chapter Sixteen

New Roommate, Old Dwellings

I woke up feeling surprisingly well rested and happy. Euphoric is not a word I would normally use to describe any of my moods, but there wasn't any other way to describe the glee bubbling up inside me. I couldn't remember the last time I woke up feeling this content; almost as though all was right with the world. It made me wonder if I was bipolar. The day before I had been immersed in misery and anguish. There was no way a bit of stretching, balancing and toning could possibly change a person's frame of mind so completely. Regardless, I wasn't going to question this feeling of relaxation; I was going to savour it for as long as it lasted. "Uncle Ryan called last night while you were out," Calleigh announced as I sauntered into the kitchen. She was up, dressed and ready for the day, which made me wonder if I had forgotten about driving her to school early for a field trip or something. I checked the calendar with a quick glance, but there was nothing scheduled.

"Was he calling to say good-bye?" I asked. I would not let thoughts of Ryan pierce my happy bubble. Thoughts of

Ryan inevitably led to thoughts of his brother and there was no way I was going to dwell on the past today.

Calleigh shrugged her shoulders, "I dunno. He just left a number and asked for you to call him as soon as you got in. I would have told you last night, but I was asleep."

I nodded. She had been sound asleep when I had checked on her last night. Things were certainly changing in this house. "I know. You surprised me. I'll call him from work since I doubt he would appreciate an eight am phone—"

The doorbell rang, cutting me off. Who on earth would be at the door at this time on a Tuesday?

Chris made it to the door first as she was passing by it just as the bell rang. Ryan entered the house with a burst of crisp winter air and bright sunshine. I couldn't imagine why he would be on my doorstep at this time of the day. I had thought he would be catching a flight to head out on his next big adventure.

"Hey Ryan," Chris said as she took his jacket. There was a light dusting of snow in his hair which he shook off before it could melt.

He smiled in greeting and leaned forward to kiss her cheek. "Long time no see," he said.

"We were just talking about you, were your ears burning?"

He leaned over to kiss my cheek also. "Nope. But I do hope you were saying good things about me."

"We don't actually know enough about you to talk about," I said in all honesty. Ryan was family, but beyond sharing DNA with my daughter, a striking resemblance to my late husband and a last name, there wasn't all that much we knew about him.

"Well, hopefully we can change that," he said with a smile. Chris offered him a cup of coffee and it seemed to me that Calleigh and Ryan exchanged a secretive, knowing glance. I could have been mistaken, but I was pretty sure the two of them were up to something.

"So, when are you heading out on your next adventure?" I asked him. I had assumed he was only in town for the weekend, but his visit this morning made me think differently.

"Actually, that's what I needed to talk to you about." I looked at him expectantly. Ryan was an adventurer. He took photographs and made documentaries about far-off places. I couldn't imagine what he would want to talk to me about with regards to his work.

"Shoot."

"I'm taking a short hiatus. I have a lot of material I need to work through and organize. I need a place to call home for a few months and I was wondering if I could stay here."

His request nearly knocked me off my chair. "Huh?"

"Calleigh said you have space. Damian's office is empty, so I can set up my work in there, and you have that spare room… I can't afford to stay in a hotel indefinitely, and I don't want to enter into a lease when I only need a place for a few months."

"Uh huh," I nodded, trying to process what he was saying. So that's why my daughter was up and ready for school at the break of dawn this morning. She was conspiring with her uncle.

"Please, Roxy. I don't really have anyone else I can ask." Well, he had me there. Damian and Ryan's mother was currently in a nursing home with Alzheimer's and their father lived in a lovely retirement community that would not welcome a bachelor for any length of time.

I sighed. Did I really need another roommate? When Chris had moved in, the arrangement was supposed to be temporary. Seven years later I couldn't imagine living without her. I knew it was selfish of me to make it so easy for her to stay, but I had come to rely on her so much. Ryan would be a daily reminder of days gone by. Days I had worked so hard to set aside so I could continue with my own life.

"I suppose we could work something out." I'm sure the hesitation was evident in my voice, but I just couldn't help it. He had to know seeing him in my house everyday was going to be very difficult.

Calleigh jumped up from her seat, threw her arms around me and kissed my cheek with a loud smacking sound. "I knew you would let him stay!"

Well, if nothing else, I had managed to please my daughter today.

Despite my uninvited houseguest, my good mood prevailed throughout the day and into the next. Lucy managed to convince me to try another spinning class Wednesday morning. I figured if I could survive the first one, I should be able to make it through the second one that much easier. At first, I was mildly concerned about asking Chris to make sure Calleigh made it off to school, but then decided that it could easily become Ryan's job a couple times a week. After all, it wasn't like he had to pay rent or anything and one of the reasons he wanted to stay with us was so that he could spend time with his only niece.

The hardest part about the workout was getting up so early. For as long as I could remember, I have not been a morning person. When Calleigh was very small and prone to rising early, Damian would get up with her. Because he was naturally an early riser, this would be their special time of the day to hang out, play quietly and spend some real quality time together. Her habits were more like mine now but I wondered if this wouldn't be the case had Damian.

"I saved you a bike," Lucy indicated the bike directly beside her, which was sporting her towel and water bottle. All the bikes in the spinning studio were the same make and model, however some had seen better days. The earlier one arrived for the class, the better the bike one could claim; the theory being the better the bike, the better the workout.

"Thanks," I handed back her water bottle and towel before replacing them with my own. Glancing around, I saw the studio was rapidly filling up. I recognized a number of faces from the previous week. I was somewhat relieved to see a certain dark-eyed vision missing from the group. Maybe last week's class had been a fluke and it wasn't something he attended with regularity. Or maybe he only came on Fridays. If that was the case, I could avoid Fridays and stick to a Wednesday class.

"How is the new roommate working out?" Lucy was already warming up. After adjusting my bike, I felt obligated to follow her lead, even though I knew I would have a hard time keeping up in the class later.

"It's alright. I put him in charge of Calleigh this morning so I could make the class."

Lucy nodded. "Good plan. He can take charge on Friday too and then you'll be able to fit in two spinning classes."

"The only problem is that this is supposed to be a temporary arrangement. He's not staying forever."

"Right." She increased her tension and raised herself into a standing climb position. "How long did he say he was staying?"

I shrugged my shoulders. Ryan had not indicated an exact timeline. He had only said he needed a place to complete his current project and that it would take a few months. I guess I should have pressed him for more details, but I had been so surprised by his initial request that my mind couldn't formulate all the right questions. "A few months. He needs to put the finishing touches on his project."

"Is he paying rent?"

Now that was a strange question. I didn't need him to pay rent, not really. The one thing Damian and I had done right was make sure we had good insurance. Upon his death, our mortgage had been paid off, and I was left with only the daily expenses of life to deal with. One of the reasons Chris had been so happy to move in with us was because her only monetary contribution was food and electricity. She made a decent salary as a teacher, but she still had a few student loans to pay off.

A movement at the back of the class caught my eye. The dark-eyed man had returned and was taking his position towards the back of the class. So much for avoiding him today. Maybe he wouldn't recognize me or even notice me in the class. Last week he had been too focused on his workout to give anyone else any thought.

"Hello? Earth to Roxanne. . ."

"Oh, sorry. No, I'm not asking him to pay rent. It's not an issue."

"Well, then, he'll never move out," she went on to list all the various reasons why Ryan should be helping with the household expenses, but I was too distracted by the man at the back of the class to pay attention. Absently, I nodded when she paused to take a breath, but I had no idea what she was going on about.

The spinning studio was set up with mirrors on three sides so you could watch your form to ensure you were holding all the positions correctly so you could get the best possible workout. This meant that you could clearly see yourself and every other participant in the class. I watched him as he adjusted his bike, laid out his towel and fiddled with his tension. Perhaps he caught a glimpse of me in the mirror, or perhaps he could feel my gaze— either way he looked up and caught my eyes in the mirror. I held my breath, waiting to see if he would recognize me. After all, several years had passed since the last time he had noticed me and it was entirely possible he had forgotten me altogether.

"Roxy, are you even listening to me?"

Abruptly, I brought my attention back to Lucy, but not quickly enough. She followed the direction my gaze had taken in the mirror and smiled slightly. "He's cute," she acknowledged.

I'm sure I blushed, which didn't help matters, since the object of my attention was openly staring back. "Yeah, I might know him from somewhere."

"Might? Or do?" she asked. Lucy was too astute by far.

I shrugged my shoulders. "Did—from a past life best forgotten." Even though I had spoken the words aloud, I knew the past was about to invade my present. Who was I kidding? It already had with the arrival of Ryan. Why should the sudden appearance of Harper surprise me?

"Anyway, he probably doesn't even remember me," I continued absently, forcing myself to dismiss his presence so I could carry on with the business of getting through this class.

"If the way he is staring at you is any indication of his memory; I would hazard a guess that he hasn't forgotten you."

I chanced another look just in time to see him quickly turn away from the mirror to make more

adjustments to his bike. "Terrific."

Lucky for me, the music started and the instructor started shouting directions to us. Easy riding, stretching, light tension—all orders I was all too eager to obey so that I could forget about the man in the back, my new roommate and the conversation I was going to have to have with Lucy sooner than later.

Lucy and I decided to reward ourselves with lunch at a local Italian restaurant. My efforts with the cabbage soup diet were quickly disappearing with the rich lunches and desserts I craved. Two spinning classes and a bit of hot yoga were not going to melt the fat away, no matter how much I sweated. I promised myself, today's lunch would be a rare treat and that I would look for a new diet plan and stick to it. Obviously, I was able to stick to a diet, I just wasn't able to maintain any weight loss upon completion.

"So," Lucy said through a bite of Caesar salad, "tell me about the mystery guy."

I shook my head. Until now, Lucy had not questioned me about anything that would upset me. I guess she was tired of waiting for me to open up. She had been privy to a number of my moods; everything from tears, to anger, to avoidance and now she was looking for answers.

"Oh, just someone I used to know." Somehow, I knew this was not going to be enough for her. She only raised an eyebrow in response and waited patiently for me to continue.

"He used to work with my husband."

She continued to eat her salad in silence. The only sound coming from her was the crunch of the crisp lettuce. I took a sip of water and picked my fork through my own leafy green salad. I was sure the manicotti I had ordered would be far more satisfying when it arrived. Briefly I wondered why her salad looked so much more appealing than my own heap of slightly wilted lettuce.

Lucy took another bite and looked at me meaningfully. I sighed.

"They worked for an advertising firm. Damian was a project manager and Harper is a graphic artist. I only met Harper a couple of times. Damian wasn't one to share his work with me."

"So why would you want to forget about Harper?" she asked, obviously recalling my comment in the gym.

"Just old memories surfacing all over again. I know that Damian died several years ago, and I should be over it now, but some things are still very painful for me." I hoped this would be enough for her. I had never shared the details of the accident or the drama that had emerged shortly afterwards. In fact, just admitting that I even knew Harper was a giant step for me.

"Okay. But you know, you should talk about it. You'll feel better and maybe all those memories won't be so unbearable to you if you share them." I considered this for a moment.

"You're probably right," I acknowledged with a nod. "But it took me years to get to a place emotionally where

I can be content with my life and where it's going. I'm not sure I want to look backwards just now."

The look Lucy gave me sent shivers down my spine.

"Are you really in a place where you're happy with who you are?"

How had she done that? She had taken my words, gave them a little twist and pointed out exactly what I had not said. Thankfully, when I didn't answer she decided to change the subject to talk about her one of her boy's hockey game on the weekend.

Menu du Jour

Breakfast: hardboiled egg, toast, coffee

Morning Snack: apple

Lunch: Leafy green salad, manicotti, espresso, and half of a heart to heart conversation

Afternoon snack: small bag of chips

Supper: surprise—chicken breasts, mashed potatoes and green beans prepared by my newest roommate

Dessert: ice cream

Evening snack: glass of much needed white wine

Calories consumed: 1827

Calories burned: 1426.75 + 774 (spinning) = 2200.75

Chapter Seventeen

Master Cleanse

I decided to try the Master Cleanse diet. I know it's an extreme measure, and I know it's probably not good modeling for Calleigh, but Spring was quickly approaching and I needed to do something. Fast. Otherwise, Calleigh and I would be spending another Saturday at the mall, only this time I would be the one in tears.

The thing I just couldn't understand was that I was exercising more than I ever had before and I was consistently gaining weight. Lucy insisted it was because I was gaining muscle and that I should stop worrying about the numbers on the scale. Chris insisted I looked better than ever, but I still had a mirror and the last time I checked all the wiggles and jiggles were firmly in place. I wouldn't even allow Ryan to comment on the situation. Every time he overheard snippets of conversation regarding my weight he would simply raise an eyebrow and leave the room as quickly as possible, his discomfort evident.

In some ways, the Master Cleanse Diet was very similar to the Cabbage Soup diet. If followed, it promised to shed unwanted pounds, detoxify your digestive system and balance your body. The diet guaranteed to cleanse your body of waste products it may have stored for months, years or even decades. Celebrities were doing it; and they looked and felt amazing. Some of the beautiful people at the yoga studio were also doing it; and their bodies were something I had only ever seen in magazines. The fact that none of them were a day over twenty-two probably had a little something to do with their physical perfection, but I wasn't even going there.

"I think you're a nutcase to even consider it," Lucy commented as we enjoyed what would be my last solid meal for several days. "You won't even have enough energy to get through the day."

"According to some of the literature I've read, you should be fine. My body has plenty of energy stores, so I'm sure I can last a few days without too much trouble."

Lucy shook her head. "You've been working out for a couple weeks now, you'll miss it."

I laughed at that. Exercise was a bit of an addiction, there was something to be said for getting your heart rate up, working muscles and then stretching them out. In the moment, I might be cursing the instructor for making me push myself, but afterwards I genuinely felt good, both physically and mentally.

The problem with exercise was that it made me hungry. Sure, my energy levels had increased and I had more stamina. But after a solid hour of cardio I was ravenous and could inhale as much as an elephant in one sitting. There had to be a way to regulate that and the only thing I could come up with was to shrink my stomach. The Master Cleanse Diet would take care of that. Unlike the Cabbage Soup Diet, I would not be eating any solid foods for several days, which, in theory, would make the hole smaller so I would be less hungry.

"Have you seriously looked at the diet? I mean, one of the required elements is to take laxatives twice a day. If you aren't eating anything —" she shuddered in distaste. "I just can't imagine."

"It can't be that bad," I insisted. "Celebrities do it, healthy yogis do it, even one of the personal trainers at the gym mentioned she had done it. It's only for ten days or so, it can't be worse than Cabbage Soup."

She looked at me with so such scepticism I could only laugh. For the most part it was lemonade and maple syrup—how hard would that be to stomach?

"The Cabbage Soup diet made you cranky," she pointed out.

"It couldn't have been too bad," I shot back. "You're still my friend."

"Oh—that's just because I want to know all your secrets. I'm in this friendship for the juicy gossip."

I laughed, "Well then, you might want to go looking somewhere else for your entertainment—the best gossip I have is that my daughter might have a boyfriend!"

"Wow, your thirteen-year-old has a boyfriend?"

I nodded. The worst part about it was I had found out through Ryan. She had been asking him a lot of questions about boys, and what they like and how to tell if they like you. I guess having a man around the house was probably good for her. "It seems my thirteen-year-old has a more active social life than I do."

"You have me," Lucy pointed out, which made me smile. Lucy was a pretty new development as far as friends go. Most of my friends from school and the early years of my marriage disappeared shortly after Damian died. I'm not sure if they just didn't know how to handle his death, or if they weren't mature enough to understand that there wasn't a right or wrong thing to say at the time. Regardless, they showed their support in the months following his death, but slowly started to fade away into the background. At the time, I had been too engrossed in caring for my daughter and dealing with my own grief to even notice their gradual disappearance.

"I do, and I'm glad for it, even if you are bossy and think I'm crazy for trying this diet."

Lucy shrugged. "I just think there are better ways to manage weight and diet. I go to the gym so I can eat whatever I want."

"I know—but that doesn't seem to be working for me. I go to the gym and I'm starving afterwards so I'm eating more than ever before."

"You need more protein."

"I need some self control!" I laughed. "Anyway, we'll see how it goes. I can quit at anytime." "But you won't," she noted.

I shook my head. She was getting to know me well.

"What the hell are you reading?" Ryan asked. He was leaning over my shoulder while I sat at my computer doing some research. I didn't even know he was home. The problem with him being a temporary guest was that he didn't own a car, so unless you saw him, there was no way of knowing if he was in the house.

"Just doing a bit of research," I was mortified that he had seen the page I was reviewing. I couldn't have been more embarrassed had he caught me watching pornography.

"You aren't considering doing that to yourself, are you?"

Well, I was, but I wasn't about to share that with him now. "It's just research, Ryan. Relax."

He took the mouse from me and started scrolling down the screen, muttering as he read the ins and outs (quite literally) of making it through the Master Cleanse program.

"That's some sick stuff. It can't be good for you."

"It can't be that bad, either," I argued. "It's all the rage in Hollywood."

Ryan shook his head, as though trying to rid himself of an annoying buzzing sound. "Yeah—and celebrities are always the brightest bunnies in the bush with their crazy religions like Scientology, various eating disorders, drug addictions and ridiculous sense of style. Great people to emulate." His sarcasm washed over me like a torrential downpour.

"Oh, what do you know anyway?"

"I know that drinking salt water is a recipe for making yourself violently ill. But, suit yourself." He sauntered into the kitchen, opened the refrigerator door and started pulling all kinds of vegetables out of the crisper. One good thing about having Ryan around, I hadn't cooked a meal in days. Coming home to dinner nearly prepared, a glass of wine poured and Calleigh settled into her homework was a bit of heaven. I should have started looking for a house-husband eons ago. I didn't want the emotional attachment that might come with one, but I was certainly enjoying the creature comforts of domestic chores being completed by someone other than myself.

However, I could also do without the silent judgements and know-it-all attitude that often exuded from him.

I returned my attention to the diet plan—if you could call it that. Although the program was fairly simple, it might actually take more effort than the Cabbage Soup one had. The most complicated thing in following the Cabbage Soup diet was ensuring you always had enough soup on hand, that was fresh and hadn't fermented as it was apt to do.

This diet would take considerably more preparation and will-power, but I was fairly certain I could survive it.

My biggest concern was the salt water flush. People weren't meant to drink salt water and the reason for it was obvious when the website explained in disgusting detail exactly what to expect from the concoction. Maybe I would skip that part and stick with the laxatives twice a day. Of course, if I was going to do the cleanse, I would do it by the rules; I'm not one to take short cuts or cheat on something.

Before even starting the cleanse, a number of websites recommended preparing your body so it would easily adapt to fewer calories and a liquid diet. The running theme was detoxification. According to much of what I read, we fill our bodies with all kinds of pesticides, herbicides, chemicals and poisons just by eating regular food from the grocery store. The first order of business is to eat more healthy foods, like fruits and vegetables that are certified organic. The organic part made me laugh, because this cleansing diet was supposed to be easy and economical. Everyone knows that certified organic produce costs about twice as much as regular food.

On the second day, you're supposed to take those same veggies and fruits and reduce them to juice so that your body can be prepared to consume only liquids. The purported upside to this is the delivery of easily processed macro-nutrients directly to your system. That's just a whole lot of big words stating you won't have to chew your food. The third day, you skip the veggie juices and head straight for the fruit juices—one suggestion was to make two litres of orange juice, dilute it with water and then add maple syrup to taste. One of the things that attracted me to this diet in the first place had been the liberal use of maple syrup. Apparently, maple syrup tastes great with everything!

If you can survive the lead-up to the diet, then you're prepared to take on the challenge of the Master Cleanse. After the bland, calorie reduced diet of Cabbage Soup; I had no difficulty getting through the three days leading up to the Master Cleanse. I wasn't hungry because there wasn't any real limit on how much you consumed; they were only limitations on what you consumed and its solidity. The most difficult day was the orange juice blitz. I have a small aversion to orange juice at the best of times; it has a slimy texture I can't get past. Adding the maple syrup to it only made it that much stranger for my already deprived palate.

I was very careful with the timing of starting the Master Cleanse process. Everything I read suggested you have a bathroom handy with unlimited access, especially after doing the salt water flush. I decided it would be best to try the first full day on the weekend, so as not to run into any potentially embarrassing moments at work. If Calleigh, Chris or Ryan wondered why I had locked myself in my room, I would just tell them I had a gastro and that they might want to keep their distance. I didn't want any of them to know I was doing this extreme diet in an attempt to quickly shed twenty pounds. I was surprised they hadn't noticed that the only thing I consumed yesterday was orange juice. But then, everyone was so busy in this house we hardly took notice of each other at all.

The recommended duration for the cleanse was ten days. Ten days of drinking a lemonade-like concoction, complete with maple syrup, and flushing your system free of toxins and other waste products that had been stored for years. This waste build-up was allegedly the root of all evil in weight management and I was going to be rid of it once and for all. Well, maybe not "for all", since as soon as you return to a regular diet the cycle of storing toxins starts all over again, so the Master Cleanse was something that would need to be repeated periodically.

In a word, the salt water flush could only be described as abysmal. Try to imagine chugging a litre of sea water in five minutes or less. Aside from the revolting taste, my oesophagus' instinct was to close up and my stomach to expel its contents. I imagined it was similar to dosing a person with syrup of ipecac. The desired effect was to flush your system from the top down—in some circles the salt water flush is known as a "top-down enema". My stomach didn't even give my body that option. No sooner had I downed the ghastly mixture than it was coming back up. I didn't even make it to the bathroom, which was only steps away.

I had read that this could happen, and that if you weren't successful on the first try, you should try, try again. I wasn't so sure I was up for that. I already had a headache from lack of substance, I was dizzy from violently hurling the contents of my stomach all over the carpet and to add insult to injury, I think my intestines were trying to turn themselves inside out. Willpower or not, this was not something I was about to repeat.

I guess I made some noise, because three very concerned individuals were banging on my door.

"Roxanne," Chris called through my door, "Are you alright?"

I didn't have the energy to respond, but didn't want them bursting into my room.

"Mom, can we come in?"

"I'm alright," I mumbled as I tried to pick myself up from the floor. How the heck had I ended up there?

"Mom?"

"I'm alright," I called out, trying to sound calm and composed.

"Doesn't sound like she's alright," Ryan's deeper voice penetrated through the door. I didn't need him in here to be witness to my folly.

"I… I just have the flu and got a bit dizzy. You might want to keep your distance." I was on my hands and knees and the room was swirling around me. If only the room would stop spinning, I might be able to get some sort of control over my tumultuous insides.

"Let me in," Chris insisted. I had forgotten that I had locked my door—not something I was in the habit of doing and Chris knew it.

In that moment, I was torn. Part of me wished I could let her in, in more ways than one. Another part of me was so glad I had barred the way. I would let them all in when I was good and ready.

Menu du Jour

Breakfast: Sea Salt Flush

Calories consumed: 0

Calories burned: however many a body needs just to breath because that's about all I could do.

Jennifer Bogart

Chapter Eighteen

Tides of Laughter

I felt like spending the rest of Saturday in bed, curled into a fetal position, feeling sorry for myself. My house has these stupid locks on the bedroom doors. You can use a thin nail to release the catch and voila, the door will easily swing open. Chris and I had kept a nail handy for when Calleigh was smaller because she often locked herself in her bedroom and bathroom. When I didn't get up fast enough to let my concerned family into my misery, Chris searched out the trusty nail and before I knew it the three of them were standing over me. I have never been so embarrassed in my life. The worst thing about it was I still couldn't peel myself up off the floor.

"Christ, Roxanne! What the hell have you done to yourself?" Ryan was staring at the puddle of orange liquid that was quickly seeping into the carpet. The stain would never come out, no matter how hard I scrubbed it away. I would have to cover it up with an area rug.

Even after Damian died I don't think I had ever lost my composure quite like this. Mortified, I rolled into a sitting position, which proved to be a horrendous mistake. I had manage to keep some of that vile potion down, and it needed to come out. Immediately. In all my life, I have never moved so fast. I was beyond grateful my bedroom had an ensuite bathroom.

When I emerged from the bathroom, I'm sure I looked like death, I sure felt like it. Chris had set Calleigh to work scrubbing at the carpet while she straightened my bed and fetched clean pyjamas from my dresser. Ryan had fled the scene, probably relieved he couldn't be of use.

"Are you going to be alright now?" she asked me as she handed me the clean clothing. I dropped my towel, not caring who was in the room and slid into the comforting flannel.

"I'm fine," I said quietly. "Leave that, Calleigh. I'll get it steam cleaned."

Calleigh stood and looked at me with concern. "We just didn't want it to smell too much." She rung out the rag she had been using and draped it on the side of the wash bin. "I can't get all the orange out." She shuddered with visible distaste. My poor daughter, she should never have been witness to that. What the hell had I been thinking?

The problem was, I hadn't been thinking. I wanted a quick fix to rid myself of years of emotional eating. I was tired of being frumpy and dumpy with no friends or social life. At my age, I should know there is no magic cure for a run down, middle aged, haggard, widowed mom. No pills or diets would magically transform me into a fairy princess. Fairy tales, like dreams are nothing but pixie dust, too easily scattered in the slightest of breezes. I would never recapture mine, they were just too far gone.

"Mom?" Calleigh gently touched my arm. "I think you should sleep for a bit. Uncle Ryan is making a nice chicken soup for lunch. It should help you feel better."

When had she turned into such a lovely young lady. Her eyes reflected a maturity older than her years. In this instant, I felt like I was the child and she was the adult. How I had let our roles get reversed like that?

Chris guided me to the bed, and carefully tucked me in, as though I were made of the finest china and might easily shatter into a million pieces if not handled with extreme caution. I felt fragile, even though I knew I was fine. The last of the salt water flush had worked its way through my system, leaving no real lasting harm. I was too tired and emotionally drained to wrap my head around it.

"Just rest for a while," Chris said quietly. "When lunch is ready, I'll wake you. You need food."

Calleigh leaned over and gently kissed my forehead, just as I had done for her, for years and years when she wasn't feeling so well. Tears stung my eyes and shamefully I turned my face away. She had already seen me completely degraded, I didn't want her to see the weakness of my tears.

When I heard the door shut with a soft click, I couldn't stop myself, the floodgates opened up. These were quiet and confused tears, not the tears of grief and pain I had shed a few days ago. They felt warm on my cool skin and just flowed freely, pooling on my pillow to form a salty puddle. These tears were almost cleansing in their purity. I wasn't overwrought with emotion, if anything I felt somewhat void of feeling. I just couldn't help this physical release of tears and I was just too exhausted to try to figure out where they came from. Calleigh deserved better than this. I deserved better than this. That thought made the tears fall faster and harder until they multiplied into hiccupping sobs.

Here was the crux of the issue. I did deserve better than this. From the outside in, I'm sure it looked like we were walking on sunshine. My job was flexible, paid well and I did enjoy it. Calleigh was a good student and natural leader. I even had the luxury of my sister living with us to help offset some of the stress of single-parenting. There wasn't anything we didn't have that we couldn't go out and buy.

On the inside, nothing was so neat and tidy. I missed Damian, even after seven years. I'm not sure if I missed him, exactly, or if I missed the thought of him. We were supposed to be doing all of this together; raising our daughter, having a successful life. At the same time, I was so angry with him. He had done and said things that will forever tarnish my memories of him and I hated him for it.

I must have drifted off to sleep, because the next thing I knew, Chris was back in the room, sitting on the side of my bed. She had brought a tray laden with delicious smelling soup and fresh bread. If nothing else, Ryan was an excellent cook.

"You're awake, good."

I struggled into a sitting position and wiped my eyes like a small child. "I'm so sorry."

Chris shook her head as she laid the tray across my lap. "Don't worry about it. We all do stupid things."

At least she wasn't sugar coating my idiocy or trying to make me think what I had done to myself was perfectly normal. "Yeah, but that was a bit over the top, don't you think? How did you figure it out, anyway?"

"Well, we were wondering what you were doing with all that juice, since you weren't sharing it." She chuckled. "Then Calleigh mentioned she had seen something on the internet about juice diets and colon cleanses. I thought she was crazy and talking nonsense, but Ryan said he had seen you researching something. It didn't take much to pull up your Google history."

"Super Sleuths. CSI has nothing on you guys," I commented dryly. The soup smelled fabulous and my stomach rumbled in response to my senses wakening because of its mouth watering aroma.

"Seriously, though, Roxy—you have to stop doing these things to yourself."

"I know." The soup tasted even better than the scent had promised. Its warm comfort slid down my throat and warmed me from the inside out. "I'm all done with crazy diet fads."

"Are you sure? We found other diets in your browsing history. The raw food diet is one that really stands out in my mind."

I shook my head. "That one probably isn't what you're thinking. It's not like you eat raw meat or anything— that's a totally different diet. Besides, that one takes a lot of work and is expensive."

"I didn't realize things were getting so far out of hand with you," Chris stated. "I feel like I was falling down on the job."

"You're not my keeper. And it's not like I have an eating disorder or anything. I need to lose weight; I don't feel good about myself. Obviously, it's going to take years to take off what took years to put on."

Chris looked at me in surprise. "Why do you think you need to lose weight? You aren't fat by any stretch of the imagination."

I laughed at that. "I have a mirror—I know what I look like."

"You look fine to me," Ryan said from the doorway.

"You haven't seen me naked," I pointed out. "And that isn't an invitation," I added for good measure.

He smiled. "I didn't think it was. But seriously, Roxy, you're perfect. Stop trying to kill yourself."

"I'm all done with extremes, trust me." I took another bite of the bread, savouring its yeasty goodness. "This is awesome, by the way."

He shrugged his shoulders. "I've learned a few things on my travels."

"Lucky for us, we get to benefit from it," Calleigh said as she ducked under his arm. "I'm glad to see you looking more like yourself."

All this attention was starting to make me uncomfortable. "I think I'm alright now and should get up and do something."

"No," Calleigh and Chris protested in unison.

"We've decided you need a pamper-me day." I gave Chris a warning look. I wasn't into feeling sorry for myself and I wasn't about to spend the day wallowing in everyone else's pity.

"Not a sit on my ass and feel-sorry-for-myself day," she clarified. "An at home-spa-celebrate-me day. We have even called in reinforcements."

"Who?" The fewer people who were aware of today's fiasco, the better.

"Lucy," Calleigh stated. "You spend so much time with her, she's like your best friend. If I were having a bad day that needed to be turned around, I would want to spend it with my best friend."

I could feel those annoying tears tickling the back of my eyes again. These were tears of gratitude. Calleigh was a beautifully sensitive child and I hoped she never changed.

"I like this one," Lucy said as she selected a bright pink nail polish from the selection on the table. We were sitting in the living room, feet bare and pampering our toes. I couldn't remember the last time we had spent quality time like this together. It used to be a monthly ritual, much like having our parents over for dinner. We would soak our feet in a warm bath, and then use a paraffin wax melt that our mother had given us one year for Christmas. It wasn't as good as a real spa, by any stretch of the imagination; but it was time spent together without a TV or computer getting in the way. I had thought adding Lucy to the mix might be a bit awkward, but she fit right in. She even insisted that she needed this girl fix more than I did since she lived in a house full of men.

"Oh—that's bright," Chris commented. "How about this one?" She held up a lovely shade of coral.

Calleigh wrinkled her nose. "That's an old lady colour, I like the blue…"

"Calleigh! I'll have you know your Grandma loves that particular shade."

Chris and Lucy started laughing hysterically and then I clued into what I had just said. "It's a good thing she's not here. Okay, Chris, no coral for you."

"Well, I'm not wearing blue, either."

I shook my head. At this rate, we would have rainbowed toes, only because none of us could decide on a colour.

"Why don't we choose for each other?" Lucy suggested. "But you have to wear whatever is picked."

I shrugged my shoulders. Why not? Worst case scenario, we would all be bathing in acetone later in the evening.

"Can I refill your glasses, ladies?" Ryan asked from the kitchen. I had almost forgotten he was in the house.

The moment Lucy arrived, he had disappeared into the kitchen, muttering something about preparing snacks and dinner.

"I'll have a Cosmo," Calleigh piped up.

"And I would love another martini," Lucy chimed in.

"One virgin Cosmo and one Lychee Martini coming right up," he announced with a flourish as he scooped up their glasses and headed back to the kitchen. "I'll be back to refill your glasses in a minute."

Something wasn't right between him and Lucy. She had a look about her that indicated she wasn't too pleased about something but was keeping it to herself.

"Do you know Ryan?" I asked her outright. After all, she would have just asked me. She might not have pressed for an answer if I wasn't forthcoming, but she would have asked.

"Yeah, I met him through my brother, Pete."

I didn't even know Lucy had a brother. Was I so self-obsessed that I have never taken the time to learn about her family?

"Really? Small world."

"Ryan was dating one of Pete's friends. They met while mountain climbing. I just thought it was strange to see him here."

"Ryan doesn't stay in one spot for very long," Chris pointed out. "His job is all about travel and adventure."

Lucy sighed, but didn't say anything. I decided to play it her way. When she was ready, she would tell me what was bothering her.

Instead, I said, "You have a brother?" I was genuinely interested in learning about her family.

"I actually have two," she responded. "I'm the spoiled baby sister in the family."

"Now that explains a lot," I said. Lucy threw a pillow at me as we all dissolved into laughter. The awful start to my day was being washed away on a tide of laughter and teasing.

Menu du Jour

Breakfast: Salt Water Flush

Lunch: Homemade chicken noodle soup, fresh bread, tea

Afternoon snack: spice cake, Cosmos

Dinner: Pasta, salad, coffee

Dessert: Fruit Salad

Calories Consumed: 1388 Just the right amount

Calories Burned: 1426.75 Plus, many through laughter.

Jennifer Bogart

Chapter Nineteen

Hide & Seek

"Tell me about the guy you keep staring at in the mirror?" Lucy asked during Tuesday morning's spinning.

I shrugged, "I don't stare at anyone."

She gave me a look that indicated this was one subject she wasn't going to drop so easily. Up until this past weekend, Lucy had never pressed me when I refused to elaborate on a subject. I don't know if Chris had shared a bit of history with her, or if she just felt it was time I opened up, but I did know that this Lucy was a bit more insistent on getting answers.

"Every time you look up, and meet his eyes, you start to push yourself harder." She slid her saddle into position and tightened the screw into place. "I can almost feel the tension between you."

"Every time I look up, I see that I'm not working as hard as everyone else, so I increase my speed. I don't want to look like a slacker."

She obviously wasn't going to buy that, even though it was partially true. Lucy sighed and clipped her shoes onto her pedals. They were really cool shoes, and I was seriously considering getting myself a pair. They would be a reward for all the efforts I had been making to get fit and lose weight. Of course, first I would have to get fit and lose the weight.

"You know, he keeps watching you too. So, there is definitely something going on between you two. And even if you want whatever it is to be buried in the past, I think it's starting to surface and won't go away until you actually deal with it."

"Since when did you become the all knowing one of great wisdom and advice?" I asked her. I didn't want to be pushed just now. I just wanted to get through this class, and then continue with my week. I had dealt with enough unsettled emotions on Saturday and I wasn't about to have another melt-down if I could help it.

Two minutes later I realized how rude I must have sounded. "I'm sorry, Lucy. I just –"

"Don't worry about it, it's not my business." I could tell she was hurt by her tone of voice.

"He was a friend of Damian's."

She nodded. "Really, you don't have to tell me. I shouldn't have pried."

"I shouldn't have pushed you away. I'm not used to talking about things… from… well, before."

"I know," she smiled. "Maybe if you did, you could put it behind you, instead of keeping it all locked up inside."

"Yeah… you're probably right."

"I'm pretty much always right," she smiled. I laughed at her. Only Lucy could get away with making a statement like that!

On our way out of the gym, I took a moment to glance around. He was getting into his car. It was a Santa Fe: black, four doors and very clean for winter driving in the city. The kind of car he drove told me nothing about him, not that I expected it would. I shouldn't have been surprised to see him at a gym. He was a bit of a health freak, if I remembered correctly. His ex-wife had once muttered something about flavourless wheat-germ and organic foods. He had the same light brown hair and hazel eyes that I found so captivating. Not in a romantic sense. They were just the kind of eyes that draw you in because you just know there is a depth of character in this person you might never come across again. I guess the cliché "old soul" comes easily to mind.

"Go talk to him," Lucy said from behind me. I had nearly forgotten she was there. "Grab a coffee or something. I'll cover for you at work."

She was probably right. Something was eating at me from the inside out. Seeing him with such regularity was only feeding that anxiety. Throughout the day I would find myself drifting into the past, my mind wandering along paths best forgotten. But I couldn't forget, and I couldn't let go. It was time I stopped lying to myself and opened the door for a long overdue conversation.

"Okay," I said with a sigh. Lucy gave me an encouraging pat on the shoulder; at least I'd like to think it was a pat and not a push in the right direction. "I'll do it, but if I don't show up at work, you'll have to do my work as well as your own."

"I'm an editor, not a writer," she pointed out dryly. "Despite what some people think, there is a difference."

I watched as Harper unlocked his car door, half hoping he would disappear before I would have a chance to talk to him. Lucy gave me a little push. "Go on, or he'll be gone and this will just be lost opportunity."

I sighed, straightened my shoulders and started to weave my way through the parked cars towards him. He glanced up as I approached, almost as though he could sense me closing in on him. I strengthened my resolve and continued towards him; I would not shirk before him no matter how uncomfortable I was feeling.

When I reached his car, we just stood and stared at each other for a few minutes, taking in all the changes the years had wrought. His hair had the lightest dusting of grey just above his ears and peppering where his sideburns would start if he were to let them grow. The lines in his face were only slightly deeper and he had the tanned look of someone who spent many hours outside, despite the cold of the winter. I drank in the familiar sight of him, wishing he were someone else, or at the very least, wishing this was a different time.

"Hello, Harper," I said at last. I couldn't believe how fast my heart was beating. If I wanted to lie to myself, I could have blamed the incessant pounding on my workout. However, I had decided to exchange self-deception for open honesty, at least where I was concerned.

"Roxanne," he returned with a curt nod. You could practically taste the silence that hung between us. There was so much to say, and yet neither one of us was willing to start the conversation. Doubtless, neither one of us really knew where to start.

"I… uh… do you—"

"Do you—"

We both broke off at the same time with nervous laughter. "Do you have time for a coffee?" I asked, my nervousness abating only slightly.

"I have time for a tea," he countered with little smirk that made me smile.

"Right, a tea, well that'll do too, I guess." I looked away, trying to think of an appropriate place we could meet. I'm a coffee drinker—I love all coffees, lattes, espresso, cappuccino, flavoured, and of course, best of all—special coffee. Those would-be ones laced with Bailey's, topped with whipped cream and garnished with chocolate shavings.

In the end, we decided to meet at a local coffee shop that easily accommodated both our needs. It boasted free Wi-Fi, fresh pastries and every sort of hot beverage you could possibly imagine. It was a bit busier than I had thought it would be for eight o'clock in the morning, but then again, I'm sure there were a number of people who were squeezing in that last cup of java and toasted bagel before dashing off to the doldrums of their office.

"It's been a while…"

"Seven years." I wrapped my hands around the comforting warmth of my ceramic mug. There was something soothing about the heat that emanated from the steaming cup of reassurance. It was familiarity in an unfamiliar world.

He nodded in agreement. "Calleigh must be quite the young lady now."

"She is. Smart, funny… beautiful. She's the light of my life." We needed to get past the small talk, but it was a safety line we were both clinging to, struggling to keep our heads above water. "Molly must also be growing up fast."

"Yes—she's in grade three now. She's eight going on eighteen, it seems. It's hard to keep up with her."

"And you and Olive…"

He smiled in a self-deprecating way and shook his head. "Things didn't work out between us. She's living in Toronto, working as a freelance web designer."

"Oh, that's too bad," I said, but somehow, I had known this would be the case. I didn't know Olive well, but whenever I had seen her, she didn't look terribly content in her life. She was always tense or on edge—sometimes even to the point of being strung out. I wondered how long their marriage had lasted, but wasn't about to dig deeper into that subject at this point.

"So—are you, uh, enjoying the class?" he asked me. "Yeah. I didn't think I would, but the more I go, the more I like it. I'm horribly out of shape, but it feels good afterwards to know that I can survive the class."

Harper looked at me quizzically. "You look fine to me and seem to know what you're doing. I thought you had been at it for a while."

"Really?" He couldn't possibly believe that. "I only started going a couple weeks ago. The first time I went I thought I was having a heart attack, but I was too embarrassed to admit it or say anything. Now I know it's good to get your heart rate up, but there are times I still worry it might explode right in the middle of class."

He chuckled, but his laugh didn't quite meet those arresting hazel eyes. "After all you have been through;

I'm thinking you have a pretty strong heart."

Here was the opening I had been waiting for. The invitation to discuss all that had been left unsaid between us for the past seven years. All I could do was look away, glad we had chosen a seat next to the window. Maybe coffee hadn't been such a great idea after all. A woman outside the window was struggling to juggle her coffee, a pastry, her purse, and a couple of tow-headed boys. For a moment, I was tempted to dash outside the door and offer her a hand. Anything to avoid this moment, now that it was finally before me.

"I won't say it's been easy," I said quietly, my gaze still fastened on the woman outside the window. Somehow, she had managed to extract her keys from her purse and she was now struggling to unlock the car door while the younger of the two boys danced up and down beside her, clearly unhappy.

"I can't imagine what you've been through," he offered. I could feel Harper's eyes watching me, but I still couldn't bring myself to look directly at him.

"You know it wasn't your fault."

"It wasn't yours, either."

I looked back at him. It was my turn to offer up a self-deprecating smile, as though we were reflections of each other in a mirror. "The last few days with Damian were hard, and I know he said a lot of hurtful things, but that wasn't really him talking."

Harper took a long sip of his tea. He looked as though he wanted to say something he had been holding in for the past seven years, but then he looked into his cup, and sighed over the steaming liquid. It rippled as a pond would if one were to throw a stone into it.

It was his turn to look away. I reached my hand across the table and lightly touched his, feeling the fine hairs on the back of his hand.

"For the past seven years I have done everything possible to try to forget the last few days of Damian's life. I locked all those memories away in what I thought was an impenetrable strong box. I needed to escape from those awful memories so that I could get on with the business of raising Calleigh and giving her something of a normal life. I was lucky—I had my sister and my parents who willingly supported the two of us in any way they could. My sister still lives with me; maybe she thinks I'm just too fragile to live on my own." I thought back to the weekend, and how she had gotten me through that dark moment when I was ready to give up on myself completely. There wasn't a doubt in my mind about how much I still needed her.

Harper just looked at me, his face expressionless, but at the same time I felt as though he were urging me to continue. "I don't think anyone else has any idea of what actually happened the day of the accident."

"You haven't talked to anyone at all?" he asked me, this time the expression on his face was incredulous. His eyebrows disappeared into the light brown curls that caressed his forehead.

"There wasn't any point."

"Roxanne, that's crazy. You need to talk to someone. Something like that can eat away at you and your self-esteem."

I shrugged my shoulders in response. Of course, my self-esteem and self-worth had been reduced in my own eyes. I didn't need to see those feelings reflected in the eyes of everyone around me. I'm a private person by nature, I always have been. Letting the rest of the world even get a glimpse of the acute anguish I had suffered, no matter how long ago it was buried in the past, was completely out of the question. Talking around the incident was difficult enough. I was doubtful I would ever be able to address it directly.

"Seriously, you could have talked to me," he insisted earnestly.

Again, I shrugged. I had lost the ability to talk in the last fifteen minutes.

"I thought I could handle it on my own." The confession came out in a whisper.

"I'm sure no one expected you to."

"It was awful. But we managed."

"I see that," his tone took on a note of appreciation. "But something has made you come out of hiding…"

"It's been seven years," I stated, without emotion. "Aren't all debts forgiven after seven years? I think I've paid my dues and it's time to start living in the real world."

Menu Du Jour

Breakfast: yogurt, banana, cereal bar

Mid-morning snack: coffee, bagel & cream cheese
Total Calories consumed before lunch: 793 (and to think there's hardly and real food here)

Total Calories burnt: 774 + whatever one burns in less than half a day.

Jennifer Bogart

Chapter Twenty

Broken Telephone

The conversation I had with Harper stayed with me throughout the day. There were so many things I should have said; so many different ways that conversation could have gone, but I hadn't found my centre of strength until that moment when I realized just how much time had passed. Seven years is too long to mourn what could have been, and certainly too long to hold onto regrets. In Calleigh's case, it was an entire lifetime. She had now lived longer without her father than with him, and her memories were fading into nothing but fragmented dreams. Even those dreams were made of someone else's memories which had been painted for her in hues of happiness and contentment.

My memories were not so skewed. They were harsh in their starkness. Since I had never shared them, they had sat like an old forbidden tome, buried deep under the chaos of daily life, collecting dust and waiting to be revealed for what they were. Examining them now would be no less painful than they had been the day they had been locked away.

When Harper had said: 'After all you've been through; I'm thinking you have a pretty strong heart', I'd wanted to reply: 'How could you possibly know what I have been through? The moment the casket closed, you disappeared, along with a select few other people, leaving me to deal with the entire mess on my own.'

When he had said: 'I can't imagine what you've been through'; I had wanted to scream at him: 'Of course you can imagine what I've been through! You were the one who helped put me in this situation in the first place!'

His concern, although touching, had been ill-placed: 'You need to talk to someone. Something like that can eat away at your and your self esteem.' I already knew what toll the entire situation had put on my self-worth. There were days when I felt as though I should have been the one to be struck in the head. At least then I wouldn't have had to deal with all the after effects. Of course, with my luck I would have lived and who knew what kind of mess we would all be in now.

The real kicker had been when he had suggested I could have talked to him. It's pretty hard to talk to someone who is virtually unreachable. No cell phone, no e-mail address, no listed home phone number. The only things I knew were his name, he was married with a baby daughter, and worked with my husband as a consultant. How the heck was I supposed to talk to someone who barely existed on paper? I was surprised to see he had a gym membership, since he didn't like to give out any personal information that could possibly track him. In my opinion, he was borderline paranoid about things like conspiracy theories. Granted, now that I thought about it, he hadn't been mistrustful of the rest of the world without reason.

I kept replaying our little chat in my head. Each time I had something new to add, so I would rewind and start again. I could have told him about the days between the accident and Damian's death, his delirium and the gibberish he spilled. I could have told him about the guilt I had suffered, all because I had forgotten to relay an extremely important message—one that would have perhaps prevented the entire fiasco. I should have told him that I had not been hiding at all, that rather, I had been surviving.

My mind wandered past the morning's conversation, to find itself replaying a scene that was supposed to be magically deleted. It's too bad that the human mind is very like a computer. You can try to remove all traces of files, but somewhere, deep within the memory system there will exist a link, or some bit of code that can mysteriously revive all you thought you had lost, deleted, or otherwise obliterated.

I was sitting with Calleigh in Damian's office. It was a Thursday afternoon, and we were waiting for him to finish up with a client. We were supposed to be going out for dinner to celebrate his new contract and my new job. The phone rang, which was nothing new in a busy marketing firm. I ignored it, knowing it would just roll into voicemail—which is more reliable than a human memo. Calleigh and I were colouring in her new princess book I had just purchased to keep her busy in the restaurant. The phone started to ring again, and once more, I just let it roll into voicemail, not thinking anything of it. This happened once more before I decided to take note of the number on the caller id display. I didn't recognize it, so again—I let it roll into his voicemail. The fourth time it rang, I looked once again at the display to see the same number flashing on the screen. That was strange.

I picked up on the fifth try. Obviously, whoever was trying to call was reluctant to leave a message and was looking for a human voice. I should never have answered that phone.

"Damian Burnberry's office."

"I need to speak to Damian."

"I'm sorry, he's in a meeting. May I take a message?" I was trying to use my best receptionist voice without dissolving into giggles.

"I need to talk to him now."

"If you could just let me know what it pertains to, I'll be happy to have him return your call." I wasn't sure if I should pull him out of his meeting. If it were a real emergency, the person on the other end of the phone should have gone through reception. I knew that Julie was at the desk because she had greeted us less than five minutes ago when we walked in. Julie was usually the last to leave the office, even when Damian and Harper worked late.

"Pull him out of the goddam meeting, and put him on the phone! What the hell kind of secretary are you, anyway?" The voice on the other end of the phone was laced with tones of anger and frustration.

I took a deep breath, and in my most reasonable and calm voice I responded, "I'm sorry sir, if you wish him to be pulled from his meeting, you'll have to go call back and go through reception. I'm afraid I don't have the authority to interrupt his meeting."

A string of vulgarities echoed through the phone lines and I cringed, hoping Calleigh couldn't hear the barrage through the ear piece. "What the fuck kind of secretary are you-you stupid piece of sh—"

I hung up on him. No one could be paid enough to take that kind of abuse from anyone. Calleigh and I went back to colouring in her book, and promptly forgot about the caller. If it were that important, whoever it was, would surely call back.

Thinking back on that phone call, so many years ago, I now know I should have pulled Damian from his meeting so he could deal with the surely man. They say hindsight is 20/20, but even years later I'm not so sure my vision is all that clear. Had I not answered the call, and had the mystery man still not bothered to leave a voicemail after numerous failed attempts, would I still feel as guilty? Or, was it possible Damian would have returned to an office, and a ringing phone? Was it possible the caller would have kept trying until he reached Damian? There was no way to know for sure. But I was certain, had I followed a different path, Damian would be alive and well today.

I do believe that events in life follow a specific path. If you chose to stray from the designed route, your life is upset forever, tossing you into a forest of unknown twists and turns. Like those mystery books I used to love as a kid: *if you choose to open the door, turn to page 43; if you choose to turn back the way you came, skip to page 62.* They were great books, with the possibility of a new story and ending each time you read it. Unfortunately, real life wasn't quite so tidy. Choosing to open a door, turn to the left or answer the phone could change your destiny forever, there isn't an option to go back to make the choice all over again. If I could go back to that moment in time, I would never have answered that phone.

But I couldn't go back, and as much as I did remember every detail of that phone call, and every moment afterwards leading up to the accident, there was nothing I could do to alter my reality. I answered the phone, and Damian wound up dead. It was that simple.

"You've been off in another world all morning," Lucy commented as she perched herself on the edge of my desk with familiarity.

I nodded. "I have been. I can't focus on getting any work done."

"Let's go out for lunch and get some fresh air. It's pretty stale in here." I could tell she was dying to ask me how my conversation with Harper went. She just knew me better than to ask outright.

I shook my head, I was already too far behind in my work as it was. A long lunch out would not help me concentrate, and talking about something better left forgotten would only bring on another wave of old memories I wasn't ready to deal with.

"I'm really not all that hungry. I had a bagel at The Bonny Bean with my coffee."

"Suit yourself, but a change of scenery might help you clear your head."

I didn't want to admit it, but I knew she was probably right, at least in some respects. Even my office held unpleasant memories for me. The fact that we couldn't display any personal effects worked to my advantage. There were no happy family pictures mocking me as I tried to get through the work of the day. I didn't even have to acknowledge I had a family or life outside of my little cubicle for the eight hours I sat here.

The Friday after our celebratory dinner was typical of any Friday. Damian was up early so he could beat the traffic into work. We usually enjoyed breakfast together before getting Calleigh up for the day. She needed to be dropped off at the school daycare for 7:30am so I could be at work for eight. Harper would pick her up from school this afternoon as he usually finished work early on Fridays to make up for all the extra hours he put in throughout the rest of the week.

"Any plans for tonight?" I asked as I poured his coffee. He was busy at the stove, making omelettes.

"Harper and Olive are in town. They might come over for a bit later this evening, if they can get a babysitter."

"Why don't they just bring their daughter? Calleigh can entertain her," I suggested. Their daughter was only about a year old and Calleigh was totally fascinated by babies.

"I'll suggest it."

He flipped the omelettes onto our plates and presented mine to me with a flourish that never failed to make me giggle. He was such a goof sometimes.

"I have a hair appointment tomorrow," I told him. "And then don't forget my parents and Chris are coming over for dinner."

He nodded. "Your parents are on my calendar."

"Roxy, do you think you could ask Chris to pick Calleigh up after school this afternoon?" he asked hesitantly. Chris had picked Calleigh up from school on several occasions for us. Normally Calleigh would go to the afterschool daycare program until I was able to pick her up at 4:00pm. We tried to keep to her usual schedule as she enjoyed the social aspects of daycare, but Fridays were special and she was always picked up at the bell.

"I'll ask her when I drop Calleigh off this morning, but I can't promise. What plans do you have this afternoon?"

He looked a bit uncomfortable, but I didn't think very much of it at the time. He hated to ask family for favours, while I had no issues with it whatsoever. That was probably because his brother was hard to pin down for any length of time and his parents were a bit on the quirky side and not open to offering to help with Calleigh. "I was waiting to hear back from someone about a contract, but the guy didn't get in touch with me. I'm still planning to get away from work early, but thought a back-up plan would be a good idea."

"Well, I'll ask her and then give you a call at work to let you know. If it's a problem, and she can't, I can always send her to daycare."

"That might be a good idea."

He left the house in his usual flurry: collecting papers, notes and various paraphernalia from around the house. He never seemed to be able to keep everything in one place. He spent five minutes just looking for his car keys, which he had left in his coat pocket the night before instead of hanging them on the rack just inside the door. If he was more disorganized or unfocused than usual, I didn't notice as this was his usual morning routine.

Christine taught grade five at Calleigh's school, so it wasn't any trouble for her to pick Calleigh up after school, provided she didn't already have plans. I tried not to take advantage of her too often, but it was just too convenient, having her right there. Besides, Chris did adore Calleigh, since she didn't have any children of her own. She was usually thrilled to have my daughter to herself for an hour or two. Chris would take her for ice cream, or get her some other treat that would no doubt spoil her dinner, but I didn't mind. I loved the fact that the two of them had such a strong bond. There was comfort in knowing your child connected well with another adult. She would always have someone else to rely on or talk to as she got older.

As predicted, Chris was thrilled to keep Calleigh after school if Damian wasn't available. The two of them would go to the local library where there was a craft session planned. The librarian was going to introduce the works of Eric Carle and then have the children create their own masterpieces following his unique style. There was no doubt Calleigh would love that.

This was the true beginning of my dependency on Chris. Had she known how much I would come to rely on her from that day on, she might not have been so eager to spoil my daughter.

Jennifer Bogart

Chapter Twenty-one

Head Games

Damian's accident wasn't fatal. It had been a simple matter of poor timing and oversight on his part. He had naively walked under some scaffolding to enter through the front door of a client, totally ignoring the signage that indicated he should walk around to the rear of the building. At the exact moment he stepped under the scaffolding, the mason above him got butter fingers. The first brick hit his shoulder; the second landed squarely on his head and knocked him unconscious. The impact should have killed him, or at the very least, it should have left him a vegetable.

When I arrived at the hospital, he was propped in an upright position and lucid, if a little dizzy from the concussion he had just received. An intern was busy stitching his shoulder where the brick had left a nasty gash.

"Oh, Damian," I was so relieved to see he was alright I burst into tears. Embarrassed, I wiped them away before too many people noticed. "You're alright?"

He smiled, looking a bit dopey. "I'll live." He winced and raised his free arm to his head. "Unless this headache kills me first."

"Don't say things like that," I whispered, horrified.

I'm sure he would have shrugged his shoulders if he hadn't been in so much pain. "I still have to go for a head CT, but the doctor assured me that since I am already up and about, I'll probably be just fine."

"Good," I nodded as I took a seat in the chair beside the bed. Hospitals made me nervous. I had watched too many television dramas that focused on the all the things that could go wrong. Even having a young intern performing something as simple as routine stitches made me nervous.

"That should do it, twelve stitches in all, so that was quite a gash," the intern rolled her chair back so the nurse could finish the dressing. His shoulder looked like it had practically been ripped off and then pieced back together. I couldn't bear to look at it and was glad it would be covered.

"He'll need to have those stitches removed in a couple of weeks. Also, try to keep the wound dry and clean for as long as possible. You can change the dressing as needed, but don't use any anti-bacterial creams. I think Ellen here is going to give you a tetanus shot just to be on the safe side, and Dr. Anderson has already prescribed an antibiotic in case of infection."

I nodded, even though I knew I wouldn't remember anything she had just said to me, I was too worried about Damian's head, which had also been bandaged. Obviously, any stitches he had required there had been taken care of before I arrived.

"Don't worry so much, Roxy," he insisted. "I'm fine. Really."

I didn't have a chance to respond because Harper came into the room, looking flustered and concerned.

"You're alright?" his voice was incredulous, as though he fully expected to find Damian otherwise.

"I'll be fine," Damian insisted again. But he didn't look so good. His skin had very slowly started to take on a greyish pallor and his eyes were slightly unfocused.

"I think he needs to rest now," I said to Harper. I knew his partner would be concerned, but now that he had seen Damian alive and stable, he should have been able to go on with his day, taking care of both his and Damian's business.

"Yeah, yeah," Harper said with a wave of his hand. "Did the guy call?"

Damian shook his head, but I could see he regretted the motion. Surely work could wait at least until tomorrow.

"Harper –"

"You must have missed him," Harper cut in, not heeding my warning. "He must be pissed if he hasn't been able to reach you."

Something about what he said triggered the memory of the phone call I had taken the night before; but the man on the other end of the phone hadn't left any kind of real message. Surely if something was so important, "the guy" would have left a message, or called Damian's cell phone after I hung up on him.

"No doubt," Damian answered wryly.

"Could he have called your cell?" I asked, thinking perhaps Damian may have missed the call while in the hospital.

"What the hell would you know about it?" Damian snarled at me.

I recoiled from him. "I was trying to help. There's no need to be snarky with me."

"Stupid bitch," Damian muttered. I couldn't believe my ears. Who was this person who had taken over my husband's body? There was definitely something wrong. I looked from Damian to Harper, but they both seemed to have forgotten I was there.

"Did you tell her?" Harper was asking. Tell me what? What on earth was going on?

"I can't trust that fat slob," Damian muttered. "I wouldn't tell her anything."

I was trying very hard to stay calm. Even during our most vocal arguments, Damian had never said so many nasty things about me. Now they were pouring out of him, reminding me sharply of the phone call I had taken in his office.

"Damian," I was hesitant to say anything, but honestly thought that if I told him something useful he might calm down a bit. "Someone did call last night, but he refused to leave a message."

The stream of curses that spewed out of his mouth was unbearable. At first I just stared at him in shocked awe, and then I couldn't help myself, I fled the room. In that moment, I didn't even care if Harper badgered my husband to death with his incessant questions. I didn't deserve that kind of treatment under any circumstances.

"Roxanne?"

I looked up and hastily brushed the tears from my cheeks. Lucy was standing over me, looking concerned. I hadn't even realized the tears were leaking from my eyes. All I did anymore was daydream and cry.

"Sorry," I mumbled. I would have like to use the excuse I had something in my eye, but I knew the lie wouldn't cover the fact that my cheeks were blotchy and my nose was running. I grabbed a tissue from the box on my desk and noisily blew my nose so I wouldn't have to look at her right away.

"Are you alright?" I could hear the worry in her voice, as though it were coming over a loud speaker. I glanced around the office, wondering if anyone else had heard or seen me sobbing. Our cubicles only afforded a miniscule amount of privacy.

"I'm fine," I sniffed. "It's all good."

"Maybe you should take the afternoon off," she suggested. "I can let Markus know you have the flu or something. It's not like you're getting any work done anyway."

I shook my head. The last place I wanted to be was at home—alone, with no escape from the past or the memories. "I'm fine, really."

She laughed dryly at that, "You do know what fine means don't you?"

I shook my head. She had me completely baffled. If I said I was fine, then I meant I was fine.

"It means: feelings inside not expressed. . ."

That got a tiny smile out of me. Lucy had some pretty funny expressions. "I think maybe I'll go for a walk and clear my head."

I hoped a change in environment would shake the melancholy out of me so I could get on with my day.

The walk helped. The air was crisp and cool, the sidewalks were clear of slush and snow, and I detected a hint of spring in the air even though it was only the end of February. Damian's accident and subsequent behaviour had all happened during the fall, so there was nothing outside to trigger more unnerving memories. I walked past the market and remembered I needed to pick up some root vegetables for the soup I was planning to make. A healthy soup, not the ghastly cabbage soup—although the cabbage soup wasn't necessarily unhealthy, it just should be integrated into a normal diet rather than be the focus of a diet. My friend Maria had e-mailed the new soup recipe to me last week, and I thought I would give it a try. It would go well with fresh bread and cheese.

My walk took me past a park where a few moms or possibly nannies were taking advantage of the beautiful weather with toddlers and preschoolers. I could smell fresh bread wafting through the air from a nearby bakery and turned in the direction of the inviting aroma. Food had always been my friend. It never criticized me, I had complete control over it and it almost never disappointed me. Cooking was a passion I had embraced, it took hours of effort and thought, which meant I wouldn't have time to dwell on the past, the present or dream about the future. It was a here and now pastime without room for negotiation. Leave a soufflé for too long and you end up with a dish of slop instead of the intended masterpiece. As long as I stayed focused, I found it pretty difficult to mess up a recipe. One thing I had mastered over the years was the ability to put unpleasantness out of my mind so I could focus solely on the task at hand.

I would pick up a loaf of fresh bread to have with the soup, an assortment of cheeses would also be nice, but I should be able to get those at the fruit and vegetable market. When I entered the bakery, the warm, yeasty smell enveloped me, reminding me of a time when I was very young and sitting in my grandmother's kitchen. She was a first-class baker. Pies, tarts, pastries, cakes, cookies, muffins, quick-breads, yeasty breads—you name it, she could make it. If she didn't have a recipe for something she would either find one or make one up herself. The best was when she had made spudnuts. They are donuts made using mashed potatoes. After deep-frying the dough to a lovely golden brown she would dredge the steaming treat through a tantalizing mixture of cinnamon and brown sugar. The memory made me smile and also made me want to try to make them with Calleigh. It would be something fun we could do together.

The woman behind the counter looked vaguely familiar, but then everything I saw today was resonating with echoes of the past. I asked for my bread, along with some chocolate éclairs for dessert. I couldn't resist adding a scrumptious looking Danish to my order. The bakery was like a small slice of heaven and I was reluctant to leave its moist warmth and sweet-smelling aroma behind.

When I returned to the office I felt much more like myself. The fresh air had cleared away the cobwebs, and the scents and comforts of the familiar bakery had returned me to my happy place. I was ready to take on the world. Well, maybe not the world, but I was ready to tackle my growing pile of paperwork and rapidly approaching deadlines.

"Hey Roxanne," Ryan greeted me as I came in the door. He was standing at the stove cooking up something that smelled divine. I was beginning to miss cooking. Since Ryan had moved in, he had basically taken over the task; it was almost like having a house-husband. In some respects, it took a lot of pressure off me because I wasn't worrying about meals or grocery shopping, but in other ways I felt as though I were losing a bit of control. I like to cook, it was something of a stress-release for me. I would have to talk to him about it. But not tonight. Tonight, I was going to put my feet up, enjoy a suitably girlie-movie and savour a much-needed glass of wine.

"You look annoyed with something," Ryan said as he stirred a delicious looking sauce.

I shook my head in response; I didn't feel like talking to anyone just now. "Where's Calleigh?" Normally I would find her sitting at the kitchen table working on her school assignments.

"Oh, she's working on a group project with some friends. I told her it was alright."

"Did she happen to mention which friend's house she was at?" And why hadn't she called my cell? I wanted to add. I'm her mother, and the last time I checked she needed to check in with me before making after school plans.

"Uh… Sandra or Sophie—I'm not too sure." He tasted his sauce and then made a face that showed his appreciation of his own efforts.

"Sarah?" If he was going to give her permission to be somewhere, the least he could do was get the message straight! "Is she at Sarah's? Did you at least get a phone number?"

He shook his head and returne his attention to the bubbling pots, adding spices here and there. "Nope, she hung up before I could get a chance to ask for it."

"Did she mention which project she was working on? Is she planning to be home for dinner?"

Ryan dropped his wooden spoon and turned to look directly at me. "What's with the twenty questions?"

He wouldn't understand, I reminded myself. He doesn't have a daughter, he barely even knows Calleigh outside of the occasional e-mail and MSN chat. "She's thirteen. I need to know where she is, who she's with, what she's doing and how to reach her. When she moves out, she can have the freedom to do as she pleases."

"Right, well that's one way of pushing the poor girl out the door."

Exasperated, I turned away from him. I didn't need this drama right now; I had enough on my mind. "When you have a daughter of your own, you might understand. In the meantime, you don't get to parent mine!"

I grabbed the phone book and phone from their home on the table and started punching in Sarah's number. I wasn't sure who I was angrier with—my daughter for not calling me directly, or my brother-in-law for not being responsible enough to know thirteen-year-olds need guidance.

"May I speak to Calleigh, please," I said to the disembodied voice on the other end of the phone.

"I'm sorry, you must have the wrong number," the voice was pleasant enough, but obviously annoyed by the intrusion of a stranger.

"I'm sorry, is this number for Sarah Glass?" I asked, just in case I had misdialed.

"Yes, Sarah lives here," the voice confirmed.

"I'm her friend Calleigh's mom, the girls were supposed to be working on a project together. I just wanted to know what time I should come pick her up." There was a silent pause on the other end of the phone, and then an audible sigh. "Sarah is at the mall, she called from school and said she was going there for ice cream with a few friends and would be home before dinner."

"Okay," I said, not sure where to go from there. "Well… uh… thanks for your time." I hung up and dialled three more friends' numbers and got the same response from each parent.

Unbelievable. Calleigh knew the rules and I couldn't believe she had lied to me. Actually, she hadn't lied to me at all, she just hadn't bothered to tell me anything. I grabbed my coat from its hook, picked up my car keys and told Ryan I would be back in fifteen minutes with his niece.

"When I get back the three of us are going to sit down and have a discussion about a few rules," I told him before walking out the door. I didn't miss the incredulous expression that crept across his features. He looked like he was the teenager who knew he was about to be grounded for life.

Chapter Twenty-two

Pecking Order

Calleigh wasn't at the mall. She wasn't at the library, the school or any of her friend's houses. I was going frantic with worry over her. No one knew where she was or who she was with. Damn Ryan for not insisting she call me for permission. I had to admit that even if she had called me, she could have lied about her whereabouts. The only difference would have been that I would be blissfully unaware of her deceit instead of frantically worrying about her.

"Has she called?" I asked frantically when Ryan answered the phone. I couldn't think of anywhere else to look. I had called all her friends who were safely ensconced in their homes with their families, I had searched all her usual haunts. It was obvious the girl just did not want to be found. At what point should I call the police and report her missing? She was only thirteen, anything could have happened.

"Relax, Roxy," Ryan said, it sounded like he was chewing—how could he be eating at a time like this?

"What the hell is wrong with you?" I screeched into my phone. "She is a thirteen-year-old child—she could be laying dead in a ditch!"

"Roxy, you need to calm down."

I couldn't calm down; I was literally beside myself with worry. A vivid movie of all the horrendous possibilities of what could have happened was playing itself at top speed in my mind. Reel after reel of terrible and graphic scenes, each clip more detailed and horrifying than the last played through my imagination.

"We are talking about my baby, here. And I can't even reach Chris—I've been calling her cell but she's not answering. It's just not like her!" Even I could hear the panic in my voice, but I couldn't get control. I hadn't thought I was prone to hysterics, but I must have been mistaken.

"Chris called here already."

His words sank in slowly. Chris had called the house and not my cell? Now that didn't make any sense at all. When did I lose control of this situation and when had Ryan assumed command?

"When did she call?" Just hearing my sister's name put the brakes on my panic mode. "What did she say? Has Calleigh called her?"

"She said she's on her way home and she has Calleigh."

"Why didn't you say so when you picked up the phone? Why didn't you call me immediately?" My panic should have been replaced with relief, but instead I was hot with anger.

"She only just hung up when your call came through. I didn't even have time to put the phone down. Calleigh is fine, so there's nothing to worry about."

Nothing to worry about? My daughter had lied about where she was going and who she would be with. My brother-in-law was too obtuse to insist the child contact her mother, and my own sister couldn't be bothered to call me directly to let me know she had my only child. I felt like I was on one of those tilt-a-whirl rides at an amusement park. My world had gone all topsy-turvy and I just wanted to get off the ride so I could plant my two feet firmly on the ground. I wasn't sure how much more I could take.

"I'll be home in five minutes," I hung up the phone, put my car in gear and made my way through the familiar streets. The movie in my mind had come to a screeching halt, and had been replaced with a completely different series. I was reviewing all the things I wanted to say to Calleigh, but I knew I also needed to be calm and in control when I saw her. It was bad enough Ryan had been witness to my moment of crazy-mom; Calleigh didn't need to see me out of control because of a teenager prank.

If this is what her disappearance had been.

When I came in the door, Calleigh was sitting at the kitchen table, her homework spread out in front of her like a force field, protecting her from the wrath of her mom. Both Ryan and Chris took one look at me and fled the kitchen. I would have to deal with the two of them later.

"Well," I said as I approached the kitchen. I hadn't even bothered to take my coat off. "Do you want to tell me what was going through your head?"

Calleigh just shrugged her shoulders and returned her attention to her school work. I stared at her in disbelief.

"Do you have any idea what you just put me through? First you called your Uncle Ryan to ask permission to go somewhere, and then you lied about where you would be! I was frantic with worry when I couldn't track you down!"

Calleigh sighed, finished writing her sentence and then very calmly looked at me. She looked so much like

Damian in that moment that it hurt to gaze into those familiar blue eyes. "I didn't lie to Uncle Ryan. I was at

Sarah Parker's house. Aunt Chris knew where I was."

"You should have called me, Calleigh. I'm your mother." I insisted. This was the part that probably hurt the most. She was accountable to me first, and then the rest of the adults in her life. How had I ended up last on the list?

"I thought you might be at the gym and didn't want to interrupt your workout."

Now that was a lie. She knew that I went spinning this morning, so there was no way I would have energy for another workout tonight. "Try again."

"Uncle Ryan –"

"Uncle Ryan is a guest in this house. He doesn't have a say in what you do, who you do it with or where you go. The least you could have done was leave a phone number."

"I guess I forgot, and he didn't ask for one."

I sighed. This conversation was going nowhere. She obviously didn't feel as though she had done anything wrong.

"Calleigh, you're thirteen years old—"

"So, you keep saying," she pointed out. Now was not the time to be snarky with me, my patience was worn thin, I was tired and the adrenaline rush I had had while looking for her had run out the moment I walked in the door.

"Who is Sarah Parker?" I asked, instead of launching into a lecture about showing respect for me and watching her tone of voice.

"We are working on our Science Fair project together. She lives close to the mall. Aunt Chris said she would pick me up on her way home from work if I needed a ride. We were doing homework, not just hanging out."

I sighed. So, all the time I had been panicking, Chris had known exactly where my daughter was. "I get that—I just need you to understand that you need to talk to me first. If I wasn't available, and neither were Uncle Ryan and Aunt Chris, what would you have done? Would you still have gone home with Sarah? I don't even know who this girl is."

"I probably would have just come home and we would have had to work something out. Look, mom, both Aunt Chris and Uncle Ryan said it was okay. I don't see what the big deal is. Other than you had a panic attack over nothing."

"Calleigh, I love you. You mean more to me than you could possibly know. If anything had happened to you, I… well… I just couldn't bear it." I stopped talking to give myself a moment to compose myself. I was angry and hurt, but I needed to be the adult here. "You need my permission to go to a friend's house or to invite a friend over. I appreciate all that your aunt and uncle do for you, but ultimately, I am responsible for you and you are accountable to me. They love you, and they're important too, but they're not your parents."

Calleigh's only indication that she had even heard what I was saying was to give a brief nod. She knew better than to pull a stunt like that. I'm not sure why she had done it, and maybe in time she would let me know, but in the meantime, there had to be consequences for her reckless behaviour. "I think maybe you should be grounded for the rest of the week. No computer, except for homework, and no TV. I would ban the phone too, but that would be going against what we just discussed and I don't want to give you any excuses not to call me when I expect it."

I left the kitchen before she could acknowledge or more importantly, argue about her punishment. Maybe it had all been an innocent misunderstanding, but I couldn't just let it go.

Once Calleigh was tucked into bed for the night, Ryan, Chris and I sat at the kitchen table, nursing steaming cups of herbal tea and wishing they were laced with something somewhat stronger than raw sugar.

"I'm sorry, Roxanne," Ryan said quietly. "I really didn't think it was that big of a deal when she called."

I stared at the tiles on the kitchen floor. They were off-white with a beige marbling pattern running through them. I'll never understand why we chose these particular tiles. The white showed every mark and crumb that made its way to the floor. The floor was already in need of washing and we had just done a thorough cleaning of the house on the weekend.

"I can't believe the two of you," I said at last. "It's like you're both keeping me locked out of my own daughter's life. Maybe not purposefully, *but I'm her mother and I need to know where she is all the time!*"

"Roxy, Calleigh is a very responsible girl. She knows the rules and she follows them." Chris sounded like she was trying to reason with one of her student's parents who had received a bad report card.

"Why would she call you and not me? And why didn't you think to call me to let me know her plans?" I was hurt by Calleigh's actions, and I was confused that everyone else seemed to think that nothing too horrible had happened.

"She called the house and left a message, and she made sure she had a ride home with a reliable adult," Ryan pointed out. "What more did you expect her to do?"

"Are you two dense? *I'm her mother!* She is supposed to call *me*; she is supposed to check in with *me*.

"I know you both love her and mean well, but she's not a Barbie doll for you to practice your parenting skills on."

"You keep repeating you're her mother, but you don't always show the best example of parenting," Chris pointed out. I felt as though I had been punched in the stomach and all the fight went out of me.

The three of just sat there, staring at each other, the only sound was the rhythmic ticking of the kitchen clock as it counted out the passing seconds. I thought back to just last weekend, when the three of them had peeled me up off the floor. I also thought about the time I kept Calleigh home from school just because I wanted company when I had had a stomach flu. Maybe I didn't make the best choices for her, but I was doing the best I could, and her needs always came before mine. I watched as a spider made its way down an invisible thread, slowly, but steadily until it reached the safety of the countertop. I couldn't even begin to fathom where it had come from since it was still far too cold for creepy crawlies to be out and about.

"You've been a bit preoccupied, lately," Ryan said. "We thought you might need a break from all your responsibilities so you could sort out where you're going."

"You can't take a break from being a parent," I shot back at him. "I wouldn't want to, anyway."

"You just seem sort of lost, lately," Chris added. "We thought if we could lighten your load a bit, you might get out there, maybe date a bit, and engage in life outside of Calleigh and work."

"I like things the way they are."

"Then why have you been trying to kill yourself with crazy diets and extreme workouts?" Chris was not going to let this go.

"I have a mirror, Chris. Over the past five years or so I have done nothing but gain weight and get flabby. I decided it was time to do something about it. Calleigh doesn't need to be known as the kid with the fat mom."

Ryan snorted. "You're hardly fat. Curvy, but definitely not overweight. Men like women with curves."

I gave Ryan a look that clearly stated I didn't need his opinion on my appearance, or anything else for that matter.

"The workouts are not crazy. They're good for me. They help to relieve stress. You should try it sometime. Next week Lucy is going to introduce me to a weight class; I can hardly wait."

"We're glad to see you doing things outside of work and Calleigh—it's normal and healthy," Chris pointed out. "But you need to be careful and smart about it."

"Are you honestly giving me a lecture on nutrition and exercise?" I laughed. "Nothing I am doing takes away my ability to parent my child. Please don't assume I need you to interfere until I ask for your help." I didn't want to insult either one of them, but at the same time, I needed them to understand the kind of help they gave tonight actually did more harm than good.

"Roxy, I've been helping you parent Calleigh for the past seven years. I love her as much as you do," Chris insisted. "I would never put her in danger."

"What you're not understanding, is that I need to know what's going on. Think about it for minute. I didn't have any idea where she was or who she was with. I couldn't find her and everyone I called didn't know where she was—no one had seen her since after school. I was frantic. All you needed to do was tell her she needed to check with me first before you could offer her a ride home."

Chris nodded in understanding. At least, I was hoping it was understanding because I was beginning to feel like this conversation was going around in circles.

The two of them were making me dizzy.

"We never meant to cause any problems," Ryan said by way of apology.

"I know," I smiled. "But at least now I think we are on the same page. I just don't want to ever go through that again, I thought my heart was going to break."

Menu du Jour

Breakfast: yogurt, banana, cereal bar

Mid-morning snack: coffee, bagel & cream cheese

Lunch: skipped

Dinner: Asian Chicken on Basmati Rice (it should have been delicious, but it tasted like straw)

Total Calories consumed before lunch: 1088

Total Calories burnt: 1426.75 + 774 (was that spinning class only this morning?) = 2200.75 (and probably more because of the stress of the day).

Jennifer Bogart

Chapter Twenty-three

Dreamland

Chris had moved in with us as a temporary measure so I could be with Damian at night and basically have a live-in babysitter. Her bond with Calleigh was as strong as mine and I knew she loved her with the possessiveness a parent has for her child. I could understand how Chris would feel she was entitled to parent Calleigh, but she also had to understand that we needed to have better communication. As for Ryan, he had no rights at all.

Shortly after Damian's accident, Ryan had disappeared from our world. He took a contract to film a documentary in some far-off land and we only heard from him on holidays and special occasions. At first, I had thought he just needed to get away so he could process all that had happened in such a short amount of time. I knew that everywhere he went he saw reminders of Damian, as did I. The difference was I had the responsibility of Calleigh to consider, so there was no way I could vanish into thin air for any length of time at all. I had to deal with the situation head on.

What I didn't know when Ryan decided to take off was that he wasn't necessarily trying to escape the loss of his brother. He was also trying to escape all that followed in the aftermath. In trying to build up his business, Damian had made a few shady business deals. Nothing that would have caused any real problems had he continued to live to see them all through. But life is never so neat and tidy.

"So, do you want to try that weight class on Saturday?" Lucy asked. She was munching on a bagel and cream cheese, which reminded me I had skipped breakfast this morning. After the drama of last night, I couldn't settle down to sleep, and when I finally did, my sleep was filled with unsettling dreams. Needless to say, I had slept in and not had time to even grab a granola bar on my way out the door.

"I do, but I need to check on Calleigh's schedule first." I hadn't shared the events of last night with Lucy, even though I was certain she would have understood my point of view perfectly. Chances were, she would have been even more upset than I was.

"You look awful, by the way."

I grimaced. Of course, she would have picked up on the dark circles under my grey eyes. When I looked in the mirror this morning, I thought I resembled one of those vampires that kids are worshipping these days. Pasty skin, bloodshot eyes that looked sunken into dark, bloodless skin—in all, not a very pretty effect. Even make-up couldn't completely hide the remnants of my restless sleep.

"Thanks. I didn't sleep very well last night. I kept having strange dreams."

"Everyone had strange dreams last night," Lucy noted. "Cameron said he dreamt about a giant hamburger that was a spaceship. But when he went inside to check it out, it was some high-tech cover-up operation, but he couldn't figure out what exactly they were trying to hide."

Caroline popped her head around the side of her cubicle. She was the sweetest thing, really, with curly red hair and freckles all over. We rarely heard from her, but when she did speak up she would have us melting with giggles in no time.

"I had an interesting dream last night too. I dreamt I was in an ordinary grocery store, but then all of a sudden there were dogs everywhere. They were wearing tutus and evening gowns; I think one even had a top hat. Every time I turned a corner with my shopping cart, I ran into another dog in some strange getup. It was weird. When I finally got to the checkout, there was a cat sitting on the conveyer belt, snoozing away in the middle of all these dogs."

"Maybe there was a full moon or something," Lucy commented with a shrug. "What did you dream about, Roxy?"

I wished I had the ability to make something up on the spot. Dreams are nothing but a series of surreal events that our psyche has somehow linked to our subconscious. They are interwoven with our daily lives, but only on a metaphorical level. My dreams weren't surreal enough to satisfy the curious.

"My dreams were about my dead husband," I admitted after a pause. Neither Lucy nor Caroline quite knew what to do with that tidbit of information. Actually, I didn't know what to do with it, either. I hadn't dreamed about him in so long I wasn't sure I even remembered what he looked like without having a photograph directly in front of me.

My dreams had been about Damian. However, true to dream sequences, nothing in the dream was quite how they should have been. He didn't look right: his eyes were too blue, bluer than Calleigh's which struck me as very odd because I had always wondered at how much they resembled each other. His hair was thicker and longer with a curl that he could never lay claim to. And yet, despite the obvious differences, there was no doubt in my mind that this character in my dream was Damian. The laugh lines around his eyes that deepened with his easy smile and the dimple in his left cheek were unmistakable. His height and build were proof he was the man I had married and slept beside every night for several years. We were married young; probably too young by many people's standards, but we had been happy.

I dreamt we were in a park, strolling along a gravel path while brightly coloured autumn leaves drifted past on an unseen wind. He looked down at me and smiled in a way that never failed to make me catch my breath. The swirling leaves picked up momentum, creating a vortex of leaves, and debris that quickly escalated into something resembling a twister. At first, Damian held me tight, squeezing my hand until the pressure of his grip began to hurt. The winds were too much, and no matter how desperately we tried to hang on to each other, we were violently torn apart.

The scene switched abruptly, before my anxiety could take hold and wake me from my own subconscious. Calleigh and Damian were sitting in a family room— it wasn't in our house, but it was vaguely familiar even though I know I had never seen it before. They were working on a puzzle, as they had done a thousand times before. As I approached the happy scene, they looked up and presented me with twin smiles. My own smile faded as I took in the scene depicted on the disturbing puzzle. It was a gruesome display of bloody body parts that looked as though they had been torn to pieces by a savage animal. Why would Damian expose Calleigh to something so horrendous?

No sooner had that thought entered my mind then the scene faded into the hospital room where Damian had spent the last couple days of his life. He was sitting up in his bed, looking vigorous and healthy, despite the infection I knew was ravaging his body. There was an innocent smile pasted on his face, but it didn't reach his expressive eyes. His eyes were dark blanks, void of emotion and life. The moment those vacant eyes made contact with mine, insults started spewing from his beautiful mouth. I cringed each time he hurled a new and more descriptive expletive, but I would not bolt in shame. This was not the Damian I knew and loved. The neurologist had explained to me that Damian's personality had been altered with the head injury—that once the swelling subsided, and with some rehabilitation, things should settle down to normal. For now, he needed time to heal and, of course, my unending patience. But a small part of me wondered if there was perhaps some underlying truth in those insults he threw my way. After all, they had to have come from somewhere, perhaps buried deep in his subconscious and only now allowed to escape because the lock on the box had been broken by the impact of the brick. Slowly, others started to appear around his bed. Harper, Ryan, Chris, my parents, Calleigh and even Lucy; they all pointed and laughed as Damian continued his diatribe of hurtful words.

I woke up to find my pillow wet with tears, the blood in my veins thundering and my heart feeling as though it had been ripped in two. The LDC display on my alarm clock read 3:28am. The house was quiet except for the gentle hum of the refrigerator. It clicked on to join the foggy sound of the furnace fan which ran constantly through the winter months. Outside I could hear the gentle tapping of either rain or wet snow against the windows. There were no human voices or sounds of mocking laughter.

I wiped my tears, flipped over my pillow to the dry side and snuggled into my comforter in an attempt to chase away the chills that were now plaguing my body. I needed sleep. The past was in the past, and my skewed perceptions did not need to play themselves out in my head. Damian had suffered terribly because of an unfortunate accident. This was all years in the past and it needed to stay there. No doubt the anxiety of Calleigh disappearing had brought up many of the repressed memories.

On my way home from work I picked up a magnetic notepad for phone messages, thinking it might remind both Ryan and Chris they need to ask for details and then pass them on to me. I also picked up a cheap cell phone for Calleigh. Since Calleigh started high school I had been resisting the urge to conform to the masses and provide her with a cell of her own. There were phones everywhere—the school, the mall, friend's houses and most of her friends already had cell phones. There was no excuse for her not to be able to reach me at any given time. I hadn't thought about me being able to reach her; I thought I always knew where she was. Last night had clearly indicated otherwise.

As I expected, when I walked in the door, Calleigh was sitting at the kitchen table working away at math problems. Beside her was a steaming cup of hot chocolate and plate of freshly baked oatmeal cookies. No wonder she preferred to go to her Uncle Ryan over me. The only time I baked anymore was when I took a day off to deal with what I thought was an impending crisis. And even that seemed to have been a fleeting thing.

I tossed the cell phone on top of Calleigh's work, and she looked up at me with surprise.

"I thought you said you would never pay for a cell for me." I could see she was trying to contain her excitement.

"Oh, I'm not paying for it," I assured her. "I set up the contract, but you're responsible for your own bills."

"Huh?"

"Obviously we need a better system to keep in touch with each other. You have the smallest plan possible which you should be able to afford once you start babysitting or finding other little jobs to do."

"Huh?"

The look on her face was priceless. She was torn between being thrilled with the unexpected privilege and being horrified at the thought of having to pay for it herself.

"You're thirteen. When I was your age I was making a bit of money by babysitting. Chris had a paper route. I'm sure even your Uncle Ryan found a way to make himself a bit of money—maybe by cutting grass or shovelling driveways…"

I looked over at Ryan who was at his customary perch near the stove. He had pulled a high stool over to the counter and was pretending to study a cookbook while obviously eavesdropping on our conversation.

"Uh… no… at thirteen I was more interested in comic books, skate boarding and trying to avoid work than trying to make any money." Now, *that* was helpful.

He could have lied, just this once, to help me prove a point.

"Right… but you must have had chores or something to earn your spending money?" This was all new to me. Damian and I had only just begun the parenting journey together. For the most part, we had always been on the same page, but adolescence was unchartered territory. Not that I needed to follow anyone else's values but my own, but still, it would be nice to know how Damian might have felt about forcing Calleigh to be more financially independent at such a young age.

Ryan shook his head and gave me a wry smile. "Nope. My parents gave us a weekly allowance. Our only jobs were to make our beds, keep our rooms decent and go to school. We went to school but the other two jobs rarely happened. I think my mom thought it was just easier to take care of it herself."

"Right." So much for getting background information from Ryan. I still thought Calleigh needed to take on the responsibility of paying for her phone. It was a consequence of not communicating better with me. She would have the means, but she would also have to pay for the privilege. Besides, I knew if I paid for it myself, I would get roped into doling out for all the extras teenagers thought they couldn't live without, like unlimited texting. The plan she had, allowed for unlimited texts and calls to five numbers only. I had already listed those numbers with the service provider.

"Well, I'm sure you'll figure it out before next month when your bill comes due," I announced. Then

I disappeared into my room to change into something more comfortable than my work suit. I could hear Calleigh grumbling to Ryan about how unfair I was being. Although I couldn't hear him clearly, it sounded as though Ryan was trying to commiserate with her while convincing her that having her own spending money wouldn't be so bad.

Menu du Jour

Breakfast: skipped

Mid-morning snack: coffee, bagel & cream cheese

Lunch: Deli Sandwich

Snack: two Oatmeal Cookies

Dinner: Large Shell Pasta with Spinach with Ricotta, Sharp White Cheddar and Asiago Cheese and topped with Béchamel Sauce

Total Calories Consumed: 972 (how was that possible—something must be wrong with the counter)

Total Calories burnt: 1426.75

Jennifer Bogart

Chapter Twenty-four

Puzzles and Pizza

Something was eating at me. I had this all-consuming desire to throw myself into a terrific rage, but I wasn't sure why I was so angry. Over the past few weeks, pieces of my past had started to come together, like the forming of a puzzle. Except this puzzle would always have something vital missing from it. First Ryan appeared on my doorstep, followed by Harper and then finally Damian. Damian wasn't here in the flesh, but for all the space he took up, he may as well have had a physical presence. I couldn't get him out of my head no matter how hard I tried.

"Roxanne Burnberry," I said absently into my phone. As a technical writer, my phone rarely rings. Most of my directions come either through meetings or e-mails. I knew it couldn't be Calleigh because she had already called my cell twice, just to see if hers would work.

"Roxanne, it's Harper." I nearly hung up the phone. We had had coffee, I had dealt with my need to speak to him, and there wasn't anything left to say.

Liar, a little internal voice sneered at me. *The last time you spoke you didn't talk about anything.*

"Hello, Harper," I answered. "How did you get my work number?"

"Your Linked In profiles lists where you work."

Oh yeah. I guess I had momentarily forgotten the power of the internet. It wouldn't have taken much more than the click of a mouse to find me, not to mention the convenience of the company directory being readily available to all those who call in.

"Right, well, I'll have to remember to change that." I'm pretty sure that didn't come out sounding very nice. It was so much easier to say what I wanted when we were separated by miles and miles of telephone wires.

"I meant to call you... afterwards... but, well, you know."

"No, actually, I don't know." I'm guessing that whatever had been eating at me had gnawed its way through and was now ready to have a go at Harper. "In all seriousness, nothing in your life could have been quite so catastrophic as what I was dealing with at the time. I don't care that you lost your job; I don't particularly care that things might have been difficult with Olive. I lost my husband. Gone. Kaput. Finished. Dead is forever, it's not like I can send him a text, or an e-mail, or call him up the phone for old time's sake whenever I am missing him."

"Roxanne, I never—that is—I know it was hard for you. I just—"

"Don't bother being all sorry about it now, Harper," I interrupted him. It didn't sound like he was going anywhere important with all that stuttering anyway. "You could have—no—you *should* have called me the day he died, and then every day after that for as long as it took for everything to be straightened out. Instead, you went into hiding, along with Ryan. You quit your job and made damn sure that I couldn't find you even if I wanted to." "I wasn't that difficult to find," he reasoned.

"The point is I shouldn't have had to find you. You should have been there!" I sighed. This conversation wasn't going anywhere, which is probably why we hadn't had it at the coffee shop. "Listen, Harper. I'm not sure what you're looking for at this point. I have managed to put the past behind me, and it was no easy feat. I'd kind of like to leave it forgotten so I can get on with the business of living my life."

"I heard that you have a new house guest."

Now that comment was out in left field, and how on earth would he know who was living in my house and how recently?

"Huh?"

"Olive told me that Ryan is living with you."

I chuckled wryly at that. Trust Olive to know someone else's business, even if she had no real connection to them. "How on earth would Olive know something like that? And what does it matter to you, anyway?"

"Olive's stepsister is Ryan's girlfriend. They met while she was mountain climbing in British Columbia," Harper explained briefly.

"Ryan has a girlfriend?" Funny, he hadn't mentioned anything about her. Not that his personal life mattered to me, I just thought she might have called or something. It was all rather strange to me. "Never mind about that. Why would you care about who is living in my house?"

"I don't, not really. Ryan has something I need, so I have been trying to track him down for a while."

Oh, now that just sounded creepy. I wasn't sure how much more I wanted to know at this point. "Why don't you just ask him for whatever it is you're looking for?"

I sat and waited patiently for his response which was a long time in coming.

"It's not that simple."

"Well, Harper, if you have my work number, no doubt you still have my house number and address. Whatever it is you want from Ryan you'll have to ask him for it yourself because I'm not interested in this game you're playing."

Harper hesitated. "Every time I try to reach him he disappears to somewhere more exotic and more difficult to reach. It's almost as though he's doing it on purpose."

Maybe he was doing it on purpose. "Look, you're all grown men. You're going to have to figure this one out on your own because I don't do secrets and drama."

At least, I don't do them anymore, I added silently to myself.

"I just thought perhaps you could talk to him for me..."

"Pretty difficult task when I don't even know what you're talking about in the first place," I countered. Did he think I was a mind reader or something?

"You know exactly what I'm looking for, Roxanne. You were there when he took it."

"Huh?" My ability for intelligent speech was limited today, and I feared I sounded more like Calleigh than the professional writer I was. "I'm not following..."

I couldn't imagine Ryan taking anything, he wasn't a thief. At least, I hoped he wasn't a thief since he was living in my house for the time being. So far, the only thing he had taken away was my enjoyment of cooking, which I was going to rectify this weekend.

"Listen, I have to get back to work. Just talk to Ryan for me, please."

And then he was gone. Lovely. I still had absolutely no idea what he was talking about.

When I arrived home, Ryan was strangely absent. Although it was unusual to not find him stirring up some concoction at the stove, I felt a small glimmer of relief. I wouldn't have to ask if Harper got in touch with him today, that conversation could wait. My stomach rumbled and I grimaced, thinking of the salad and tuna I had eaten for lunch hours ago. During my afternoon meeting, a scrumptious array of pastries and delicacies had been laid out before us, but I had been so busy taking notes and talking about the project, I hadn't had an opportunity to choose my favourite from the parade of sweets. By the time I got a break, all that was left were custard-filled puff balls. Not being a fan of custard, I grabbed a water bottle and settled back into my seat. Usually I would come into the board room and immediately select one of my favourites, knowing how quickly they can disappear. I guess being busy with this project saved me from myself.

I opened the fridge and contemplated what I could whip up for dinner. I wasn't even sure what ingredients we had in the house as it had been weeks since I had done more than pull up a chair and compliment the chef.

I found some veggies, pepperoni and an assortment of cheeses and decided that tonight we would indulge in one of Calleigh's favourites: homemade pizza. I would get started on the dough, and when she came in, she could help with the "decorating" as she used to call it. I smiled at the memory. There was a time, when Calleigh was very small, that we did practically everything together. Cooking had been a family activity before it became an escape route for me. I thought hard for a moment and couldn't remember the last time Calleigh and I had prepared a meal together. In recent years, it had become a job for one. She was often close by, but usually somewhere in my peripheral: as a small child she would work on a puzzle or muck in playdough, as she got older, the toys were replaced by studying and homework.

The phone rang and I jumped, startled by the noise. I hoped it wasn't Harper trying to track down Ryan. For a moment, I contemplated letting the answering machine pick it up so I wouldn't have to deal with him again, but I knew that was childish, so I quickly wiped my hands on a dish towel and grabbed the phone.

"Hello?"

"Hi Mom," Calleigh's voice was bright and cheerful on the other end of the line. I glanced at the clock and realized that she should have been walking in the door within the next five minutes. Even with a new cell phone, communication between us wasn't getting any better.

"Shouldn't you be on your way home?"

A very loud sigh answered my question. I waited patiently; obviously she had called for a reason.

"Sarah and I haven't finished the project we were working on the other day. Can I go to her house to work on it? I'll be home by five-thirty. Her mom can drive me back."

It was my turn to sigh heavily into the phone. At least this time she had called the right person. There was no way she could know I had made plans for us to spend some quality time together, and homework does come first.

"Besides," she continued cheerily, "Uncle Ryan told me this morning he would be in late this afternoon, so supper will be late, anyway."

I gritted me teeth, trying desperately to bite back the first snarky remark that came to mind. He could have said something to me, too.

"Fine, but be home by five thirty at the latest, supper isn't going to be late. I'm cooking."

I hung up the phone and returned to my pizza dough. So much for a little quality mother-daughter time while the house was quiet. As I pulled open the fridge door, the magnetic message pad caught my eye. Ryan had left me a quickly scrawled note, after all.

I pulled out all the veggies, intending to spend my frustrated energy on chopping and dicing but my attention was drawn to a lonely piece of chocolate cake. It was just staring at me, begging me to eat it. My stomach rumbled again. Determined, I grabbed the bag of baby carrots and decided to snack on them, instead. I didn't need the cake. I wanted it, and I was hungry, but it wouldn't satisfy all that I was craving, it would just be a bandage for what I really needed.

At five-thirty on the dot, Calleigh wandered in the door. She looked happy and relaxed as she tossed her school bag in the corner and shrugged off her jacket.

"I thought you said supper would be ready?" Confusion marred her pretty features.

I smiled. "It will be ready, after you help put it together. How do you feel about "decorating pizzas" with me?"

She shrugged her shoulders, looking perplexed that I would ask her. "Uh—I guess that would be okay."

She wasn't nearly as excited as I had hoped she would be. Disappointed, I started to unwrap the bowls of toppings I had spent the past hour rinsing, chopping and dicing. I had even had time to make my own pizza sauce.

"Don't you remember doing this when you were little—it was always one of your favourite dinners." I tried not to let my disappointment in her lack of enthusiasm slip into my voice.

"I think I was about five, then. I hardly remember doing anything with you in the kitchen." Calleigh commented absently. She was spreading pizza sauce on her pizza and didn't even look at me, almost as though she knew her remark might have been painful.

Not sure how to respond to her, I chose to ignore her statement.

"I was going to make a lemon meringue pie for dessert, but noticed Uncle Ryan made cookies again, so we'll just have those instead." Silently, I added to myself, *not to mention I would probably end up eating the entire thing.*

Calleigh's response was little more than a nonchalant shoulder-shrug. She started picking through the veggies, scattering them haphazardly over her pizza without much care. Years ago, I would have had to wait for her to complete her masterpiece. Where had my little girl disappeared to?

"Look," I showed her my pizza which I had turned into a landscape of flowers and awkwardly shaped butterflies.

"Okay," she muttered. "You know, I'm not five anymore."

"I know," I answered her quietly. "I just thought it would be fun doing something we hadn't done in a while."

"We haven't made pizza like this since before Dad died." Her comment was simple and matter-of-fact, as though she were pointing out nothing more than the milk had gone sour and needed replacing. "I'm done."

I looked at her pizza. She had carefully covered it in the thinnest layer of sauce and then topped it off with the vegetables I had prepared.

"Don't you want cheese?" I asked. Cheese was a very integral part of pizza; I had even grated more than one kind to make it more interesting.

Calleigh shook her head. "I prefer it without."

Since when? I thought, but didn't say anything. If she didn't want the cheese, that would mean more for me. I looked at my daughter, longing for the days when she was small and we had shared that special mother-daughter bond. So much had happened when neither of were equipped to deal with it. I only hoped my efforts to reconnect with her and myself weren't too late.

Menu du Jour

Breakfast: yogurt tube, banana, granola bar and 2 cups of coffee

Mid-morning snack: apple

Lunch: Supper leftovers

Afternoon snack: 2 of Ryan's oatmeal cookies, coffee

Supper: Homemade pizza

Early evening snack: popcorn

Total Calories consumed: 1141 (I guess homemade really does make a difference)

Total Calories burnt: 1426.75 + 176 (walking) = 1652.75

Jennifer Bogart

Chapter Twenty-five

Picture Perfect

For the second evening in a row, the house was strangely silent when I unlocked the front door and came in. The sunlight was slowly fading into darkness, casting long shadows and creating soft edges. Both Ryan and Chris were obviously out, which meant Calleigh was probably hiding in her room. Moments of quiet solitude are rare in this house. It's almost as though we keep the lights on and noises blaring so we don't have to sit in contemplative silence.

I had become so accustomed to the inviting smell of dinner cooking that I found the plain odour of the house almost offensive. We didn't have a pet or a fish tank that would cause any stale smells to linger, but with four very different people living in the house, there was a definite lived-in aroma to it. Funny, either I had never noticed it before, or I had never taken the time to think about it.

Through the crack of Calleigh's bedroom door, I could see the faint glow from her bedside lamp. Calleigh must be reading or doing homework. If I were her, I would have chosen the comfortable sanctity of my bedroom over the vast expanse of the empty kitchen also. Her door was just slightly ajar, letting me glimpse a sliver of the picture within.

She sat in the middle of the floor, her hair spilling over an old banker's box, creating something of a curtain. In her hand was a piece of paper, or perhaps a picture. She was studying it so intently, she didn't even notice when I pushed the door open just a bit more so I could get a better view. The expression on her face was both sad and happy, if those two emotions could exist in tandem. Her eyes had a dreamy quality to them, almost as though she weren't looking at the photograph, exactly, but was somehow entranced by it.

I must have made some sort of noise that alerted her to my presence because she jerked her head up and snagged her hair on the ragged side of the old box. Grimacing, she set the picture on the floor beside her and gave her golden locks a vicious tug. Her hair came free, but not without a few delicate fatalities.

"Where did this come from?" I waved at the box which I could now clearly see was filled with a jumble of photographs and old documents. Some of the papers were yellowed with age, but others appeared to be more recent additions.

Calleigh shrugged her shoulders. "Uncle Ryan gave it to me earlier today. He said he needs it back, but thought I might be interested in looking at some of the old pictures."

That was reasonable enough.

"Mind if I take a look with you?"

I settled myself on the ground beside her, glad I had chosen to wear loose-fitting slacks this morning instead of a less forgiving pencil skirt. Calleigh's answer to me was another shrug of those delicate shoulders. When I looked at her in the faint light, I could see slight track marks on her cheeks, as though she had been crying.

"Is everything alright?"

"It's just that I miss him so much," she whispered as she looked away from me. "I don't even remember him. What he looked like, what he sounded like, what we did together. But when I see pictures, a part of me…"

Her voice trailed off and she wiped away the tears she was struggling to keep under control. I didn't know what to say. Pictures of Damian and me had slowly been replaced by pictures of Calleigh, Chris and me. Even our wedding portrait had been replaced by an adorable self-portrait Calleigh had painted when she was in grade two.

I picked up the photo she had been staring at and frowned. Damian wasn't even in the picture. It was a picture of Calleigh and me when she was about three. It looked a bit like something you might find in a magazine, our identical blond hair blended into each others'. Grey eyes smiled into brilliant blue ones and our matching smiles mirrored a kind of happiness that can only be found in the most special of mother-daughter relationships. Calleigh was breathtaking in her innocence. Happy, adorable, not a care in the world—exactly the way a three-year-old should look. But more astounding was the image of the glowing, young mother. I couldn't even identify with her; she looked like a complete stranger to me.

"Daddy's not even in this picture." My voice was laced with confusion . "But I do remember the day he took it; we had spent the day at the park and your dad was playing with his new camera."

Calleigh shook her head and bit her lip. A flash of guilt swept across her features, but was gone before I was sure I even saw it.

"I know," she whispered. Gingerly, she took the picture back and stared at it thoughtfully, lost in the dream-world I had found her in only moments before.

"It's not really him I miss."

I caught my breath; not at all sure I had heard her correctly. She gave me a rather self-deprecating smile, the kind you usually see on adults, not pre-teens.

"When I think of him, I only see little snapshots in my head, usually of things we've talked about. Those aren't real memories; they've just been planted there over time, and now they sort of feel like they're real."

"Oh, Calleigh—"

"In the end, it's not Daddy I miss. It's you."

The words tumbled out in a rush, falling over top of each other just as the tears started to trip over my own cheeks. "I remember feelings more than actual events. I remember laughing, and snuggling and chatting. I remember kisses on booboos and teasing and having someone there to chase the monsters away from out of the closet. I remember feeling safe and loved and protected..."

"Calleigh—"

"I don't feel safe anymore. It's not this house, or having Uncle Ryan here or even you going back to work. It's just this feeling that's sitting inside of me, and no matter how hard I try, I just can't control it. I feel like we're running away, when what I really want, is to be running towards something. I feel a bit like Dorothy in the Wizard of Oz, and I just want to stay on the yellow-brick road so I can find my way back to... well... to you."

I took a deep breath, unsure of what to say or how to respond. Calleigh was looking for something I knew was in me to give. I glanced again at the photo she still clutched in her hand. Who was that self-confident young woman laughing with my daughter? Where had she gone? At what point had she disappeared? Was it before or after Damian's death?

"May I see that for a minute?" I held my hand out for the photograph, reluctant to just take it from her. Calleigh handed over her treasure as though she were offering up her first born for sacrifice. "I'll give it back, don't worry."

I did not remember myself as this happy, confident young mother smiling in the picture. Damian had taken it with the sun behind us, so the two of us were wrapped in a halo of light. Nothing but sunshine and smiles in this picture—it was astounding. He had captured the perfect moment, not knowing it would be buried in a box until it was desperately needed. This photograph was a reflection of who we had been; it could also be seen as a reflection of who we wanted to be. I sighed and gave Calleigh back the picture.

"Calleigh, I'm sorry. I was so young when your dad died. I was angry, confused, stressed…" I shook my head and leaned in close to my daughter. "I think it might be possible I lost a little piece of myself when I decided I could brave my way through the entire situation."

Calleigh gave me another one of her very adult-like smiles. Her expression was soft and calm, almost as though she had yet again taken on the role and responsibility as parent, but I knew better. She was only as strong as I could be for her. "Don't apologize for things you had no control over. I know you always do what you think is best for me."

I nodded. I did always try to do what was best for her, but I was starting to realize that putting her first all the time had harmed us both.

"That doesn't mean that the choices I make are always the right ones." I spoke quietly, half hoping she wouldn't hear what I had said.

"What do you mean?" The question reminded me that she was still very much my little girl.

"Well, sometimes I do things without thinking everything through to the end; like going back to work fulltime, or letting Uncle Ryan move in with us."

"But then you wouldn't have met Lucy, and I like her," Calleigh pointed out.

"True."

"And I like having Uncle Ryan around."

"Right." I took a deep breath and tried to compose my thoughts into something that would make sense to both of us. "The thing is, the past few months have been pretty miserable for both of us. Sometimes I wonder if the road would have been a bit less bumpy had I just continued working from home so I could be here for you. I made the decision to change jobs so I could start to move on with my own life without taking your needs into consideration."

Calleigh shook her head and inched closer to me. "Remember a few weeks ago, when we did the at home spa day?"

I nodded.

"That is my favourite memory of all time."

Tears started to well in my eyes. I had to admit, it was quite high on my list too, despite its horrible start. We hadn't done anything all that special, but it had been memorable in its simplicity.

"We spent an entire day, just sitting around, telling funny stories, acting like a normal family. I loved that."

I put my arm around her and inhaled the special scent that has always been my daughter. "Are you okay with me working fulltime and not being home for you?"

She nodded and smiled a real smile. "I am. Mostly because you seem to be more alive than you were before.

I'm a little jealous that you have new friends, and that you go out at night and stuff, but I'm glad you're starting to live your life again."

"Calleigh, you are my life," I insisted. I hugged her close to me, afraid that if I let her go I would lose this rare moment of intimacy with her.

"I know, mom. But I don't want to be your everything," she whispered. "It's too hard."

I thought about that for a moment. Had I really put so much pressure on her by making her the centre of my world? Was it possible that by seeing to her every need and anticipating her every want I was smothering her instead of mothering her? This was something I was going to have to work out, and I knew it wasn't something I would be able to work out in this moment.

"Okay," I hugged her back, and reached behind her for a tissue off her night table. There was nothing else I could say to her. "Let's see what else is in this box your uncle left with you. I bet there are all kinds of treasures."

I reached into the box and took out a handful of pictures. Some, I remembered, others were completely foreign to me. I wondered where Ryan had been storing this box. The pictures on top were primarily of Damian, Calleigh and me, further towards the bottom of the box were pictures of Ryan and Damian as children. Those ones made perfect sense; of course, he would have pictures of the two of them. I just wondered where he had gotten so many pictures of my immediate family and why he would even have them.

Jennifer Bogart

Menu du Jour

Breakfast: peach, yogurt, granola bar, coffee

Mid-morning snack: banana

Lunch: apple, Deli sandwich

Mid-afternoon snack: coffee

Supper: pork chops, rice, steamed broccoli

Dessert: Spice Cake

Total Calories consumed: 1406

Total Calories burnt: 1426.75 + 477 (express yoga lunchtime) = 1903.75

Chapter Twenty-six

Projects, plumbing and painkillers

That the weekends always crept up on me when I least expected it. I know that sounds absolutely ridiculous, but there were times when I wished there was just one more day in the week so that I wouldn't have to deal with my extended and varied family.

Of course, this weekend would be a little different as we were expecting guests for the first time in years. Having Lucy and her family over was completely different than having my parents. I knew what my parents expected when they visited: fine wine, good food and homemade dessert. As for Lucy, I had no starting point with her. Her work habits told me she was meticulous, so I wanted the house to be as perfect as it could be. Her gym routine indicated that she was very scheduled, so I wanted everything to be ready for five o'clock on the dot. I had no idea about her family, not having met any of them. I did know she had three boys, all younger than Calleigh. I just hoped they wouldn't be too bored in our very girl-oriented house.

"Stop stressing," Chris said as she calmly sipped her coffee. I was buzzing around the kitchen, trying to remove stains left from Ryan's zealous sauce-making blitz the night before. He was an excellent cook, but not exactly very tidy about it. Unfortunately, I was pretty sure the tomato stain was not going to wash off the wooden chopping block and would have to wear off in its own sweet time.

"I just want to have as much done before I leave as possible." I was already dressed for the gym. I had come very close to cancelling so I would have more time to clean and prepare, but I didn't want Lucy to know that I was a bit stressed about her family coming for dinner. Perhaps we shouldn't have lived like hermits for so long.

Chris sighed, shrugged her shoulders and went back to sipping her coffee and reading the paper. Obviously, she wasn't going to be of much help to me today. The groceries were done, the main course was marinating in the fridge (thanks to Ryan), dessert was sitting on the counter and all that was left was a run to the liquor store. Chris didn't worry so much about the condition of the house, it wasn't her style to let things like tidiness get in the way of having a good time.

"It's not like she hasn't been here before," Chris pointed out as I continued to fuss with papers and countertop clutter.

"I know, but that was different."

"How? If I remember correctly, the house was a pigsty that day."

I glared at Chris. I didn't need a reminder that Lucy had seen me at my worst. "That was different, I was unprepared."

"Whatever," she muttered. When I turned back to her, she was already engrossed in the entertainment section of the newspaper.

I glanced at my watch and realized if I was going to make it to that weight class I had better get moving. The idea of lifting weights for an hour was a bit intimidating, but I figured it wouldn't hurt to try. I had already conquered hot yoga and spinning—both of which I discovered I quite enjoyed. It was entirely possible this class could also win me over.

Lucy was waiting for me at the gym when I arrived, wearing my customary workout attire. With the workout schedule I had been keeping, I would need another shopping excursion soon. Washing the one outfit everyday was getting to be a bit tedious.

"For today, you can keep your weights pretty light—just so you can learn the routine and get used to the movements. The most important thing to remember is to watch your form—you don't want to hurt yourself."

"Right," I nodded. Lucy helped me select a variety of weights and showed me how to set up the bar. She also suggested grabbing a couple of handheld weights to use during the shoulder track as they would be easier to hold.

The women in the class were like robots as they gathered their equipment and set up their space. Some of them were very particular about their set-up, as well as their placement in the class. Most were dressed in classic workout outfits, similar to mine. In fact, many of the conversations floating around the class were about where they had bought what and what was newly available. It was a very different dynamic to what I had experienced in both the spinning and yoga class. Everyone simply got down to business in the spinning class, probably because it was early in the morning and it was more of a pit-stop before going to work. The yoga class was completely silent; presumably because the drill-sergeant instructor wouldn't allow for any chatting before the class and afterwards we were all so drained that chatting just wasn't an option.

The warm up was easy enough. As instructed by Lucy, I loaded my bar up with two 2.5 kg weights. Not too heavy to start, but enough weight that by the end of the track I could certainly feel my muscles working. Then we moved onto squats, so as per instructions, I doubled my weights. About halfway through the song, my thighs were on fire and I wasn't sure I would be able to make it to end of the song. Just when I was certain my legs were going to give out, the song came to a grinding halt. Feeling exuberant because I thought I had made it to the end of the track in one piece, I prepared to put down my bar. Imagine my surprise when the music started up again—there was still one more set!

I struggled through the class, following Lucy's cues and watching the instructor carefully. The last thing I needed was a back injury, but I did find holding certain postures difficult, especially as my muscles got tired and started to scream in agony. By the end of the class, I was once again ready to kill the instructor.

"That was insane," I said to Lucy as we started to clear away our equipment.

She laughed at me. For the most part, her weights had easily been double mine, but she didn't even look out of breath. I know she had worked as hard as I had during the class, I could tell by her intense facial expressions. However, once again, as we left the studio together, she looked fresh and exuberant while I looked sweaty and exhausted. Maybe one day I would get to the point that a simple class would be like a walk through the park. Maybe—but I had a feeling it might take years to get to that point.

"It's actually better if you can get to a weight class two or three times a week."

I looked at Lucy as though she were a complete nutcase. Spinning twice a week, plus hot yoga and now three weight classes? I would never be able to fit all that in my week, maintain a full-time job and look after Calleigh. Not to mention the sheer exhaustion I felt after a workout. Typically, I felt like I needed a nap after each workout, even though I had heard repeatedly that exercise was supposed to increase your energy.

"I don't know when I would fit it in," I answered honestly. "My schedule is already pretty crazy."

"It's not that bad, you could do it. We could probably fit in a lunchtime class if you're up for it."

Workout instead of eating lunch? Food was my comfort in life. Obviously, I wouldn't look like I did if it wasn't. I wasn't so sure I could survive swapping out lunch for a workout—especially on the most stressful days.

"I don't know, it would mean taking a longer lunch and then having to stay a bit later to get everything done."

"Yeah, but that's better than going after work when you're already tired and getting home even later. At least if you go at lunch, it is just part of your work day." She picked up her bag and headed for the door. "Think about it and let me know. If you want, we could do weights Monday, Wednesday and Friday, then spinning Tuesday and Thursday mornings. We could still do hot yoga Wednesday nights. Then your weekends and most of your evenings are free to do as you please."

Wow. She had thought this through. Of course, this could have been her usual routine before she started spending so much time with me at lunchtime. I had no idea what her schedule was like before she came to work for us, but it was obvious she was able to fit in a regular workout routine because she was in excellent shape.

"Right, I'll let you know." I bent down to pick up my own bag and moaned. By tomorrow I would be a mess of knots and screaming muscles.

She smiled. "Okay, so I guess I'll see you at five o'clock? I hope you're ready for all my boys!"

I nodded in response as I slowly made my way to an upright position. "Calleigh has some video games they might like, and we can always put on a movie."

Although the drive home was short, by the time I pulled into the driveway, I knew my thighs were going to give me trouble with the stairs. Going up wouldn't be so bad, but the muscles that stretch across my quads screamed in agony during every downward motion. Part of me thought that if I just kept moving, I would be fine. Another part of me was insisting I was going to die an agonizingly slow, horrendous death. There wasn't enough Advil in the world to ease this muscle pain.

To make matters worse, Ryan had emerged from his temporary quarters and for some reason had decided to set up shop in the middle of my family room. I know I had told him to make himself at home, but today was not the day to be messing up my house.

"What's all this?" I swept my gaze over the clutter of photographs and bits of paper that now littered the previously immaculate room.

He looked up and smiled at me, the similarity to Damian was breathtaking, but it didn't ease my frustration. "I needed space to spread everything out so I can organize my book better. Don't worry, I should have it out of the way before your guests arrive."

"Should?" I held my breath, waiting for his response.

Ryan shifted a few pictures, moved one pile from the sofa to the floor, and shuffled a few scraps of paper around before looking at me, surprised that I was still waiting for an answer.

"Well, that's my plan, anyway."

"Seriously? This can't be here when they arrive."

He shrugged his shoulders. "I'm sure they'll understand that I'm working here. It's not like I've left my underwear hanging from the chandelier."

I bit my lip. I thought having Ryan in the house would be good for Calleigh, but I was beginning to realize that it might not be so good for me. At what point could I send him packing? This was supposed to be a temporary arrangement, and while I had told him to make himself at home, I'm not so sure I meant that literally.

When he realized I was still just staring at him, waiting for a better response he sighed heavily. "Okay, it will be cleaned up by four-thirty. I'll even vacuum for you."

I nodded and made my way, step by agonizing step, to my ensuite bathroom. I would take a bath and try to soak away some of my aches and frustration. Hopefully when I emerged, the family room would look less like a recycling bin.

"Oh, Roxanne, I'm glad you're back." Chris met me in the hallway. The expression on her face didn't match her words.

"I'm almost afraid to ask…"

She bit her lip nervously. "I think we're going to have to call a plumber. We don't have any hot water."

"Huh?"

"Calleigh and I just checked all the taps, a few sputtered drops, but no real water. I'm guessing that old hot water tank just gave up the ghost. Either that; or we have a leak somewhere."

"Crap." *Could this day get any worse?* I took a deep breath and nodded. The best I could do was make a few phone calls and hope that someone could come out within the hour to rectify the situation. At the very least, I needed a shower.

"I'll make a few phone calls and see what I can do. Worst case scenario, I guess I cancel dinner for tonight."

The thing is, I was worried that if I cancelled, I would never get up the courage to reschedule. As it was, my nerves were already fried.

"You could always sponge-bathe, if that's what you're worrying about. You should have showered at the gym."

"Should-have-would-have-could-have," I muttered. I could barely lift my arms to shoulder height, how was I going to manage a sponge-bath and hair-washing in the sink?

"Mom!" Calleigh's voice echoed through the house.

Now what? I wondered.

"Mom!" she called impatiently.

"I'm upstairs," I called back.

"Oh—I found the leak. It's in the basement, dripping hot water down the wall in the back room." I know she was trying to be helpful, but I would rather have heard the element in the hot-water heater had burnt out than the fact that I had yet another mess to clean-up.

"Thanks, love. Chris, will you turn off the water while I call a plumber?"

"You don't need to call anyone," Ryan called from where he sat in the middle of his own chaos. "I can fix a leaky-pipe."

I sighed. If he fixed the pipe, it would save me a few dollars, and might even be done faster, but then I would still be left with his mess in the family room. "What about your project?"

He shrugged. "It can wait, or you can help me with it …"

I looked at the piles he had created; I could see some sort of order taking shape.

"Okay, you can leave your stuff there. Thanks, Ryan." At least he would save me a few dollars on an emergency service call.

In the end, the house was orderly, dinner was perfectly prepared and we were all waiting with time to spare for our guests to arrive. Even Calleigh had pitched in on the basement clean-up, helping her uncle with the simple repair and then volunteering to mop up the mess. Luckily for us, there wasn't much water damage—just a few boxes of old photographs and papers that were so old, I didn't even remember storing them there. Anything of any real value had been stored in plastic bins. We would go through the soggy papers Sunday afternoon and no doubt end up tossing the lot of them.

Jennifer Bogart

Chapter Twenty-seven

Everything happens in threes

Lucy's brood arrived promptly at five o'clock, just in time for cocktails and I was sorely in need of one. Ryan appeared with his usual casual elegance to serve up drinks and put Lucy's husband at ease in our female dominated household.

As the boys entered the house, politely and quietly removing their coats and shoes Calleigh stared at them in awe. "One, two, three—are there anymore?"

"No, thank goodness!"

"They're all the same." I don't think Calleigh meant to voice her thoughts aloud. The moment the words left her mouth, she blushed and mumbled, "Sorry."

Lucy laughed and simply proceeded to introduce her eight-year-old triplets. How she could tell them apart was beyond me. "These are my boys: Sebastien, Alexander and Maximillian. And their dad, Cameron."

The boys sat quietly on the couch in identical silence. They didn't appear to be nervous or shy, just calm and relaxed. Weren't eight-year-old boys supposed to be rambunctious and boisterous?

"Calleigh will show you where the playroom is, and if you want, she can set up a movie, or the Wii." Perhaps if they could escape the adults they might behave more like children and less like robots. As one, they stood and filed out of the room, following my daughter like baby ducks.

"Are they always so well-behaved?" Ryan asked in awe. Perhaps he was remembering when he and Damian were young.

Cameron shrugged his shoulders but didn't say anything. His blue eyes came to rest on Lucy who gave an identical shrug of her shoulders.

"It won't last," she said dryly. Somehow, I doubted that.

Cameron was the stuff of movies. Sometimes I do think they take all the pretty people in the world, lock them away into one room and then only set them free for special occasions. Lucy must have her own key to that room. Blue eyes, blond hair, muscular body that showed clearly through the designer shirt he wore. Clearly, he spent as much time at the gym as Lucy did. I was sorely tempted to ask if he had a brother.

Dinner started out lovely and calm. I wasn't used to having so many children in the house and I'm not sure what I had expected, but they were better behaved than any of Calleigh's friends had been at that age. Well, at least they started out that way.

"Mom, Alex won't pass the potatoes."

"Well, you won't pass the salt." I would assume this comment came from Alex.

"You don't need salt if you already used butter," quipped the third.

Lucy let the bickering go on for a couple minutes, but when it was obvious they couldn't work things out on their own, she intervened. "SAM—that's enough. If you want to leave the table, then carry on, otherwise behave yourselves."

Who on earth was Sam? Was there a fourth one I had missed? I could see Calleigh and Chris were clearly having the same thoughts as they started to silently count the boys, and tick off the three names. Sebastien, Alexander, Max—right, got it. Cute and efficient, just like Lucy.

Unfortunately, the calm didn't persist. As the meal progressed, so did their behaviour. I could clearly see why calling them by one acronym was easier than spitting out all three names. They were either all good, or they were all bouncy, there was no in between and there was never a point when one was behaving while the other two were getting into mischief. Lucy certainly had her hands full. Cameron was relaxed and laid back, pretty much the polar opposite to his wife.

A loud crash summoned the adults to the family room, where the boys were supposed to be playing on the Wii with Calleigh in attendance. She was quietly sitting in a corner, trying to read a book while the boys looked as though they were playing a game of don't-touch-the floor. They had cushions and blankets strewn across the carpet where the gaps were too large to jump from one piece of furniture to the next.

"SAM—I told you this game wasn't allowed here," Lucy said. Her voice was stern, but her eyes were tired.

"Really, it's not a big deal," I said as I picked up the pieces of broken glass. They had knocked over a picture frame—something I had probably purchased at Walmart or Zellers years and years ago. I just didn't want them to cut themselves on the shards.

"Roxanne, I'm so sorry—they'll replace the frame."

"No worries, really. I'm just glad no one was hurt." Chris handed me a plastic shopping bag to dispose of the glass and Ryan appeared with the dust-buster to suck up the remaining bits we couldn't see. The picture was still in the frame, not even scratched—so no real harm done.

"Maybe we should go…"

I shook my head. "Why don't we have Calleigh put a movie on for them? We should have something that will hold their attention."

"They're eight-year-old boys. Nothing holds their attention for long," Cameron commented. He looked mildly uncomfortable.

"It's not like they put a hole in the wall, or anything—"

"Yet."

It was Calleigh who finished the sentence for me. She looked mildly frustrated. "So far, they have cracked one Wii remote, ripped a hole in the cushion, broken that picture frame and wrote on the wall. It's only a matter of time before they do some real damage."

"But, they've been so quiet. Why didn't you say anything?" This I said to Calleigh, she was supposed to be watching them so the adults could enjoy an evening together.

"You told me to watch them, so I've been watching them. I didn't want to disturb you."

"It's getting late, anyway—the later they are up past bedtime, the more mischief they will get into," Lucy pointed out.

"But mom, we're having fun."

"We'll be good—we promise!"

"Please, mom. Just five more minutes?"

The SAM trio were tripping over each other in their attempt to regain order. Sitting on the couch they looked so deceptively innocent.

"One, two, three—let's go." The steel in Lucy's voice was a clear indication that these boys weren't going to get away with anything.

As one, they stood, bottom lips jutting out just a bit and marched to the front door to collect their boots and jackets.

"Thank you for having us over," Cameron said as he shook Ryan's hand, and then leaned over to kiss my cheek. "Dinner was terrific."

"Boys?" Lucy raised an eyebrow and looked at them pointedly.

Still pouting about having to leave so abruptly, they muttered politely, "Thank you."

Cameron opened the door and shooed them along, before they could damage anything else.

"Sorry about that. It's been a long day for them. "Lucy leaned over and gave me a quick hug. Dark circles were starting to appear under her tired eyes. Maybe they had always been there, and I just hadn't taken the time to notice.

"It's fine, really. They're little boys, and there's not much here to keep them occupied." I returned her hug, feeling the slightest twinge of guilt. For the past few months she had been an excellent friend while I sorted through my own issues, never once asking her how her life was going. I just assumed the facade she presented to the outside world was the real deal. "Next time, maybe we'll do a girls' night out—no kids, no men."

"Sounds like a plan."

Once they were out the door, I started putting the family room back together again. Ryan and Chris were arguing like children over which pot should soak and which should be scrubbed. The chaos of the family room would be much more inviting than their squabble.

In all reality, the triplets hadn't done all that much damage. The Wii remote could easily be replaced, the pillow might have already had a tear in the seam and the room was due for painting anyway, so a little marker on the wall wasn't an issue at all.

I picked up the picture frame from the coffee table where Calleigh had left it earlier. The photograph was a school portrait of Calleigh from grade one—just two years younger than the boys who had been here. She was missing her front teeth and had straggly blond hair, but was beautiful just-the-same. At six, she had already lost her father, but the picture didn't reveal sorrow and loss. Instead, it showed a happy little girl with a twinkle in her bright blue eyes. It was possible this picture was taken before Damian died, but I couldn't remember.

When I started to dismantle the frame, another photograph slid out from underneath. It was similar to the one Calleigh had been looking at the other night in her room. The difference being this one was with her dad, not me. Bright blue eyes met equally electric eyes, her light blond hair swept into his sandy shade. In the background was the last project Damian had worked on. Ryan had been there taking pictures for insurance purposes and had spontaneously snapped this one, just days before the accident. I can't imagine why I would have covered it up with a school photo; it didn't make any sense. In fact—I couldn't even remember it ever being on display. If it belonged anywhere, it was in Calleigh's room. This would be one of her last happy memories of her dad.

"The kitchen is done, anything we can do in here to help clean-up?"

Ryan came into the room and stood over me, his voice overly loud in the quiet of my reflections. I smiled and shook my head.

"I think everything is under control." I held up my treasure for him to inspect. "Look what I found."

Gingerly, he took the photograph from me, but didn't smile when he looked at it. He just stared at it, as though seeing more than his brother and niece sharing a happy moment together. I wondered what he saw that eluded me.

"It's a good picture of the two of them. I can't imagine why it was hidden behind an old school photo." Ryan continued to silently stare at the picture, not responding to me. "It's probably the best picture that exists of the two them. They're both happy and relaxed. You did a great job."

When he still didn't respond to me I began to wonder if he was ok. Ryan talked about Damian about as much as I did—which was basically not at all. Perhaps seeing the photograph was particularly jarring for him, despite the box he had allowed Calleigh to sort through. Suddenly, his eyes focused on me very intently.

"Where did you find this?"

"I told you; it was behind her school picture in the frame SAM broke." He looked almost angry, but I couldn't figure out why. "It's a shame it was hidden away all these years—"

"Who hid it there?"

"I guess I did?" I didn't remember ever seeing it in this frame, or any other for that matter. "After Damian died, things were a bit of a blur."

"Do you know how long I've been looking for this?" His tone was accusing, as though I had purposely hidden the photo away.

Anger started to boil up from within me.

"No. I don't know. Even if it had been blown up and on display in the front entrance, you still wouldn't have seen it. After Damian died you disappeared so fast, I thought you were angry with me too. I couldn't figure out what I had done to make both of you hate me so much."

"What are you talking about? All the time that Damian was in the hospital I was here, trying to keep our business afloat. After he died I made sure everything was closed up the best I could before I 'disappeared'—if you can call it that. I left you several ways you could contact me, if you had wanted." He took a deep breath in attempt to calm down; it was an action I recognized from years of living with his brother.

He was right, I knew it, but I didn't want it to be true. I just wanted to blame someone else for all that had gone wrong in my life. Except, my life was actually pretty good. Sure, I had been widowed young and left to raise a small child as a single parent. I had had to work to keep a roof over our heads and food on the table, and I had given up a lot of my life to be everything to my daughter. On the flip side, I have a beautiful, intelligent daughter who means the world to me. My parents and sister have offered endless support and even my job has been lenient to my single parenting needs. Financially, Damian left me in a good and solid position. I work so we can have all the extras and luxuries, not because we were left destitute.

"I'm sorry, I'm just tired and frustrated."

Ryan shook his head and handed the picture back to me, obviously finished with his study of it. "I'm sorry too. I did run away pretty fast afterwards. I just didn't know how to cope and seeing you every day… well, it was hard."

My lips quirked, trying to hold back a smile and I raised an eyebrow at him. "You should have tried being me. I had to look at myself in the mirror every day."

Ryan had been there to witness my meltdown the day before his brother's death. He was the only one who knew what had happened between Damian and me, which is probably one of the reasons he couldn't stand to be with me directly afterwards.

"If you want, I could probably clean that picture up a bit for you, and get it enlarged. Calleigh should have it in her room." It was a peace-offering, one I would be foolish not to accept. Ryan was one of the good guys.

I handed the picture back to him and smiled. "She would love that. We were talking the other day about how she hardly remembers the physical presence of him. Having this picture will help."

"You know, Roxy, what you said to Damian, just before he… uh, just before?" I nodded, trying to ease Ryan's discomfort. Even though I'm pretty sure I didn't want to hear what he had to say, sometimes you just have to let a person spit it out for their own sake. "Well, you shouldn't feel guilty about it. It's one of those moments in life when you should get to hit the delete button and forget about it."

"Logically, I know that. But psychologically, the damage has been done."

"You're a tough cookie, Miss Foxy-Roxy," Ryan said as he draped an arm around me. "Tougher than you look, and probably tougher than you think.

"It's all the time I've been spending at the gym," I quipped in an attempt to lighten the mood. "Lucy has been whipping my butt into shape."

Jennifer Bogart

Chapter Twenty-eight

Objects in the Mirror are Closer Than They Appear

I sat at my old-fashioned dressing table and stared into the slightly warped mirror. Damian had bought this antique set for me shortly after we were married. I had a love of antiquities, and while we couldn't afford much at the time, he had been very handy and talented when it came to woodworking. He purchased it at a flea-market; stripped off layers of white and pink paint; sanded it down to fresh wood and stained it dark mahogany to match the rest of our reconstructed bedroom furniture. It had been a wedding gift; the only thing left to do was to replace the ancient glass when we had more cash on hand. Even as our money situation improved, he never did get around to repairing the mirror. In all reality, it didn't matter. I didn't use it to apply make-up or style my hair; mostly I had used it as a place to think. After he died, I couldn't bear to part with it, but I couldn't remember sitting on the dainty little chair anytime over the past seven years.

I leaned forward and tried to catch a clearer image of the woman staring back at me in the mirror. If I let my imagination go, I could almost see the young woman I had been—the one that had been smiling in the photograph with Calleigh. The grey eyes and dark blond hair were the same, but the woman staring back at me was sad and a tiny bit lost. Even in the warped glass, I could see the denial of the past reflected in those eyes. It was time to take a deeper look and acknowledge all that had happened so it could finally be put to rest.

Like all marriages, ours wasn't perfect, but we were mostly happy. Our parents had only mildly objected when we told them our plans fresh out of university. Damian was going to start up his design business and I would find work as a technical writer. Our wedding was a quiet affair, with only close friends and family in attendance. Calleigh hadn't been part of our initial plans. We wanted children; we just expected them to come along much later in life.

After having Calleigh, I was so in love with being a mother, I wanted another baby. I didn't want her growing up to be a lonely-only child, but Damian wasn't ready. His work was just starting to take off, and we needed both incomes in order to stay afloat. When Calleigh had been an infant, my mom had watched her for a few hours each day so that I could do the bulk of my work from home— one of the many advantages of being a writer. Now that Calleigh was in grade one, she was gone for most of the day and I missed her terribly.

"I told you the timing is all wrong," he had stated when I told him I was pregnant for the second time. He didn't believe me when I said I hadn't planned it. We were in our bedroom, I was sitting at my dressing table, running a brush through my long blond hair and he was adjusting his tie in the mirror. We presented the perfect picture of married harmony to anyone looking in through the window.

"I can't help that the pill failed." I was blinking furiously, trying to keep the tears at bay. I would never have deceived him into having a second child when he wasn't ready. Mother Nature just had different plans.

He snorted derisively and turned away, as though he couldn't bear to look at me. "More like you forgot to take it."

"No, no. I told you, I wouldn't do that to you." Those tears were about to create a waterfall. I knew if even one escaped I would be swept into an emotional abyss. Even then, I didn't cry often, but when I did I had a hard time getting myself back under control.

"Well, it's done now. I hope you're happy." He picked up his keys and walked out the door to work. I just slumped down into this very chair and stared at my reflection in the warped glass. I knew he just needed to blow off steam and that work was particularly stressful just now. I knew I shouldn't have taken his anger so personally and that he would come around. He loved Calleigh and he would love this baby just the same. Life was just a bit overwhelming at the moment.

When I had told Damian about the pregnancy, I was only about five weeks along and there weren't any signs or symptoms. In light of all that happened afterwards, I should have just kept my mouth shut and maybe our last few days together would have been a bit better.

I heard Damian leave the house, and decided I wouldn't let this conversation bother me too much. He needed time to think, and I had better things to do with my day than sit in self-misery and loathing while gazing at my warped reflection.

I lost that baby, a few weeks later. Part of me wondered what would have happened if he had survived. We were given just enough time to become accustomed to the idea of another child in the house. Damian had warmed to the idea and Calleigh was equally excited at the prospect of becoming a big sister. Even though we hadn't told anyone yet, all the signs were there. At just ten weeks I was already starting to expand at the middle, probably because this was my second pregnancy. Damian started working longer hours so he would be able to take some time off when the baby arrived. Life was good, not perfect, but good.

Occasionally, I would catch him with a strange look on his face, just staring at me. It made me wonder if perhaps he still thought I had planned the pregnancy all along. Shortly after I miscarried he asked, "So, are you expecting to try again?"

I shook my head, thinking that his question was hugely insensitive. "I really don't want to talk about this right now."

"We should, I need to know what to expect from you."

I took several deep breaths, trying to remain calm. Fair enough, although he had warmed to the idea of another baby, he was still not exactly ready to plan for another one. I knew where he was coming from, but he had to understand that I wasn't in the right frame of mind to have this discussion. I gazed out the kitchen window, trying to collect my thoughts. In losing this baby, I felt I had lost a small piece of my soul. And even though it was a very tiny piece, it was so very painful, I just wanted to cover it up with a bandage and carry on with my life. I certainly didn't want to talk about it just now.

"Are you kidding me?" I snapped. "I just had a miscarriage. Maybe it's different for men, I don't know, but in my heart, that baby was as much a part of this family as it was a part of me. He wasn't a goldfish, it's not like we can just go out and replace it. So, no, to answer your question—I'm not thinking to try again anytime soon!"

Was this the sweet and caring man I had married? Something more than another mouth to feed had to be upsetting him. Damian was generally mild mannered, a little quirky, very hard working, but lately he was full of pent up angst. Whenever we were together I felt like an explosion was imminent. He sat there staring at me, as though he were looking at a stranger. Looking back at him, I felt as though I were suddenly married to a complete stranger.

After this, things didn't get better. We tried. For Calleigh and for ourselves, we made an honest effort to make life more pleasant between us. I faithfully took my birth control, and he never brought up the subject of babies again. We showered all our love and affection on Calleigh, and sprinkled our own relationship as needed, in the hopes of repairing all the unseen damage. Perhaps, if we'd had more time…

Well, we didn't have more time, and I held those last few weeks we'd had together in a little box, locked up in my heart. We should have taken the time to talk to each other and work through all the things that were niggling at us. As a couple, we were fine, instinctively, I knew this. Whatever was causing the invisible elastic of tension to pull taut was something outside of our relationship: perhaps his work or my preoccupation with the miscarriage. Whatever it was, it was too late to ruminate over the should-haves and could-haves. Those few tense weeks, although living vibrantly in my memory, shouldn't be so strongly imbedded in how I remembered Damian. I wanted to remember the easy-going, fun-loving, relaxed man who made me smile. The man who laboured over resurrecting this vanity set so that I could have my picture-perfect antique bedroom. That's the man I needed to rediscover in my memories.

I sighed and swiped away another wayward tear. I had spent so much time mourning over the relationship that had started to fall apart, instead of mourning over the one I had actually lost. I think the last couple days of Damian's life had a larger impact on me than I had been willing to admit. Everyone kept saying to me, "it's just the head injury talking; you know he doesn't mean it." And yet, they didn't know, there was no way they could.

Every time I walked into his hospital room, I was met with a diatribe of foul language and crude insults. The medical staff insisted it was the head injury, but those poison-tipped words had to have come from somewhere deep inside of him.

After one particularly sour stream of cursing and name-calling I said quietly, "It really is too bad that brick didn't kill you."

Anyone in the room had been shocked into silence as I fled down the hall, trying to hold my tears back. Just how much was I expected to take from him before I snapped?

A few hours later my cell phone rang. I was in the kitchen, making dinner with Calleigh and Chris. Cooking always worked to take my mind off my troubles, so we were planning a mini-pizza party. Calleigh was busy mucking about in a small batch of dough, while Chris and I chopped fresh vegetables.

I didn't recognize the number, so I didn't bother to answer it. If it were important, whoever it was would leave a message, call back or track me down at the house. I had just come from seeing Damian who had been full of vinegar and spit, as my grandmother would say. The phone blipped, indicating a message—I would check it after dinner.

But I didn't check it, in fact, I completely forgot about it. Chris had rented a cute little girl movie for us to enjoy with Calleigh as we indulged in our homemade pizza in the family room. This was such a treat for her, as we usually insisted we eat at the table as a family, no electronics, phones or interruptions. A rule Damian had insisted on when my phone alerts became a nuisance while working with a company overseas. We needed at least one hour a day of family time without either his work or mine interfering.

I woke in the middle of the night to the melodious chime of the phone beside the bed. The digital clock displayed 1:00am in blaring blue. Who could be calling at this hour? I fumbled for the phone, not bothering to turn on the light.

"Mrs. Burnberry?" a woman's voice was on the end of the phone. In the background, I could hear what sounded like voices echoing though a paper-towel roll and suddenly my senses went on full-alert. Why was the hospital calling me at this hour?

"Yes."

"You need to come down to the hospital. Your husband has taken a turn for the worse." The disembodied voice was very matter-of-fact. Emotionless. Perhaps even rehearsed.

"Okay, I'll be there in a few minutes." Although wide awake, I still felt vaguely disoriented. After ensuring

Chris was fine to watch Caleigh, I quickly changed into street clothes and made my way to the car. It was a warm evening for spring, I'm not sure why that small detail filtered into my mind, but it did. Summer was definitely just around the corner.

When I arrived, the nurse in the room looked up at me as though startled. Did they think I wouldn't come?

"What—"

Damian looked as though he had aged decades in just twelve hours. Grey skin, sweat beaded on his forehead and dark circles sagged beneath his eyes. What had these people done to my husband?

"We're not sure, and need to run more tests," the nurse answered my unspoken question. "I'll let the doctor know you're here. It won't take a moment."

Alarmed, I stepped inside the room, but was afraid to go much further. The nurse wore much protective clothing; facemask, gloves and some kind of yellow raincoat like jacket. Was this for her protection or his?

"You might want to speak with the doctor before you come in," she said as she left the room.

I didn't have to wait long, although it did feel strange to be lingering in the hallway. When I spoke with the intern, a young man badly in need of a haircut and updated glasses, he was calm and hopeful.

"Your husband has contracted an infection; he has been running a fever for the better part of the day, as well, he has had some digestive issues." I nodded. Damian had mild colitis, as long as he stuck to his diet, he had few issues. Perhaps hospital food, although bland, had set it off. "We have started a course of Flagyl and stopped his other antibiotics. Baring any further complications, he should straighten around in no time."

I nodded again, not sure I understood. They had called me here because he had an infection? "Can I go sit with him for a bit?"

"Sure, but you'll want to wash your hands and put on gloves before going in. Also, be sure to dispose of the gloves and wash your hands when you leave. We don't want to spread this infection to other patients."

I didn't plan on visiting any other patients, but I didn't argue with him either. I just wanted to make sure that Damian would make it through the night to insult me all over again tomorrow.

The smell in the room reminded me a bit of Calleigh's diaper pail, awful to say, but true. This was another thing that struck me as odd to remember so vividly. He was so still in the bed, his skin grey against the bleached sheets. I wanted to reach out and touch him, but thought better of it. No one likes to be stroked with latex, not really. I should have asked the doctor what kind of infection he had contracted, but I was afraid to know, afraid I might bring it home to Calleigh, another reason I couldn't bring myself to touch him. Looking at him there, in that bed, he didn't look like he would make it through the night. A tear slid down my cheek, somehow, I knew this was going to be goodbye for us. There would be no growing old together. I blew him a kiss, gently tucked the blanket around him and like the coward I was, I turned and fled the room.

Jennifer Bogart

Chapter Twenty-nine

Throwing out the Soggy Mess

I dried my tears and tried not to think of all the things I should have said and done that night. I had wasted our last few hours together immersed in self-pity and righteous indignation instead of at his side, comforting him as he slipped away from this mortal world. My anger over his treatment of me overshadowed my impending grief. Or perhaps, being angry had been easier than being sad and acknowledging I was about to lose him forever.

Tomorrow would be another crazy day, with the sorting of the soggy pictures from the basement. Normally, I would just throw them out, since I didn't even know they were there in the first place, hidden as they were behind a pile of forgotten junk, but I didn't think that would be fair to Calleigh. If there were pictures of her dad that she wanted, then she should have them.

I changed into comfy PJs and snuggled into my bed, expecting sleep to come easily after the physical and emotional labours of the day. My brain, however, had other ideas. It kept replaying the scene in the hospital over and over again, like someone was hitting the replay button on the DVD player. Only each scenario was slightly different than the last. The all ended the same, with him not making it through the night, but my actions were more loving, more indicative of the person I wanted to be than the person I had been in that moment.

Sighing, I sat up and decided there was no use in trying to sleep. The house had that middle-of-the-night quiet wrapped around it like a comforting blanket. I may as well start sorting through the soggy mess that was waiting for me in the kitchen. Ryan had thoughtfully piled the boxes in a corner so we could get to work on them first thing in the morning. I would set anything Calleigh might be interested in to one side and then just get rid of the rest. The box had been down there for so long, it was doubtful there was anything useful or relevant in it.

To my surprise, Ryan was one step ahead of me. Dressed in grey sweats and a tatty T-shirt, he sat on the floor with piles of photographs scattered around him. The scene looked very much like the one he had created earlier in the day in the living room, only these photographs were time-worn and water damaged.

"Couldn't sleep?"

He shook his head and smiled sadly. "I've been looking for these pictures for years. The thought of them sitting here all this time was driving me insane."

"I don't understand."

Again, he paused to give me that sad smile as he gingerly peeled two wet photographs apart. "Just something I wanted to put to rest in my own mind."

I gave him that pointed stare every parent develops and waited for him to elaborate. It didn't take long.

"When we were at the job site, there's no way there should have been any falling debris. Sure, the scaffolding was still in place, but that was so we could put up the signage, as part of the contract. That last project we did was a bit shady all 'round."

"I'm really not following you, Ryan. You'll have to back up a bit and start at the beginning. I had very little to do with that business. I did a bit of copy work once or twice to help everyone out, but I had my own career and a child to raise."

"Harper was very good at keeping secrets, so no one really knew what he was up to. He made an arrangement with a company that wanted to only deal in cash. No receipts, no records. We needed the money, so Harper jumped on it, even though we didn't have any idea who these guys were. Damian found out something about them. He wouldn't say what, but he didn't want to finish the job. Harper insisted we could get it done quickly and then walk away a bit more financially secure."

Carefully, he separated a few more wet pages and laid them out in front of him. The ink had smeared and they were no longer legible. It was Ryan's turn to give me the pointed look. "The thing is, we couldn't just walk away. They kept asking for more work, at prices we just couldn't ignore. We needed that money to get us into the black. If we didn't start making money soon, the company would be bankrupt."

"Damian never said anything." He had been moody and irritable. He had worked a lot of crazy long hours, but he had never said there were any business issues weighing him down. I thought we talked about everything to do with his business, so this both surprised and hurt me.

Ryan shrugged his shoulders. "He really didn't want you know. I think he thought you would be safer this way."

"Are you saying that the Damian's death might not have been an accident?" I was suddenly feeling very confused and disoriented. Damian had died from an uncontrollable infection, not the accident.

"For a long while, both Harper and I thought that, but it really was just a case of being in the wrong place at the wrong time."

"So, what's with the pictures? And why has Harper been trying to track you down?" This conversation was quickly turning into a game of twenty questions.

Ryan peeled two more pictures apart and grimaced at their soggy state. "Harper thought I might have some incriminating evidence on film."

"I'm not following."

Ryan pushed the pile of pictures from me and looked up, finally making full eye-contact with me. His expression clearly stated he didn't want to have this conversation, but mine countered with a strength I didn't know I had. I was tired of the mystery surrounding Damian's death and wanted to put the past firmly where it belonged; a distant memory of another lifetime.

"The day I took the picture of Calleigh and Damian together, a few of the 'big bosses' were hanging around the site. I had been warned not to photograph anything and assumed that meant the building and anyone related to the job—not candid shots of family. It seems I was wrong. Harper saw me with the camera and insisted I hand over the roll of film. I'd told him that wasn't possible because the camera was digital. He wasn't aware that it held a memory card I could easily remove."

"I still don't understand the big deal. The only two people in that picture are Calleigh and Damian."

Ryan looked away and grimaced. "I took other photos. I know I wasn't supposed to, but something seemed wrong and I just wanted to have something documented.

So, while it looked like I was photographing Calleigh, I was focusing on other items."

"So, what happened to the pictures or the memory card?"

"Harper told Damian and Damian insisted I give him the card. I did—after I had the pictures printed as a safeguard. Afterwards, I thought better of it and handed the prints over to him as well." Ryan shrugged and looked directly at me. "There's nothing incriminating in any of the pictures. I was experimenting with a new digital camera, and back then, the picture quality wasn't all that great. At best, there are a few grainy shadows."

I nodded, trying to take it all in. I still couldn't understand why Ryan hadn't said anything to me sooner. "So why is Harper trying to track you down?"

"It's nothing."

"You've told me this much, there's no point in hiding anything else."

Ryan bit his lip and nodded, probably wondering when I had changed from shy little mouse to take-charge tigress. He shuffled a few photos, created a tidy pile, changed his mind and placed the photos back in the soggy box. I wanted patiently.

"The guys we did the deal with got in touch with me a few months ago. It turns out they knew I took the pictures even though I thought I was being discreet." He shrugged his shoulders, indicating he didn't have anything more to say, but I knew otherwise.

"And?"

"They wanted the pictures for some reason, but the memory card is long gone and the pictures were destroyed in your mini-flood. I guess Damian hid them away where no one would think to look, along with some other junk that's not important, as far as I can see. The only picture of any value is the one of Calleigh and her dad. Since they're the only two in the picture, I don't think anyone has anything to worry about."

I nodded, took a handful of water-damaged pictures and shuffled through them. He was right. The print quality had been so bad that the ink had run together, obliterating anything that might have been of interest.

"So, are you going to call Harper?"

He nodded as he started to gather up the soggy mess that had taken over my kitchen. "May as well get it over with. Haven't talked to him directly in years. I can only assume he was looking for me for same reason I was looking for the pictures."

I thought about what he said for a moment, my brain slowly processing his worlds. Something about the entire situation stung. "Did you only come back into our lives to find the pictures?"

Ryan froze in place. His arms were weighed down by the heavy, wet box, but he simply stood there and stared at me.

"I know this looks bad, Roxy –"

I turned away from him, not wanting him to see how much he had just hurt me. Naively, I had thought that he had returned to reconnect with us, instead his reasons were selfish.

"Just don't let Calleigh know," I whispered, as I walked away.

My aching limbs and tired mind decided a hot bubble bath was in order. I needed some time alone to reflect a bit more on the past before I could lay it all to rest. The hot water and lightly scented bubbles soothed my muscles as I tried to clear my mind. Lately, I'd been taking an awful lot of time to mull over things that had been better off left in the past.

Ryan's reappearance in our lives set off a wave of observation within me. The hurt and self-doubt I had carried around for years weren't completely an illusion within my head. Damian had been awful to me in the weeks before his death, but not because of a failing relationship, rather because he had been trying to protect Calleigh and me. His stress levels must have been phenomenal, and I only wished he had confided in me instead of trying to hide all the details of a shady business deal that went awry. I might not have been able to help in any concrete way, but at least I wouldn't have spent years wondering if his anger had truly been directed at me. In retrospect, his harsh words and distance had probably been a result of his stress and worry for his family. No wonder he hadn't wanted another child. At the time, I had been reacting to the situation, not to him. My wish for him to die hadn't been heartfelt; it had only been a careless expression of frustration. My inability to deal with his imminent death wasn't because I didn't care; it was because I cared too much. In that moment, I had needed some distance so I could deal with the entire situation. Over the past several years, I had continued to use that distance as a means to keep the full extent of my grief at bay. The past few months had proven that I needed new tools in my coping box.

Water sloshed over the sides of the tub as I stood and began to towel myself off. Glancing at my reflection in the mirror I noticed two things. The first was that all the exercise and redirected eating habits were starting to pay off. I now had muscles developing where there was once jiggly flab. The second was that I hardly recognized the young woman gazing back at me. She was calm, self-assured and looked as though she was ready to take on the world. She knew she was a little late to the party, but at least she had finally decided to show up.

Chapter Thirty

No Strings Attached

I had a plan. It was time I took back my life and my future. No more hiding from the past, no more wishing for things that would never be. I might not be able to change all the things that had put me on the path to this moment, but I had every intention of being in control of how I chose to move forward. This sensation of self-assurance was both strange and exhilarating. A part of me was wound up with nervous energy, and yet another part was all cool and calm confidence.

As I passed by the family room, I noticed that Ryan had neatly stacked the few salvageable photos on the coffee table. The rest were in the soggy box by the door, waiting to be sent to the recycling bin. I didn't bother to stop and peruse the pictures. They were part of a past I had acknowledged but didn't want to dwell on.

My destination was the bright and spacious kitchen. This afternoon I was going to cook a meal fit for the royal family, and then… well, then I would lay out my plan for my own royal family. Like it or not, there were about to be some significant changes in my house.

Humming, I set to work; pulling out various ingredients, pots, pans, whisks, mixers and utensils. I chopped, diced, peeled and grated with glee, feeling alive in the reclamation of my kitchen. Part of me wanted Ryan to wander through to see that I was once again in control of the hub of our house, and part of me was glad he had decided to disappear from sight. In fact, both Calleigh and Chris had made themselves scarce. No doubt, Calleigh was in her room. I could only hope the Chris was out doing something for herself. It was time she ventured beyond this little house and found her own place in the world.

Once I had the savoury goulash simmering on the stove, I started the rewarding process of making fresh bread. There's something to be said about the age-old process of mixing the simplest of ingredients, using your hands and getting back to basics to create sustenance and hearty goodness. This meal was one of my favourites: uncomplicated but completely nourishing and made with love.

Bread completed, I decided to add an equally old-fashioned dessert of apple crisp. The apples were a little lacking in spirit, but with a little cinnamon, lemon and sugar they were easily revived. With the supper preparations completed, I had little to do but clean up the mess and wait. Suddenly it occurred to me that Ryan and Chris might not even be home for dinner. Chris rarely ate out, and when she did she told me, but I had no control over Ryan's actions. He came and went as he pleased, although, to be honest, he mostly stuck close to home.

I don't know why I ever doubted my plan would work. Promptly at six, all three of my house mates appeared in the kitchen, drawn by the aromatic smells of home-cooking and their hungry tummies. Perhaps Ryan had heard the noise in the kitchen and just thought it best to avoid any place I happened to be. Chris arrived via the front door, looking rosy and windswept from the cold. March was clinging tenaciously to winter.

None of them were surprised that dinner had magically appeared on the table. It had been this way for years, the only difference being the addition of Ryan who had assumed cooking responsibilities when the urge came over him.

"This smells awesome," Chris said as she took her seat opposite me. Of course, she was completely unaware of the tension between Ryan and me, so the silence that greeted her words was even more oppressive.

"Did I miss something?" Her mouth full of fresh bread, she didn't stop eating long enough to look at any of us.

"Mom and Uncle Ryan had a fight," Calleigh said quietly. She had dished a modest amount of the goulash into her bowl and was using her bread to sop up the juices. At least she was eating these days.

Ryan jerked his head up and looked at me pointedly. I had nothing to hide from my family. He was a guest in my home, nothing more.

I shook my head and smiled. "We didn't have a fight; we just had a long overdue conversation this morning."

"About what?" Of course, Chris would want all the details. Big sister by only a couple minutes, she felt she needed to know all the particulars of my life.

"Just things that are probably best left in the past," I answered. Ryan gave a noticeable sigh of relief and started to eat his meal with more enthusiasm.

"For a minute, there, I thought you were going to ask me to move out," he muttered.

"I am going to ask you to leave," I said quietly.

"Roxy—"

"I'm going to ask both of you to move out." Chris dropped her spoon in complete shock, splattering vegetables and sauce all over the table.

"You've got to be joking."

I shook my head. "I'm not joking, and don't worry, I'm not kicking you both out to the street without giving you time to find something permanent. I wouldn't do that to you."

"I don't understand…" Chris looked truly perplexed. I felt the smallest twinge of guilt, but swept it aside. I needed to do this for all of us, but most importantly, I needed to do this for me.

"When Damian died I needed you. Calleigh was little and your support meant the world to me. The past few months have let me see things a bit differently. I thought I was a washed up middle-aged mom with nothing to offer the world. Going to the gym, trying all those crazy diets, and seeing Calleigh grow into an independent young woman has made me stop and take a better look at myself and what I need. I think it's time I do some things for myself, on my own."

Ryan continued to eat in silence. He didn't have much to contribute to the conversation, since he was only ever meant to be a temporary guest. Calleigh just sat back and watched the adults in the room. I had thought she would be the one to protest the loudest, given her fondness for both of them, but she remained strangely quiet.

"Seriously, Roxy, do you really think you're ready to do everything on your own?" Chris had picked up her spoon and resumed eating. I could tell she was thinking this was just a little test, to see how they would react.

I nodded my head. "I think we're both ready to start doing everything on our own. I'm not disowning you; I still need you—both of you. But there is a fine line between mothering and smothering. You're my best friend, always have been and always will be. Letting you stay here and relying on you for constant support the way I do, isn't doing you any good either. You're thirty-three years old; you need your own space so you can live your own life."

"I've never lived alone before," Chris said quietly. I had sort of forgotten that part. Before she moved in with me, she had lived with our parents, saving for a down payment for a house. In the end, she had never needed to touch her savings.

"Really?" Calleigh asked, suddenly breaking her silence.

Chris and I shook our heads in unison while Ryan and Calleigh looked at us in disbelief. Chris was tying me to the part of grieving widow, and for both our sakes, I felt we needed to have some space and independence from each other.

"Finish off the school year, so that you aren't stuck with the chaos of moving while trying to teach. I'll help you go house-hunting. It'll be fun, and maybe even give us a way to reconnect on a different level."

Chris nodded. I could tell her heart wasn't completely committed to this new idea, but she would warm up to it. Over the past few months we have grown apart. I still needed her, but not in the same way I had when Calleigh was small.

"What about Uncle Ryan?"

Since Ryan's stay was intended to be transitory, I had no qualms about giving him a firm deadline too. In the time he had been living with us, he had become an important part of Calleigh's life, and I didn't want to take that from her. However, he did need to figure out a more permanent solution as he had just about worn out his welcome.

"Don't worry about me, Calleigh," Ryan answered before I could say anything. "In another week or so I'll be off on my next grand adventure."

Calleigh could easily accept Chris moving out as she would still be a constant in our lives. Ryan was another matter altogether. I wondered if he would disappear completely again.

"But you just came back."

Ryan nodded his head. "I'm not going far. In fact, I was thinking of renting an apartment so I do have a place to call home while between projects. Your mom is right—this arrangement was terrific for a little while, but now it's time to get a few things in order, settle down… be responsible."

She nodded, relief clearly washing over her fine features. Her beloved uncle wasn't planning to disappear completely from her life.

"I think it will be weird, with everyone living in different houses."

"I know, sweetie, it will seem strange at first, but I do think it will be best for all of us. I'll tell you what— you can even have Aunt Chris's bedroom, since it's bigger than yours."

"Do you think we can leave the reorganizing for after I've found a new home?" Chris protested. "I'm still here, you know."

"Well, Aunt Chris, I do need to plan how I want it decorated. My room is a bit babyish for me; I need more mature decor."

It would take time, but this arrangement was going to work.

Calleigh and I sat on opposite ends of the couch, watching an old movie on TV and snacking on popcorn. The evening air was cool for June, but we were comfortable snuggled up on the couch, enjoying each other's company. Chris had officially moved out the week before and this was our first night of calm since the flurry of activity that had engulfed June.

True to his word, Ryan had set off on another photographic journey, promising that when he returned he would find an apartment close by. He had contacted Harper before leaving, delivered the few unfocused, water-damaged pictures that remained from one day of folly, and finally settled the issues that had been hanging over them since Damian's death. Seeing Harper at the gym was less jarring than it had been; it turned out we could be friends despite the history that drove us apart. While we would never be best friends, I had to acknowledge that he was a pretty decent guy. At the time of Damian's accident, we were all a little self-absorbed. Given the situation, it was understandable that he only wanted to escape Montreal so that he could keep his family safe.

Over the past couple months, I had slimmed down, muscled up and started feeling more in control of who I am and where I'm going. I felt the identity of being "Calleigh's dowdy mom" slipping away and being replaced with the dynamic person I'm meant to be. Lucy's influence had such a positive impact on me. She might be a bit on the bossy side, which can be hard to take if you don't know her. But she is never judgemental and is always available to offer encouragement and support, no matter what folly I embark on. Not a replacement for Chris, by any stretch of the imagination, but certainly a welcome addition to my small circle of friends.

"Are you going out on Friday?" Calleigh asked suddenly. She was getting used to my increased social schedule, just as I was getting used to giving her the freedoms of a teenager. "I saw you wrote something on the calendar."

I nodded. "Yes. I have a date."

Calleigh sat up straight, leaned forward and blinked, as though trying to clear her vision. "What?"

I laughed. "I'm going on a date. It's been a while, but I think it's time, don't you?"

"Who is this guy? Do I know him? What does he do for a living"

Playfully, I threw a pillow at her. "Who's the parent in this relationship?"

In response, she only raised an eyebrow.

"Okay, okay. His name is Connor Bryant. I met him through someone at work, he's a consultant. You don't know him, I don't know him. That's the whole point of a date. Don't worry. I'm meeting him at the restaurant so I'll have my own car."

She smiled and nodded her approval.

"Do you have plans for Friday?"

"I might sleep over at Aunt Chris's if that's okay with you. She wants to go shopping on Saturday morning for furniture."

"Sounds like a good plan."

We settled back onto the couch in comfortable silence, just enjoying the feeling of being comfortable with each other.

The End

Jennifer Bogart

~ *About the Author* ~

Reader, writer, editor, explorer, dreamer… Jennifer Bogart is having a love affair with words.

Currently the author of three women's fiction novels (*Newvember, Hot Dogs are Diet Food,* and *Money, Masks & Madness*), two romantic short stories (*Under the Stars* and *Seven Seconds*), one YA fantasy series (*Liminal Lights* and *Shadow Shifts*), and the serialized novel *Sunny with a Twist of Olive,* she can't stop writing any more than she can stop breathing. You can follow Jennifer on Facebook, Twitter, and her blog.

Links:

Facebook: www.facebook.com/JenniferBogartAuthor/

Twitter handle: @JenniferBogart

Blog: https://www.jenniferbogart.com/